a piece of the moon is missing

by the same author

James L. Johnson

a piece of the moon is missing

a new code name sebastian novel

A. J. HOLMAN COMPANY
DIVISION OF J. B. LIPPINCOTT COMPANY
PHILADELPHIA AND NEW YORK

U.S. Library of Congress Cataloging in Publication Data

Johnson, James Leonard, birth date
A piece of the moon is missing.

I. Title.
PZ4.J6917Pi [PS3560.0379]   813'.5'4   74–8579
ISBN–0–87981–025–4

DEDICATED TO

**All those willing to
risk the deeper
places**

The four-engine Navy Constellation patrol plane out of Thule Air Force Base in Greenland made its turn and flew down the length of the white hummocks of ice that form Ellesmere Island. It was March 8, exactly 2:00 p.m. The long Arctic winter was done, the six months of night past. Now the sun, hanging like a frozen star off the far horizon, cast a red haze on the ice, turning it to an ocean of flame, jabbing the winter sleep to wakefulness.

At 2:30 p.m. the plane passed down Nansen Sound and dropped two thousand feet so that the observation crew could get a better look. At 2:40 p.m. the movement on the ice was spotted by the forward turret observer. At 2:45 p.m. the pilot radioed back to Thule:

FROM NAVY FIVE FIVE SIX ZERO TO AIR COMMAND SEARCH THULE. UNCLASSIFIED. AT ONE FOURTEEN ZERO ZERO ZULU. OFF NANSEN SOUND, LONGITUDE AND LATITUDE MARK. EXPEDITION SIGHTED MOVING NORTH BY NORTHWEST UP NANSEN SOUND. AM COUNTING FIVE DOGSLEDS AND SEVEN PEOPLE. NO ACKNOWLEDGE TO OUR RADIO CONTACT. WILL HOLD FIX PENDING YOUR ORDERS. OVER.

Back in Thule, from the cluttered office of Air Command Search, a call was put out over the intercom for Admiral John Fish, Director of Operation Moon Rock, who was just finishing lunch. Fish, going on forty, was comparing notes with General Horace Buckner, Coordinator of Military Operations for Moon Rock. The call for Fish meant something significant had come up in operations, and with-

5

out so much as a glance at Buckner he rose and hurried out.

Buckner scrambled to catch up. "Something new on Thorsen?" he called to Fish's back.

"I don't know," Fish replied. "But all we have on that ice right now is a Norwegian scientific ice team. One of the patrols must have spotted something else."

"There's hardly enough light yet to see anything from the air," Buckner said. He was ten years older than Fish, with white hair and an easy grace to his walk.

They moved into the operations room. "What have you got, Lieutenant?" Fish asked the officer monitoring incoming radio traffic.

The officer handed him the message board.

"Oh, by the way," Fish added, "General Buckner, this is Lieutenant Bob Hestig." Buckner nodded at Hestig and took the lieutenant's hand quickly and dropped it, not really that interested. "Lieutenant Hestig is on special duty with us these days, released from computer electronics and interspace communications in Washington, to keep his ear on every kind of signal that comes off the Arctic ice, right down to a polar bear's yawn."

Buckner gave Hestig a second, more direct and appraising look. Hestig, perhaps embarrassed to be performing so menial a task, gave an almost bashful smile in return.

Fish meanwhile had turned to the map of Greenland and the two major land masses, Ellesmere Island and Axel Heiberg Island, on the far wall. There was only one blue pin on the map, and that was on Bradley Island fifty miles out on the ice.

"That pin is the Norwegian team," Fish said to Buckner, as the general moved up to look at the map. Fish put up another blue pin at the channel that separates Ellesmere and Axel Heiberg on the edge of the Arctic Ocean.

"And you think that's Thorsen?" Buckner asked.

"Who else would be going up that way at this time of the year?"

"We just received this a few minutes ago, Admiral." Hestig handed a yellow piece of copy to Fish.

6

Fish read it quickly. "The Russians are on the move," he said, more to himself than to Buckner. He pulled down a sliding red marker and placed it over a location far up on the Arctic Ocean to the north and east. "Which means they must know Thorsen is on his way out on the ice too. . . . That Russian activity is air traffic," he added, as he handed the message to Buckner. "They're probably going to set down by airplane just north of their SP-Six ice station and take it by sled from there."

"They surely can't know where Thorsen is," Buckner said skeptically. "We're the only ones with authorized air traffic over Greenland and radio codes—"

"Lieutenant." Fish was still studying the map. "Notify Navy five five six zero to go on classified transmission under code Zebra."

"Somebody monitoring our radio?" Buckner frowned. "Why wasn't that patrol plane on classified—"

"That Constellation is an air rescue patrol, not a military observation flight, General. They just happened to stumble on that party moving up Nansen and are checking them out as the routine dictates."

"But how could the Russians pick them up and move so fast?"

"Maybe they've got some other source of information we don't."

Buckner sniffed and peered more closely at the map. "Why is Thorsen taking that route, anyway? Why didn't he just hire a plane and fly it?"

"General, since you have been on the job as military coordinator of Moon Rock only a week, let me inform you that anything that could fly—even a kite—was locked away from Thorsen by National Security in Washington the day he disappeared from Houston a month ago. The way we see it, Thorsen probably booked a ship to Smith Sound, wintered there, and then started out a week or so ago to go up Cape Sabina here, then to Bay Fjord, and then up to Nansen Sound, where he's about ready to break out to polar ice."

"That's a long way to go."

"He's got time on his side. As long as he carries that

moon rock, there won't be any quick moves on our part to stop him. . . . Lieutenant?"

"Sir?"

"Notify all military units on Operation Moon Rock standby that we have probably sighted the Thorsen party heading north by northwest up Nansen Sound toward Arctic ice. Observe but do not close—repeat, observe but do not close. Air reconnaissance to begin immediately around the clock. Also give Home Plate on classified frequency the gist of that order. Got it?"

"Aye, sir."

"Home Plate? Who is that?"

"Apollo Security Control, the boys anchoring this party."

Buckner frowned, not sure whether to pursue the question further or not. Then he said, "I still don't understand why Thorsen is taking that specific route to the Pole, if in fact he is trying for it."

"Because it's the Frederick Cook route. You know, of course, that Frederick Cook claimed to have reached the Pole in 1908, ahead of Admiral Peary?" Buckner did not respond, because he wasn't up on polar exploration history, and he wasn't sure it was relevant anyway. Fish, sensing his hesitation, went on quickly. "Well, Cook always said it was the only way to go. His claim has been disputed, but looking at it now it seems to be a more plausible route, and Nels Thorsen is a strong defendant of Cook's claim over Peary's. So I suppose he will try—if you'll forgive my speculations—to kill two birds with one stone: reach the Pole in order to do his thing there and at the same time prove that Cook could also have made it by that route."

Buckner shrugged. Polar exploration seemed insignificant in view of the larger picture.

"Why didn't you intercept Thorsen before he got to Greenland?"

Fish paused, weighing the question as if he had turned it over many times himself. "Well, nobody knew where Thorsen went when he disappeared from Houston. It was

8

three days before anyone realized he was gone. It took another two weeks before Apollo Security figured out that he could be heading for Greenland."

"That's pretty slow."

"General, I don't run Apollo Security." Fish spoke mildly enough, but it was apparent that he had been smarting over the same point. "The fact is, before anybody could make any kind of move, Thorsen was already on Greenland territory at Smith Sound and it was too late to jump him."

"How long are you going to wait?"

Fish hesitated, staring at the map again. "Until we can get close enough for a good shot," he said finally. "It's a sure thing I'm not going to try for a duck shoot from the air—and our people won't close with Thorsen on the ice to try it either. That man is an expert glaciologist; he knows the Arctic like the back of his hand. Nobody is going to get close to him, even within cannon range, without his knowing it, and even if we were lucky enough to get in range but missed, he could explode the rock right there."

"You going to let the Russians get to him?"

"The Russians are supposed to be cooperating with us on this, remember? After all, if Thorsen does blow that rock anywhere on the ice, the effect on the world could be devas—"

"Admiral, I know all that," Buckner said impatiently. "I was briefed too, remember?"

Fish shrugged. "All right. The Russians can't risk an explosion on the ice any more than we can, that's all I'm saying. But you can be sure they're thinking that they can get both Thorsen and the rock for themselves, right? You talk about hot rocks; how'd you like to stumble onto a piece of silicon carrying enough nuclear energy to make the hydrogen bomb look like a squib firecracker? And all in a rock the size of a grapefruit?"

"I'm still asking," Buckner insisted. "Are you going to let the Russians close in on him?"

"Well," Fish replied, with a sigh, "somewhere along

the line to the Pole that Cook followed, or said he followed, we'll have to make our move. Thorsen doesn't have a team of ice experts with him. He's got maybe a couple of Eskimos; the rest are starry-eyed college kids who think this is all a lark to put a hole in the establishment. Besides that, Thorsen is running with only five sleds, and that's not enough to carry the supplies he'll need to keep them all alive on the run to the Pole. It's a good five hundred miles from where he is now. A few good snowstorms, some losses of equipment, food, ice hazards, and frostbite, and Thorsen may wind up going it alone—and that's when he becomes most vulnerable."

"Where and when are you going to intercept him?"

"That's up to Otto Dietrich to decide."

"Dietrich?"

"The man in charge of Home Plate, Houston Apollo Security. He's somewhere out in Greenland himself, but we don't know where and we aren't supposed to. Could be up at Point Alert or maybe down at Eureka on Ellesmere Island, west of us. Dietrich knows the Arctic almost as well as Thorsen, and Dietrich is an avid if not fanatical supporter of Admiral Peary's claim to the Pole, if that interests you at all."

"What has Dietrich done up to now?" Buckner was growing impatient.

Fish shrugged again. "All we know is that he got an agent from Interpol. Actually Interpol insisted on getting into it, because they were sure the Russians were making a play. The agent is an Israeli, and a woman to boot."

Buckner glanced at him quickly. "You're not going to tell me Thorsen is a dirty old man who will tumble to a woman in the end?"

Fish grunted. "Not quite, General. Dietrich probably feels a woman is low key, right now, and has a better chance to get near Thorsen than a man. Anyway, she's been dropped this side of Bradley Island at a point we can expect Thorsen to cross on his way north. Maybe within a week, if Thorsen keeps going in the poor light—which he probably will—she could intercept him."

"So she just walks up to Thorsen, introduces herself, and puts a bullet into him?"

Fish yawned. "The girl will have her own way of doing it, I'm sure. Dietrich knows how to get everything in line. At any rate, Thorsen, as careful as he is, will probably— I say probably—take a second look at a marooned girl out there, right?" Buckner did not respond. "Anyway, we better hope she can pull it off, or we've got ourselves a sticky business, wouldn't you say?" Buckner again ignored the question, so Fish continued. "In the meantime, we keep constant air recon on Thorsen, if we can. I would like five military units, skilled ice people and crack shots, trailing Thorsen all the time. When it comes down to zero, whether or not Dietrich says so, we're going to have to make a move on Thorsen and try to get him before he can blow the rock. And, of course, it'll have to be done before the Russians, or even the Chinese, get close."

"Chinese?"

Fish pulled down another sliding red marker and let it rest over Spitsbergen Island off to the east. "A Chinese expeditionary force was cleared in here a week ago. They're supposed to be studying water temperatures in the Greenland Sea. But that could allow them a lot of latitude."

Buckner stared up at the red marker, amazed, if not a little irritated, that Fish could recite all this as if it were a classroom exercise.

"So when is zero?" Buckner finally asked.

"When Thorsen reaches the Big Nail."

"The what?"

"The Big Nail, what the Eskimos call the North Pole, some four hundred thirty miles from the shore of Ellesmere and Point Sverdrup—just about where Thorsen will be in two days—and approximately forty days' travel for Thorsen with his dog teams. That is, if he can make ten miles minimum a day. Thorsen's aim, according to Dietrich, is to knock a hole in the delicate gyro of the world. And don't ask me what possesses a renowned scientist and glaciologist to do that, okay?"

11

Buckner did not comment. He could only ponder the magnitude of the problem—all that ice, that thin red line running up the white surface of the map indicating the route Thorsen was expected to take, the "old Cook route," to the Pole. With those odds, one woman seemed hardly worth betting on. When he glanced at Fish's impassive face, he was sure the admiral was thinking the same thing.

U.S.S.R.

SP-6
RUSSIAN ICE ISLAND ★

NORTH
POLE ✠

ICE ISLAND
T-3 ★

SPITSBERGEN
ISLAND

EUROPE

AXEL HEIBERG
ISLAND

NANSEN SOUND
EUREKA
SMITH SOUND
THULE

ZZZZ BIG LEAD

ALASKA

ELLESMERE
ISLAND

GREENLAND

NORTH AMERICA

➤➤➤➤ THORSEN ROUTE
--------- SEBASTIAN AIR DROP
•••••••••▷ RUSSIAN INTERCEPT
∘∘∘∘∘∘∘∘∘▷ CHINESE INTERCEPT

1

He knew he was about one hundred miles south of the Arctic Ocean's shore, somewhere on Ellesmere Island, one hundred miles or so west of Thule, in a place called the Eureka Weather Station. He remembered that much, a slice of cognition that had stuck with him in the blur of time he had spent in the air, crossing miles and miles of territory that held no familiar landmarks. He also knew that from October to February, Eureka lay locked in by the sullen Arctic, which leaned on it with relentless blasts of frigid cold as low as 70 degrees below zero. Even in spring and summer, if such seasons are worth mentioning there, Eureka huddled out of habit, its three Quonset shacks housing the few weather personnel who were game enough to take the duty, but not bothering to offer any real expectation of shelter. Someone had told him all about that too—or had he read it?

He had lost his sense of time and place. He could smell the moldy straw mattress under him, feel puffs of cold air coming up through the rustic floorboards. He lifted himself up on his elbows, opening one eye at a time, peering at the red glow of the potbellied stove in the far corner that looked like a single eye of mean intent.

He thought he had slept. But he wasn't sure. He felt the gummy pressure of the plugs in his ears and reached up with his right hand and touched the cords running down under the bed into the receiver unit in the wall.

15

There was no sound coming through this morning, but he vaguely remembered going to sleep the night before as instructed, with the plugs in place, and hearing the monotone voice:

"The polar ice north of Greenland, covering the Arctic Ocean, is a vast wilderness of frozen waste, frozen winds, and huge cliffs of choppy ice that has broken the back of many a courageous explorer. The treachery of the polar sea does not lie there readily discernible. It appears to be a flat plain of white, disarming at first in its placidity, lying cold and deathlike, beckoning the would-be explorer to taste the delights of winter sport. But, once on it, there come the nightmarish miles of rolling ice, long black patches of water breaking open from ice floes, murderous storms that whip winds up to eighty miles an hour and drop temperatures to as much as eighty degrees below zero. . . ."

He could almost recite the entire narrative just as it had been repeated over and over to him while he slept. He removed the ear plugs, glad to be rid of them, and let his neck drop back. His eyes caught the light in the ceiling again, that peculiar gyration of yellows and reds and blues melting into a montage of color that neither jarred nor comforted him. There was something about that light, the way it turned in slow cycles like a carousel, something diabolical about it, even. He remembered that when he had climbed into his bunk—what time was it, last night or the night before?—and lain back to stare at it, the ear plugs in place, he had wondered why it was there.

"It's a heat gyrator," the sergeant had told him simply. What was a heat gyrator? It seemed even more important that he know the answer now that he was awake, even more than when he went to sleep. But he didn't know why.

He lay back on his pillow again, his eyes watching that light, held to it; he really did want to know what it was all about. Then he glanced at the ear plugs on the pillow beside him.

"Worse yet is the short duration of open ice on the Arctic. From late February to early May is the only time

16

an explorer can make it to the Pole and back to Greenland's shores again. To get caught out on the ice during the thaw is to ask for sure death—either by being dumped into frigid waters as the ice breaks up without warning or by being trapped by impassable open leads of water."

Yes, he could remember most of it. But was that all? What else could have passed through his head during sleep? Was it all pure ice topography, as Dietrich said it would be? "Learn while you sleep, for there isn't enough time during the day." Dietrich had said that . . . in a room that was as nondescript as a monk's cell, somewhere in this place. . . . When was it?

"Your letters to Professor Thorsen in Houston were intercepted by our security, so we know about your concern for him. How well do you know Thorsen, Mr. Sebastian?"

"He taught me geology back in university."

"And he flunked you, correct?"

"Yes. It was because I would not accept the evolution theory of determining the origin of man. My written term report did not substantiate that principle. Instead I insisted on the Genesis creation theory. You have to remember I was pretty young then."

"That was twenty years ago, as we have been able to trace it. You have not seen him since?"

"Three years ago he wrote me to come and try to help his older son, who was mired in drug addiction."

"He had two sons with that problem."

"I know. But the older of the two was about to blow his mind."

"Why would he ask you for help if he was so hostile to you and your faith back in college?"

"I don't know. I guess he was desperate enough to try anything."

"And you did not succeed in helping him?"

"No. I just couldn't get through to that boy's mind, already so burned out by drugs."

"What did Professor Thorsen say to your failure?"

"Nothing. All he did was thank me for trying."

"But it didn't do much to convince him that your God was the God of miracles, after all?"

"If anything, I think he had even less confidence in me as God's espoused instrument for that miracle."

"You must have left an impression on him if after twenty years he should remember you."

"He couldn't stand my Christian view of the world. He thought I was ridiculously naïve, as he put it, and a poor example of a student. We argued a lot, in and out of class."

"And he became so hostile toward you that he prevented you from gaining admission to graduate school, correct?"

"If you know it all, Mr. Dietrich, why bother going on with this?"

"Would he be hostile to you now?"

"I don't think so. I don't know. . . . He wasn't hostile toward me when I tried to help his son."

"Would he consider you a friend or an enemy if he saw you now?"

"I don't see why he would consider me an enemy."

"Well, then, if he does not believe as you do, or sympathize with your theological position, why are you so concerned for him?"

"I have always respected him—"

"Or is it that you feel you can maybe score some points by trying to help him? Maybe now you feel you can snatch him from the burning and win his soul for God?"

"You don't know Professor Thorsen very well if you think that."

"But I know quite a bit about you, Mr. Sebastian. I've checked out your theological pedigree, and I think I am not too far out of line by saying that your work falls into that class of religious zealousness that smacks of exploitation, correct?"

"I would not put it like that."

"The point is that we cannot afford to clutter up any of this with ulterior motives. And I know that for you it

18

would be quite a feather in your cap if Thorsen were to become a Christian on top of his being such a renowned scientist."

"Then you really do not know me at all, Mr. Dietrich. The last time I saw Professor Thorsen he was almost broken by the hopeless problem of his son. I told him then I would help him at any time I could."

"You know he is on his way to the North Pole?"

"The papers said only that he was missing."

"And that he is also carrying a moon rock that is highly lethal?"

"The papers said he had the rock. . . . I don't know anything about its being lethal."

"Fifteen times the power of the five-megaton bomb we exploded at Amchitka Island two years ago, to be exact."

"What does that mean, exactly?"

"It means that if it blew up in Chicago, the entire city and everything within a six-hundred-mile radius would be totally wiped out. Fallout would put the rest of the continent in near disaster. The world as a whole would feel the shock, because such a blast would come awfully close to triggering chain reactions in our molecular structure."

"All that in a moon rock?"

"Yes, all that, Mr. Sebastian. When the last Apollo journey to the moon returned home with the usual load of rocks—normally they are harmless pieces of meteor deposits—these apparently were structured energy cells that remain docile in the oxygen-free atmosphere of the moon but are subject to rapid deterioration when exposed to oxygen. When the astronauts took those rocks into the command capsule, they sealed them into oxygen-free containers. But one piece, maybe a millionth of a milligram, was dropped. When it made contact with the oxygen atmosphere of the capsule, it blew up, knocking out machinery and making a shambles of the interior. The papers, as you know, told the heroic story of how those men fought to get it all back together again and return

19

to earth. We had no idea that the moon rocks were responsible until Professor Thorsen himself made the discovery."

"But why is he carrying one of those rocks to the Arctic?"

"To detonate it at the North Pole."

"Why?"

"Are you aware of the decline of Thorsen's health in the last year?"

"He wrote me after his son committed suicide—that was about nine months ago. He wrote me again two months afterward, when his wife died from the shock. I wrote him back, but I got no reply."

"All right, does this paragraph from his journal at least confirm that he is dangerously ill? I quote: 'I am convinced that man is running out of history and that science is moving in to destroy his sense of humanity and even decency. We have lost our way and must be brought back together again. If we are to survive as a civilization, it will take a colossus in nature that will bring universal adversity and thus force a banding together of all races into a new bond of community. Perhaps it is time now that I become the instrument for such renewal.' "

"That doesn't say anything about his going to the North Pole."

"Here is a photocopy of a map he had drawn only a month ago; it shows the exact route he was contemplating to the Pole. We also found a dozen volumes in his office, propounding various theories about the effects of sudden ice melt at either pole and the stress of energy release, particularly its effects on the earth's crust."

"So you are concluding that Professor Thorsen has chosen to set off a seventy-five-megaton bomb at the Pole to give the world a common challenge for survival and to bring back the values of community?"

"It seems clear enough, Mr. Sebastian. You know he always used to say that his boy had had it too easy in life, no challenge. He said many times that he should have given him something to fight for."

20

"I cannot totally disagree with him on that."

"Do you, a man of God, believe that world calamity, the deliberate destruction of lives, is the only way?"

"I am not sure that disaster of such magnitude is possible even if Professor Thorsen would dare to contemplate it."

"Allow me to enlarge in layman's terms, then: The world spins on its axis because of the centrifugal force of ice at both the Arctic and the Antarctic poles. As long as ice melts and breaks off in the amounts nature has set, that force is not affected. And even if it should suffer a freak accident in nature, scientists say there is a bulge in the earth's surface, just about at the equator, which will absorb that shock and keep the crust of the earth from cracking. We do not know how much of a shock that bulge can take, but we are sure a seventy-five-megaton explosion is far too much stress. Beyond the chain of devastating earthquakes that would result across the world, we would also have to cope with all that ice melting at once and rushing into the Atlantic. We would have hundred-foot tides on all shorelines, putting cities under water. On top of that, altered tides of that magnitude would play havoc with the delicate balance of climate, thus affecting crop production and ushering in worldwide famine. And I have not yet said anything about what an explosion of that size could do to jar the axis of the earth."

"Professor Thorsen would not be the instrument to such destruction, no matter how sick—"

"Do you want to wait and see?"

"I'd like to hear it from Thorsen himself."

"All right. In any case, that is why you are here, is it not?"

"I allowed myself to get carried off my flight to Houston at O'Hare Airport by your men two nights ago and flown a couple of thousand miles north without one word of explanation. I should think my purposes in allowing that are clear enough, even as your hijacking is now obvious."

21

"Very well, we are clear on that, then. Let us be clear on one other point. As distasteful as it may be, when you get to Thorsen—if you do—you must be prepared to kill him on the spot."

"You know I cannot do that."

"You are the one man Thorsen knows and will recognize as some kind of neutral element. Perhaps no one else in the world right now has the opportunity you do."

"If Professor Thorsen has, in fact, gone mad, I doubt he will accept me any more than his own mother."

"But there is that one chance, and if we have any odds at all, they are on you, and you must take it!"

"I do not intend to walk up to the man I have tried to reach with the love of God and blow his head off, Mr. Dietrich!"

"Then what are you going to do? Hold an evangelistic meeting out there on the ice? You claim Christianity! Then act in its spirit! One man's life is surely worth taking if it will save millions! Is that not the same sum total as the redemptive act of Jesus?"

"Don't pander to me now, Mr. Dietrich. If you want to murder Thorsen, do it yourself. He knows you too."

"He knows me as Director of Apollo Security. Do you think he will let me get within a mile of him without breaking the seal on that rock?"

"I will not murder Professor Thorsen. I will try to catch up with him, reason with him—"

"And if reason fails, what then?"

"Then I will do my best to capture him, short of killing him."

"Do you think we haven't tried to devise a way to do that? The only way to take him without killing him would be with a special tranquilizing dart that can be fired with fairly good accuracy at fifty yards. But the fastest time for a tranquilizer to work is six seconds, Mr. Sebastian. It takes only three seconds for a man bent on destruction to break the seal on that rock, and you can bet Thorsen will have it close at hand."

"I will try to catch up with him, Mr. Dietrich, but from then on I'll play it by ear."

"You are the only man, the only hope for any of us—for the world, in fact. I ask you to think carefully about that, even in the name of God."

"I said not to try to manipulate me on theological grounds, Mr. Dietrich."

"Very well! Perhaps you are not the right man, after all. All I can suggest to you is that you sleep on it; maybe in the morning you will have come to your senses. But I say again: your only recourse is to kill him, do you understand me? You must—yes, in the name of God and the saving of humanity—kill him!"

Kill him? He opened his eyes again. It seemed colder in the room. The pinwheels of light continued to dig into his brain like a giant screw working its careful revolutions deeper and deeper, each turn seeming to command some new territory within him. He felt no resistance to Dietrich's order any more. For some reason, it even seemed right. There wouldn't be another opportunity with Thorsen. . . .

There was a knock on the door and someone shouted, "Breakfast is on, sir!"

"Very well."

He got up, feeling the chill in the room. The cold from the wooden floorboards penetrated the heavy woolen socks he had worn to bed. Even the thermal underwear he had on was no protection against it.

He got up and walked to the stove and stood there by the heat. The gyrating light followed him, each turn saying over and over: Kill him . . . kill him . . . kill him.

He glanced at the side table; the gun was still there. The sergeant had left it the night before with a mumbled, "You may want to check it over, get acquainted with it, sir." He had left it where the sergeant had put it.

Now he walked over to it slowly, picked it up in both hands. It felt heavy. He knew little about weapons of any kind. This one was pistol-shaped but had a long barrel, like an air gun he once had used as a boy. He fumbled with the breech and snapped it open, the sound of it startling him in the cold, quiet room. He hefted it in his

23

right hand, then his left. Yes, maybe there was something right about the feel of it. . . .

He put the gun down on the table again and walked into the small bathroom cubicle and turned on the wall heater and stood looking at himself in the mirror, not even sure of his own reflection. Yes, it was the same face —the high cheekbones, the blue-green eyes set into slightly receding sockets, the Lincolnlike gauntness to his cheeks, the almost hawklike nose, the high forehead and tangled black hair that fell around his ears and over the nape of his neck—yes, the same. But what—God!—what was so different about him now? What illusive element would not rise for identification; what part of himself was pounded down, flattened out, and buried deep in his brain, beyond his own power to recall? Was that "something" important to him? Or was it just the cold, the change, the preoccupation of the night with the polar Arctic taught to him by tape while he slept?

He shaved with the battery-powered razor provided for him, frowning at himself in the mirror, thinking of Professor Thorsen. Dietrich had come close to the truth; there was no question that he had waited a long time to make his point about the reality of God to this scientist, this one man who had made his undergraduate years so miserable, in the classroom and out. There was no question either that he had waited equally long for the professor to come to a point of humility in his life about the ultimate mastery of God in the universe. But was Dietrich also right in his suggestion that he was chasing Thorsen mainly because he was enamored with the idea that a man like Thorsen, won to Christianity, would be a trophy the world could hardly ignore? Perhaps. But why be so beautifully idealistic about it? Was there not also a bit of holy vengeance here too? He had never before used a man's suffering or deprivation as a wedge for declaring the credulity of Christ; he left that to the skid row preachers. Yet he knew there was a strong ingredient of this in what he was thinking about Thorsen. Well, what was he expecting to happen out on the ice, once he con-

24

fronted Thorsen? That the older man would behold a man of God bearing down on him, if in fact he did recognize Sebastian, and then crack up into a blubbering, compliant, repentant pagan scientist too overwhelmed by the gesture of godly concern to resist the claims of God?

"Come off it," he said to himself in the mirror. The sound of his voice startled him. It sounded caustic, as if he were smothering a laugh over a very bad joke.

For the first time since he had put his clergy cloth aside, along with his sermon notes, and taken on the mantle of a churchman's James Bond, Sebastian felt doubt. Maybe Dietrich was responsible, with those probing, surgical words, laying him open to doubts about his primary motivations. Maybe it was nothing more than the loneliness he was beginning to feel in these adventures; the fact that those he once knew in the ministry, including his own father, had nothing much commendable to say about his exploits. To them, as one magazine put it, his "gallivanting with strange partners in international Cold War adventures was a long way around at best to declaring the redemption of Christ." In fact his own father had said, trying to make it kind, "You are offering a strange mixture of spirituality and international politics that seems to muddy your cause rather than sharpen and enlarge it."

What would "his cause" end up to be if he did, in fact, kill Thorsen out there on the ice? If he did manage to save the world its holocaust, and maybe be praised for his act, would he stand taller as a man of God? Maybe here was the pit of his doubt: there were better assassins than himself, men more capable of pulling it off, men more suitable to the task than he who was supposed to preserve life, not destroy it. Why was he even bothering to entertain the possibility?

He remembered the two letters he had received from Thorsen a couple of months back; they reflected an increasing amount of confusion and imbalance. There were words of either self-destruction or intent to destruction, sometimes coupled with phrases that bordered on paranoia. It was all so completely different from the well-controlled demeanor of this scientist, who had never before shown the slightest ripple of mental or emotional concern, regardless of the stresses of life. Would the loss of his son to drugs, and the death of his wife a few months later, affect his personality that drastically? It could. . . .

In any case, the letters were not at all identifiable with the man who was honored only three years ago at the Geophysical Congress in Denmark for his contributions to world science. They did not even reflect the man Sebastian remembered from the classroom and from that time a few years back when he had tried to help his son.

But the fact remained: *Thorsen had written to him.* That point seemed to puzzle Otto Dietrich too, because there was no reason for him to do it. Except, again, maybe Thorsen was turning in desperation to a source he felt he could trust. Maybe, unable to understand what was happening to him, he was seeking help, even as he did for his son, from an area that was free from the entanglements of science, moon rocks, the pressures of Apollo Security. Yet not once did Thorsen mention God in those letters or in any way indicate his need for divine assistance. What was he expecting Sebastian to do?

Maybe nothing. At any rate, the fact remained that he was not going to wait for help from anyone. If Dietrich was right, Thorsen was on a beeline for the Pole to blow a hole in the delicate gyro system of the earth. So it all came down to one issue: Thorsen had to be stopped, as Dietrich had put it so bluntly, and maybe it was better that he, Sebastian, be the man to attempt it, even if it did mean pulling the trigger on him in the end. It was, after all, the larger picture he had to think of—the world itself and the millions who would die if he did not.

But even with that conclusion, he could not fully rise to it, even though the idea of killing was no longer repulsive to him. He looked intently at his eyes in the mirror. Why wasn't it repulsive to him? How could he stand here shaving, performing the simple acts of com-

26

mon toilet, and accommodate himself to the death of another human being by his own hand?

He finally sought refuge in the shower, turning the cold spray on himself, resisting the shock and yet hoping it would shake loose the weblike fuzz that seemed to encase his brain.

When he finished, he dressed quickly, pulling on the warm clothing that was set out for him, although he didn't know where on his body some of it was supposed to go. Finally, when he was through, he felt the need to read from his pocket New Testament, to lay hold of added spiritual strength, to find balance and order. He hunted for it in his small flight bag. It was not there. He went through his one suitcase. Nothing. He checked the room carefully. He sat down on the bed, staring at the cold antiseptic room, conscious more than ever that something was definitely at work that was beyond him, beyond his capacity to define. He tried to get his mind to reach into memory for a scriptural passage to counteract his sense of imbalance, but nothing would come. . . .

Then there was another commanding knock on the door and the voice said, "Mr. Sebastian, Mr. Dietrich is waiting breakfast for you."

He rose slowly from the bed, scratching his head idly, knowing he had to dismiss whatever he felt because of the demands of the moment. His course, as in other times, had to be left to God. He moved to the door, passing the table where the gun still lay, its gray-black sheen giving it a metallic glow of newness and readiness and proficiency. He meant to leave it, then paused, looked at it again, and finally picked it up in his left hand and walked through the door.

Breakfast was hot oatmeal with raisins, topped off with a small chocolate bar and a cup of hot water in which a coffee cube had been melted. It was, as Dietrich put it, "the kind of meal you will have out on the ice, high in calories." Sebastian ate it without comment, but even more than he was conscious of the third man at the table,

27

he was conscious of Otto Dietrich across from him, hearing his steady stream of words, unhurried but rippling along with some destination in mind. Dietrich had a large face with a broad nose and a small mouth that remained in a pleasant line but did not carry many smiles in reserve; his horn-rimmed glasses emphasized large grayish eyes that had a tendency to stare with commanding intent. Sebastian avoided the eyes most of the time, but he didn't know why. They never smiled either, not even when the mouth wiggled in a condescending spasm; maybe that's where the mask of pleasantry ended. He was dressed in heavy brown corduroy with a red woolen scarf around his neck and a heavy yellow woolen sweater pulled tightly around his upper torso. He looked like an Alpine guide lecturing tourists on the finesse of mountain climbing.

". . . so it is good you have decided to go, Mr. Sebastian." He went on as if all he had been saying about the way to eat while moving on polar ice was a proper preamble for it.

"Good, very good," the other man said, the man Dietrich referred to as "Landau, our logistics man." Landau had a thin face with a long pointed nose that was always red from the cold and which he had to wipe continually with a soggy handkerchief while he ate his steaming oatmeal. His eyes were watery brown and small, and they blinked too often, as if his brain were always short-circuiting.

"And that is the best weapon for the business," Dietrich added, putting a spoonful of oatmeal into his mouth, indicating the gun sitting on the table with just a flick of his gray eyes.

"I don't even know how to fire it," Sebastian said.

"That will come," Dietrich replied quickly. "The main point is that you are prepared to use it . . . correct?"

Landau paused in his eating to stare into his gruel as if waiting for something.

"I will do what I must do, Mr. Dietrich."

Landau nodded, as if satisfied, and went back to his oatmeal.

28

"But you have not told me yet how I am supposed to get to Thorsen. I know nothing of travel on polar ice."

"Judging from your exploits in the Negev, your adventures with those Cubans in a midget submarine, and that fantastic episode in Berlin, lack of knowledge has never affected your success," Dietrich replied, his mouth wiggling into spasm again.

"I know how to run fast, Mr. Dietrich, but on polar ice, if what I learned while I slept is correct, that is a cumbersome way to maintain mobility."

"You have learned well," Dietrich replied, in a tone of satisfaction. "It says much for the theory that the brain absorbs whatever it gets even when the body lies comatose. . . . Right, Landau?"

Landau shrugged and wiped at his nose with his handkerchief, his eyes blinking uncertainly, first at Dietrich, then at Sebastian.

"In any case, we intend to fly you to a point we believe Thorsen will cross on his way north in a few days." Dietrich got up, dabbed at his mouth with his paper napkin, and walked to his neat table a few feet behind him. There he punched a button on a small box panel that sat on his empty desk top, and a huge map of the Arctic Ocean and Greenland descended from the ceiling. There was a black line running a weaving course north and a big blue X to mark Thorsen's position. Beyond the blue X was a red one a little farther north of it, where Sebastian supposed Dietrich meant to drop him. "The black line is Thorsen's expected route," Dietrich said.

"Frederick Cook's old route," Sebastian commented.

"You know about that?"

"Professor Thorsen's favorite lecture years ago was about Cook."

"Cook's claim to the North Pole in 1908 ahead of Peary was considered a hoax," Dietrich replied shortly, dismissing it.

"Professor Thorsen always claimed that Cook's route had less formidable ice barriers, so it was easier and quicker to travel."

Dietrich hit another button on the panel and a mural-sized blown-up photo slid down out of the ceiling, next to the map of the Arctic. Sebastian studied the jagged mounds of ice and snow; it looked like a picture of a giant boneyard witnessing to the last stand of a herd of dinosaurs.

"That is the ice barrier on Cook's supposedly easier route," Dietrich explained flatly.

"Well, at least Professor Thorsen is going to prove something about that one way or the other."

"The point is irrelevant," Dietrich snapped. "It's all part of the dementia Thorsen has plaguing him. In any case, a man sixty-three years of age is not going to prove much out there, of that you can be sure."

Sebastian thought Dietrich seemed more testy than he should be for something so "irrelevant."

"I assume you are dropping me on the big red X?" Sebastian decided to get to the point. "How do I travel from there, by snowmobile?"

"Absolutely not. That kind of equipment would be useless in the screw ice you see here. You will go by dog team and sled. Besides, if Thorsen saw you coming on motorized equipment, he would assume you were military. Dogs and sleds are the Eskimo way of traveling, and Thorsen knows it."

"I still don't know anything about traveling on ice."

"Fortunately we have an Eskimo guide for you who knows the Arctic better than anyone else. He spent five years at Thule Air Force Base here in Greenland as special guide to Air Force units. He knows English, but he has never forgotten the Eskimo ways of staying alive on the ice."

"One man only?"

"We could give you a dozen, but what good would that do? A small party will seem like less of a threat. Only the two of you, yes, with two dog teams and two sleds. It will look like an Eskimo hunting trip. I don't expect you to stay out more than a week anyway, Mr. Sebastian. You will have to intercept Thorsen, or you will have failed. If he slips by you, you will never be able to

30

approach him from the rear. He'll be looking behind him all the time from where he expects us to be in pursuit. Ah-Ming knows that too."

"Ah-Ming?"

"Ah-Ming-Ma, the Eskimo guide. The name means musk-ox, but there's no resemblance."

"And radio contact? How do I stay in touch?"

"You will have one small radio. But you are not to try to communicate with us at any time prior to getting Thorsen. He could be listening in, and once he hears you trying to raise us, your hand is tipped. But you can listen to our air reconnaissance reports of his position during the day. That way you might be able to judge his position in relationship to yours."

"How?"

"Well, we will be putting you down at eighty-four degrees, thirty minutes north, fifty-seven degrees, five minutes west. Any report of the longitude-latitude change, either to higher or lower figures along that line, will give you some idea, correct? At least you will know if he got by you."

Sebastian wasn't too sure of the navigational lingo, but he let it go.

"I take it I carry only a week's supply of fuel and food?"

"If you should need help, you will have to use the radio, but I would avoid that until you are sure your situation is hopeless."

"Are we the only ones looking for Thorsen?"

"No. The Russians are on the move here"—and Dietrich indicated a spot on the map—"the Chinese are here, and there is one Interpol agent here, about fifty miles north of your drop. We have notified her in code that she is to remain there and intercept Thorsen in case you miss him."

"She?"

"Yes, a woman. . . . Besides her, our own military units are staying back on the trail a good ten miles behind Thorsen, waiting to go in if they have to. If the Russians

31

get too close, we will have to take a chance of getting Thorsen—so you see why it is important that you don't waste any time in getting the job done. If the Russians, Chinese, and Americans all reached Thorsen at the same time—well, you can imagine what a shoot-out like that could do. Now, if there are no further questions, you need to get checked out on that weapon there; also, you need to be briefed on what you are carrying in supplies and so forth."

"How about this Ah-Ming? When do I get to see him?"

Dietrich looked at Landau, who simply shrugged again and sniffed loudly. "Right now, if you like."

Sebastian got up and followed Dietrich out the door, stopping only to pick up the gun from the table where he had left it, feeling Landau watching him as he did so. They went through an outer foyer that led into what appeared to be a supply warehouse. Stacks of boxes lined both walls, along with sleds and barrels of gasoline, and there were mounds of Arctic cold-weather clothing on tables in the center of the room. Dietrich moved on in his brisk pace to a far corner, asked one of the military men a question, then continued over to another corner where some burlap bags were piled against the wall.

When Sebastian came up behind him, he saw there was somebody or something lying on the bags, bundled up in a heavy fur parka and heavy fur pants. The odor emanating from it was a mingling of dead fish and alcohol.

"Ah-Ming-Ma!" Dietrich said in his commanding tone and reached out his booted right foot and kicked hard. The mound of fur stirred a little, protesting the prodding. Finally, after five or six kicks, the head came up and Sebastian saw a leathery brown face encased in the parka hood, looking shrunken and cracked from the Arctic weather. A strip of straight, coarse black hair, like bangs, fell across the forehead, poking out of the parka hood like bristles on a push broom. The eyes were small, almost slanted, each black pupil looking like a thumbtack

32

jammed carelessly into a sclera laced with jagged streaks of red. There seemed to be a coat of black soot on the skin, as if it had been hanging over an open fire for too many years.

"Whoopee," the voice croaked out of the fur parka, but it was only a statement of fact, not particularly enthusiastic, just a caustic commentary on what he must be feeling in his hangover.

"Come on, Ah-Ming." Dietrich prodded him again, giving the Eskimo's boot a kick. "Time to get to work."

"You're giving me a drunk to be my guide?" Sebastian asked, as the Eskimo's head dropped back on the burlap.

"Eskimos drink from the time of the beginning of the long winter night in October to the first sun in February," Dietrich replied with detachment. "That's all they've got to do. Drunk, they're useless, yes, and maybe Ah-Ming is worse than the rest of them, but not by much. Ever since he lost his wife and two children through the ice while they were hunting for seal four years ago, he's been a compulsive, mean drinker. But sober, as we expect to make him right now, he is the best there is on the ice. In fact, we would not trust this assignment to any other man up here. But as long as we are on the subject, let me remind you, Mr. Sebastian, lest I forget in the haste, to make sure he doesn't drink anything alcoholic while you are up there. If he should get the least bit pie-eyed, you've lost your one means to survive, let alone get to Thorsen. There is nothing worse than a drunken Eskimo out on the ice."

Sebastian did not comment. He looked down at the prostrate form of the Eskimo stretched there full length, no more than five feet four, bundled up in furs that made him appear like a child in a teddy bear costume. The black eyes were peering at him intently. "Whoopee," Ah-Ming said again, like a greeting, and he grinned, showing a gap in the front lower jaw where two teeth were missing. "Me Innuit."

Sebastian looked at Dietrich.

33

"Innuit in Eskimo means 'real man.' "

"You like good Eskimo broad, chief?" The voice croaked again, and the grin widened at Sebastian.

"Now, now," Dietrich cautioned and kicked the Eskimo's boot once more. "No time for Eskimo broads, Ah-Ming." And Dietrich gave Sebastian one of those meaningless spasm smiles.

"Eskimo broad very good," Ah-Ming insisted, his eyes never leaving Sebastian.

Sebastian folded his arms and smiled down at the Eskimo. "You look as if you've had too much Eskimo broad already."

The Eskimo grinned, and then a cackle came out of him.

"Hee-hee—heee! *Ka-aga!*" And he lifted one small, grubby, smoky hand toward Dietrich.

"Well, he says come on, let's go," Dietrich said, pulling Ah-Ming upright. "You must have said the right thing so far."

Ah-Ming-Ma stood up unsteadily, the top of his head coming up no higher than Sebastian's shoulder. The smell of alcohol and dead fish was overpowering. The Eskimo looked up intently into Sebastian's face again and then belched loudly. The full force of the gaseous expulsion was enough to knock Sebastian down.

"I need a drink," Ah-Ming said thickly, as if what he had seen in Sebastian's face had given him a jolt he wanted to forget.

"Sergeant!" Dietrich called across the crowded warehouse. A big sergeant came over quickly. "Get him into the steam room and keep him there until he's sober."

"Right, sir."

"Stem?" Ah-Ming repeated, resisting the sergeant's grip on his arm. "No want stem . . . want drink . . . stem kill you . . . kill ice . . . kill Innuit. . . ."

"Drink later," the sergeant said and pulled the Eskimo along. Sebastian watched as they struggled across the warehouse, Ah-Ming moving in an unsteady, bow-legged gait, not able to fight off the big sergeant's heavy

34

hand. Once at the other side of the room he turned his head to look back, and that sloppy, broken-toothed grin flashed in comical farewell.

"Whoopee! Li'e stem!" His voice rang across the warehouse, and then he turned again and stumbled on to the sergeant's prodding like a little boy trying to resist a bath.

"We could wish we had more going for you," Dietrich said.

"I'm used to his kind," Sebastian said simply. "I would be a little disappointed, I suppose, if I had anybody but him."

Dietrich, puzzled, glanced at him as they moved across the warehouse back to his office. Then he said, "All things come to him who waits, I suppose."

Sebastian didn't understand this, so he glanced back at Dietrich, but there was no intent to enlarge. The remark was harmless enough, but somehow to Sebastian it struck a false note. There was something wrong about Dietrich, or maybe even about himself, in the operation at hand. But there was no way he could make sure. Time had him by the throat, and only God knew where it was all going to end.

2

Otto Dietrich decided he would put Sebastian and Ah-Ming-Ma on the ice at 2:00 P.M. that same day, before full dark set in. It was after lunch when he told Sebastian of his decision. The winter sun would soon go below the horizon, while darkness began to show up in blotches against the horizon, putting a murky layer of misty fog over Eureka. Sebastian asked politely whether it was wise to try to land on the ice in such marginal light. Dietrich patiently, almost too patiently, pointed out that wasting another night at Eureka was only allowing Thorsen to get that much closer to the Pole. "Besides," he added, "we've got a weather buildup over Canada, and if it hits I'd rather have you up on the ice closer to the action than grounded here."

Sebastian could not argue the point. All morning he had tried to get as much information as he could on everything that was going into his equipment and materials to keep him alive on the polar ice cap. Everybody cooperated in briefing him, but, apparently because of the urgency of the operation and because Ah-Ming was going along, none of them went into details.

The two hours at the target range, practicing with the gun, were the exception. A man named Anderson explained the weapon as a "special model machine pistol, nine millimeter, suited for situations like this. The longer barrel, twelve inches, gives it better rifling so you get a

36

higher-velocity bullet traveling for you. It's made of light alloys so that it is not heavy, maybe four pounds with the magazine clipped in. You can carry it in your parka pocket, which is fourteen inches deep; it fits into a holster, here, which slides into the pocket easily. The important thing is not to show a weapon to Thorsen when you are approaching him, but to have it close enough to whip out when you have to. Since this magazine carries forty rounds and is automatic, we expect you to do your work well within ten feet of the target. On rapid-fire two-second bursts, you'll be throwing fifteen rounds at him per second. But the gun won't do much for you beyond ten feet." Anderson then fired a burst down the alley at the silhouette of the man on the platform a good twenty-five to thirty feet away. The bullet holes showed high up on the left shoulder. "And I've been shooting this thing for some time," Anderson commented. "Let's move up to ten feet and see how you do it."

It took time for Sebastian to practice clipping in the magazine and using the upward motion to get on target. Then he attempted a couple of two-second bursts. The gun bucked some in his hand, but after a few more attempts he found he was tearing the target to shreds around the chest area, which satisfied Anderson.

"You're not terrific," he finally said after what seemed a long time of working the gun; the stink of cordite was strong in the room and the noise was a ringing hum in Sebastian's ears. "But you'll do, I guess. Remember, don't try it beyond ten feet; that's the important thing. That gun was made for up close. But at short distances, I don't see how you can miss. One thing: you're kind of shaky shooting at a target up close. I guess you don't like looking into the eyeballs of your victim while shredding him with that thing, and that's understandable, considering. . . . Anyway, you get that close, you can close your eyes if you have to; the gun will do the rest."

Sebastian hardly heard him. He kept staring toward the torn target, not comprehending that he had done all that damage and unable to reconcile the fact that he would actually do that to Thorsen. Yet, he felt satisfied about it—for some reason.

He went on from there as directed, examining the material going into his survival pack. His clothing was laid out for him, each piece explained. His boots were called mukluks, the Eskimo kind, made of smoked moosehide and lined with innersoles of plastic mesh and wool felt designed to be removed and dried at the end of the day. Thermal underwear went on first, then a wool shirt and pants, followed by heavy woolen socks. Then canvas duck trousers went on to keep out the wet. The inner parka was made of light cotton. On top of that went the outer parka, which was knee length, made of poplin, and lined with Sherpa cloth. The hood was encircled with wolverine fur. Along with this came a face mask for ears, forehead, and chin; the mittens were wool-lined with an outer covering of leather.

Next came the food. There were cans of bacon and tuna bars, along with various kinds of soups, plus powdered cereals, mostly oatmeal. There were also emergency cans of pemmican, the Eskimo diet of seal blubber to provide calories and the necessary energy to withstand the cold. A few cans of chocolate were thrown in for good measure. "A bite of chocolate with that pemmican will help it go down better," Sebastian was told bluntly.

With the food and extra clothing were four five-gallon cans of fuel for the primus stoves. A couple of two-man tents, with caribou hides for the floor of each one, were included. One tent was for emergency use only, although nobody expected him to need it for that short a time on the ice and with an Eskimo guide along. In fact, nobody really told Sebastian how to set up those tents, how to work the stoves, what kind of diet was right or wrong. Everybody seemed to think Ah-Ming's going along made explanations unnecessary. It said a lot for Ah-Ming-Ma, but Sebastian felt uneasy in having to depend so heavily on the Eskimo.

It was early afternoon when Sebastian met Ah-Ming-Ma outside the Quonset where he was working with the two teams of sled dogs that would be going along. He looked the same, even when sober. His parka hood was pushed back, revealing the bramble of straight black horse-tail hair that fell around his ears. He had the stub of a cigar in the corner of his mouth, the imposed image of the American culture he had learned at Thule Air Force Base. His movements were not staggering or heavy as they had been earlier, under the grip of his hangover; they were quick and deft, and the crack of his voice commanding the twenty dogs was like pistol shots in the cold air.

"*Ingluc-tu!*" he said to Sebastian, grinning, showing that gaping parenthesis in his lower front teeth. "Cheer up!" he added, and he laughed. "Heee-heeee-he! The dogs are your friends! When you cold, they curl up with you, keep you warm. When you hungry, they make good stew. If you lost, they pull you like hell cuz they no want to be lost! He-hee-heee-he! Only thing dog needs to know who is master." And Ah-Ming leveled a sharp kick at one of the huskies which wouldn't yield to the sled harness and tried snapping at his hand. The dog yelped and settled back to take the harness line. When he got the team hooked up to the sled, he took time to find a match and light his cigar, his steaming breath mixing with the smoke, his thumbtack black eyes flicking toward Sebastian in quick observations of the man who was to be his companion on the ice.

Then he walked over to the sled and said, "This Eskimo sled called *kometic*. Best for ice, made of wood, very strong. *Ka-aga!* Come on, we go!" And he snapped a command to the dogs, which jumped into the harness and started off at a brisk pace, pulling the sled, the Eskimo pushing with them, Sebastian running alongside. "You no ride sled," Ah-Ming yelled at Sebastian after a short run. "Dogs soon hate you for giving them extra load. When it smooth ice and snow, you ride; they don't feel it . . . but most time you push and help dogs. They like you for it and work like hell to pull you to hell and back!"

Sebastian had to smile, though he felt cold to the

39

bone in the minus-fifty-degree temperature. Obviously Ah-Ming didn't know the occupation of the companion he was guiding out on the ice—or maybe it really didn't make any difference.

Sebastian took his turn getting behind the sled and shouting "Huk! Huk!" at the dogs. But the dogs seemed to sense he was an amateur hanging on behind, and they began to look over their shoulders at him. Soon they were drifting out of their fan-shaped harness link, and the two dogs directly behind the big lead husky started to fight, uncertain of command.

Ah-Ming went over and kicked both of them into submission, stripped off the harnesses, and dropped the lines into the snow. Walking back to Sebastian, he said, "Now you hook dogs, hokay?"

Sebastian found he had no rapport with the dogs at all. When he picked up the harness lines, they turned on him, snapping and snarling.

Ah-Ming stood off to one side, unmoving. "You do it yourself. If I do, they never let you touch them again."

Finally Sebastian approached the pack again, trying to ignore their snarls, trying to reach out to lay the harness lines to the lead husky, which kept its white teeth bared. He knew he had to master them now; otherwise, his chances were nil of running the necessary second dog team and sled, and there was no way to stay out on the ice for as long as they had to without it. Besides, Ah-Ming was watching him, testing him, computing just how much strength there would be in this companion so new to the Arctic. Sebastian finally reached out and grabbed the lead husky by the scruff of its brown hair back of the neck. The dog seemed surprised at the quickness of the move, and at that instant Sebastian aimed a boot into its ribs. The dog yelped, more in surprise than in pain, and Sebastian hooked the harness trace quickly before the dog could recover. He held the dog's neck by the hair and looked down into the black eyes and curling lips, saying, "You won't bug me any more, will you, Big Bay?" He didn't know why he called the brown husky "Big Bay," but for some reason the dog responded with a low whine, the lips uncurled, and the low growl faded. Then he reached out with the other hand and patted the dog on the flanks and added softly, "Okay, now we're friends."

"But not for long," Ah-Ming said from behind him. Sebastian turned to look at the Eskimo. He still had that grin on his face, the cigar stub sticking out at a comical angle, like a piece of burnt scrub. "That dog, he jump you when you no look. You keep him honest with boot and not love, hokay?"

"Hokay," Sebastian replied in the parlance of the Eskimo and tried a grin on him. Ah-Ming found a match and lit up again, ignoring the cold on his bare hands, peering at Sebastian through the smoke with those black eyes that told nothing of what he was thinking or feeling.

They made four or five runs with the dogs, Sebastian handling the sled under the Eskimo's constant reminders about guiding it for the dogs and not riding it with his feet on the long back runners. "Dogs know when you cheat!" he yelled at Sebastian. "They remember! When you need them to pull like hell, they pull like a full pup on a tit! Dogs no pull, you die on the ice! Push! Like a good Eskimo broad—push!"

At 1:30 he received a quick rundown on some "factors about the polar sea that might be helpful." Sebastian tried to absorb each word, wanting all he could get for what he felt would be needed sooner or later. "Ice drifts about two to three nautical miles a day, sometimes up to twelve nautical miles, depending on the wind. . . . Be sure you take that into consideration when you travel north on the ice. . . . Always take your fix from the sun, if there is any; you can't trust a compass so far up on the magnetic field. . . . When there's no sun, check the radio; we'll home in on your position. . . . Don't try navigating by putting an iceberg over your left shoulder and keeping it there; it's useless because that berg is drifting all the time."

The last thing on his agenda was a peculiar word test conducted by Landau in a small airless room, which

41

was simply called "psychological conditioning." Words and phrases were flashed on large white cards and he was asked to identify them. The phrase came up: "He wears his faith as the fashion of his hat."

"Would you say that is from the Bible, Mr. Sebastian?" Landau asked sharply.

Sebastian could not answer. He stared at the words, noting a familiar lyricism. "I—I don't think so," he finally said lamely, feeling that strange blurring cloud come down on his brain again. "No, I don't think so. . . ."

There were many more words and phrases snapped in front of his eyes. Some he was sure were biblical, and yet he was not sure.

"If I just had my New Testament," he finally said to Landau. "Did somebody find my Testament—or did I drop it somewhere?"

Landau just put the cards down on the table and said, "It is time for you to see Mr. Dietrich."

Still troubled and somewhat bewildered, Sebastian sipped at his coffee in Dietrich's office. It was less than thirty minutes before departure. Dietrich was busy running down the list of equipment checked out for the survival packs and the comments sent in from the various briefing centers. Landau sat off to one side, sniffing loudly and wiping at his red nose with his damp handkerchief.

"You didn't do very well at the firing range," Dietrich said almost laconically, studying the list.

"Another few hours—"

"You don't have it. The point is not to open up on Thorsen beyond ten feet."

"Suppose he doesn't let me get that close?"

"Don't try it. You are chancing a miss, even on rapid-fire, and that means he could blow the rock before you get him. The point is you have to be absolutely sure before you shoot. Is that understood?"

Sebastian waved his half-filled cup toward Dietrich. "The point has been made quite adequately already, Mr. Dietrich."

"And your handling of the dogs was clumsy—"

42

"Ah-Ming say that?"

"No. My own observer. The two most critical points of this operation are the use of the gun and the handling of the dogs." Sebastian sipped his coffee and said nothing. "So I should share one other complication that has arisen in the last half hour," Dietrich said as he carefully put the clipboard down on his desk. "Ah-Ming has found out you are a clergyman by profession. He does not want to go now."

"Who told him?"

"That is irrelevant. The point to consider is that you cannot afford to have tension between you and your guide out there on the ice."

"What's he got against clergymen?"

"You have to understand that Ah-Ming, despite his years at Thule Air Force Base, where he learned to think like us, has not lost his respect for his own religious traditions. Eskimos respect and fear the god who lives on the ice and are careful not to antagonize that spirit. Taking you out there, to him, is like taking another god, a strange one, and is the same as challenging the ice spirit to—"

"Well, do I get another Eskimo then?" Sebastian cut in, trying not to be irritated by Dietrich's overindulgent tone, as if Sebastian were a child in these matters.

"No. I talked him into going anyway. Or, more accurately, I upped the price we are paying him. Ah-Ming has a serious drinking habit that has to be fed through the long winter—so money talks. But that is the poorest reason for him to go. Everything that goes wrong out there he will blame on you. And he will be less confident, as well."

"If there's anything worse than a drunken Eskimo on the ice, it's a nervous one, right?"

"Exactly," Dietrich replied bluntly, and Landau nodded in a jerk of his head. "Just remember he is going to be thinking more of himself than of you. When things get rough, if they do, you will be more on your own."

"Thanks, it's a good time to know that—"

"But remember he is still the best man on the ice

43

we've got. He will do all he is supposed to do, but no more, for the pay. Now, I have checked everything on your list. You have more than enough supplies for a week, even ten days. You have been checked out on your radio, the gun, the dogs—"

"I have some questions—"

"There isn't time. Ah-Ming will handle everything once you are on the ice. Again, he knows your mission."

Dietrich turned and hit the buttons on the panel on his desk. The map of the Arctic Ocean and Greenland slid down from the ceiling again.

"I am going to drop you here, just the other side of the Big Lead," and he pointed to a dark stripe in the mass of white polar ice, not too far off the Greenland coast, running from east to west in a jagged, gouging line. "The Big Lead is a stretch of open water in that ice, about one hundred yards wide, maybe fifty miles long about this time of year. It coats over with thin ice every day, and I expect Thorsen will try to make his dash across there some time tomorrow, since our reports indicate a drop in temperature tonight to minus seventy-six degrees. I will drop you here." Dietrich pointed to the red mark, which was about two inches up from the black gouge. "The day after tomorrow, judging by the pace Thorsen is setting now, he will come through this area close to you, if he keeps to the old Frederick Cook route. It does offer the best path there through the rafter ice. You will be on a hummock of ice offering a good view for miles in either direction, if you use your binoculars. We will try to establish Thorsen's position in relationship to you tomorrow at this time and the day after. We will relay this to you on the radio on a special frequency and in the kind of code language we use in communications from our reconnaissance planes so Thorsen won't suspect there is another party on the ice. . . . The time of transmission, frequency, and nature of the code message are in this envelope." Dietrich dropped the manila file on the desk. "However, in no case are you to transmit to us, except for the usual 'roger' in confirmation of receiving ours. Only

44

when Thorsen is dead are you to contact us. Is that understood?" Sebastian did not respond, so Dietrich put his
pointer down and added in a precise tone, "You know
what you have to do with regard to Thorsen, right, Mr.
Sebastian?"

There was a long moment of silence, during which
Sebastian could not focus directly on the question. Finally
he reached into his parka pocket and pulled out a ragged
paperback.

"I found this in my journeys through the Quonset
for my briefings, Mr. Dietrich," he said, indicating the
book. Dietrich did not look at it. "It's called *Cook's Route
to the Pole.*"

"Some of our logistics people were reading that to
determine Thorsen's projected course."

"I imagine so, Mr. Dietrich. But I'll give you this, if
you give me my New Testament. How's that?"

Dietrich frowned, ignoring Landau's quick look. "I
don't understand, Mr. Sebastian."

"I came here with a pocket New Testament, Mr.
Dietrich, and I can't find it anywhere. I feel a need for it
right now."

"I hardly know at this point where to start looking for
it," Dietrich snapped. "But you can keep that paperback—
you might find it interesting reading during the long night
hours while you are waiting on the ice. I go back to my
original question: You know what you must do about
Thorsen?"

Again Sebastian hesitated, but he did not know why.
"I know how to use the gun well enough, Mr. Dietrich," he finally said, and the words sounded right, even
as Landau leaned back in his chair with a sag of relief.

"You realize the necessity of killing Thorsen?" Dietrich prodded further.

"Of course."

"Good!" Landau added in a tone of restrained approval.

"It is time to go then," Dietrich concluded. "Good
luck, Mr. Sebastian. Need I say again that the hope for a

45

good part of the earth's population as we know it goes with you?"

Sebastian got up slowly, sticking the paperback into his parka pocket again, feeling the bulk of the heavy woolens dragging on him. He put his cup down on the desk and took Dietrich's bony, unfeeling hand in his, then Landau's cold one, picked up the envelope, and turned and walked out of the room, pulling on his parka as he went. He sensed the other men following him.

The huge helicopter's rotors were already turning. He saw Ah-Ming out by the open cargo door, loading the dogs by throwing each of them up over the open door ledge. As Sebastian started moving out to the copter, he saw one dog coming toward him, limping slightly on its left front leg.

It was Big Bay.

"What's wrong?" Sebastian yelled at the man next to him, who was apparently there to supervise takeoff.

"Your lead dog has a split foot!" the man shouted back.

Big Bay came up to Sebastian, whining and trying to push his nose up the sleeve of the parka. "Why can't he go anyway?"

"You don't want a dog limping up there on the ice," Dietrich shouted at him from his left, above the tug of the wind that had sprung up with frigid, cutting puffs. "The other dogs will turn on him."

"What will you do with him?"

"He's no good to us either, not that way! We'll just have to shoot him!"

"Then he goes along!"

"Mr. Sebastian, he will only eat your food and turn on you in the end."

"Then I will shoot him, Mr. Dietrich, okay?"

Dietrich did not respond. The copter was kicking up blasts of snow that stung them as they stood there. Finally Dietrich shrugged. "Ah-Ming is going to be testy about that, but it's your problem from here on out!"

Sebastian turned and cuffed Big Bay behind the ears.

46

The dog sprang up eagerly and bounded ahead of him for the copter, his limp not so noticeable. When Sebastian got to the copter door, Ah-Ming looked down at him and the dog. There was no indication of a smile now. The smoky, cracked face had no expression at all; it was frozen to a kind of withdrawal, the small stub of cigar a jutting piece of pugnaciousness. But when he turned away from Sebastian, he shouted something at the two helicopter crewmen looking on and the men responded with laughter.

"What'd he say?" Sebastian yelled at one of them as he came up into the crowded cargo hold with Big Bay.

"Dog meat!" the man shouted, pointing at Big Bay.

Sebastian looked toward Ah-Ming, but the Eskimo was already buckling himself down in the seat against the far wall. Sebastian found his seat across the aisle, the bundle of supplies, dogs, and sleds heaped up in front of him. The cargo door slammed shut. He looked out the small window toward Dietrich and Landau. The snow blurred the image. It was getting darker rapidly. The pilot jumped the copter off the snow pad, as if he sensed the diminishing light too. Soon Eureka slid away in a sea of white, mere blotches of gray dissolving into nothingness.

As always, at this point of his commitment, Sebastian felt a keen shaft of loneliness. He could use Ah-Ming's jaunty cigar-wagging conversation now more than ever. But he did not get up to look over the mounds of cargo to see if the Eskimo might be ready to talk. He knew better. Dog meat. Well, maybe that's what it would be for both of them. Only God knew, finally. He shifted the long-barreled pistol around in his parka pocket holster, taking strange confidence from its feel. Big Bay curled up in front of him, growling at the other dogs, which watched curiously, knowing perhaps that he was not one of them.

And he simply sat there reading the labels on the wooden crates in front of him, feeling a temptation to laugh. But he was used to the bizarre dimensions of this kind of life by now, so he didn't laugh. He sat quietly, feeling the buck of the copter against the wind, wondering again what had happened to his New Testament. . . .

47

Otto Dietrich went immediately to the communications Quonset after the helicopter had disappeared in the murky skies to the north. There in the small room crackling with the sounds and smells of high-frequency electronic gear, he faced Landau, who had been demanding a meeting for days. Dietrich did not want to give him the time of day, but Landau, though subordinate to him in this operation, had too much position in the Kremlin to totally ignore. Besides being the head of the new program of Thought Control and Neuropsychomatics—which was a fancy term for plain hypnotism, although on a more sophisticated scale—he was also officially representing the KGB, though not directly involved with KGB activities per se. Joining them at Dietrich's request was Alec Bosman, the chief of communications operations, a fortyish, slow-moving man with a fat face, graying hair, and dimples.

"You wanted to talk, Landau?" Dietrich said, not totally able to hide the irritation in his voice, growing more impatient with this spidery man with the perpetually red and runny nose who seemed to wilt more every day from the cold.

Landau glanced uncertainly at Bosman, not sure how much he could say in the presence of someone so far down the line of command.

"He's gotten away from us," he finally began, sniffing nervously, his eyes blinking rapidly.

"Who?"

"Thorsen, who else? I programmed him, Dietrich, as you ordered, but now he's loose on five million square miles of ice."

"You did program him well, Landau, and that is all you need be concerned about."

"I did *not* program him to blow that rock."

"I know that, but you have said many times before that you can never tell how a man's mind will move when it is under someone else's control. You turned him on to run with the rock; his intent to blow it at the North Pole is one of those unfortunate by-products of neuropsychomatics, correct?"

48

"Disastrous in this case, Dietrich, not unfortunate," Landau retorted. "You gave me a man suffering from the shock of losing his son and his wife within a few months of each other. He was conditioned emotionally to commit a deranged act before I ever got to him, and don't forget it. . . . Besides, there is always the chance he may not blow it, always the chance."

"You read his log entries and analyzed them, Landau, and you interpreted them as being solid evidence of a mind bent on self-destruction. You should know if anybody does. . . . The point now is we can't afford to wait and see, can we?"

Landau sniffed, hating that quiet, overbearing sureness in Dietrich's voice. "Zukov wants to know how Thorsen got out of the net," he said, seeking to implicate Dietrich, if he could, in the growing demand for an accounting by the KGB.

"The Russian trawlers were waiting to intercept him at Smith Sound as planned," Dietrich replied evenly. "But nobody could have anticipated that Thorsen would land a hundred miles south on the lower extremities of Ellesmere Island where no ship has attempted such a landing before."

"You should have known which ship he was going to hire in New York and put your agents aboard. If you knew he was going for polar ice, it would seem to be a simple matter—"

"We did find out that he had hired the *Morning Star*, an American freighter—but he changed his mind at the last minute and hired a Syrian flat-bottomed chemical tanker out of Boston. He somehow knew we were on to him."

"So he pirates the whole ship and the crew, a man sixty-three years of age with only a bunch of college kids with him?"

"The mind that slips into psychopathic syndrome, as you said once, Landau, is much more clever than normal, correct?"

Landau sensed that Dietrich was playing with him, jabbing him with his own familiar words.

"We should have programmed him to head elsewhere then, to the desert maybe, where the danger would not be so high." Landau went on as if he were rehearsing the answers to the questions Zukov of the KGB would be asking later. "We should have anticipated—"

"Thorsen's mind would not have yielded to your control if you insisted on deserts," Dietrich countered. "He is an ice man, a man who has traveled polar ice many times and studied it all his life."

"All right, but you still have to explain how he got a full nine-hour start ahead of my programming without your knowing it. That nine hours gave him the time to get another ship."

"You shouldn't have gone to Acapulco at the time of the countdown," Dietrich replied laconically.

"I am a sick man, Dietrich, and three months of programming Thorsen in Houston took it out of me," Landau retaliated.

"All right, but it's all in my report to Zukov which you were supposed to read," Dietrich replied. His voice was growing weary, a sign he would not put up with these questions much longer. "Let me tell you for the last time: Thorsen was supposed to go out on February twenty-second; that's the way you programmed him. On February twenty-first at noon he logged into his moon rock lab. You know we don't have monitors on him to check him when he is in there, a privilege he insisted on and which NASA granted over my objections. At nine o'clock that night, when he did not log out—which is not unusual for him—we checked. We found he had gone out with the rock through the main drain pipe under the floor, a pipe no more than thirty-six inches in diameter. That pipe is not big enough to allow a normal-sized man to negotiate the one hundred yards to the outside. And Thorsen, at his normal hundred and fifty pounds, could not have done it. But by then he was down to under one hundred forty because he hadn't eaten a full meal for the five months since the death of his wife. That we did not anticipate, Landau, because we had sufficient confidence in your neuropsychomatics to expect him to go out a day later."

50

"Then you should have tried to carry the rock out yourself," Landau snapped, feeling the bite of Dietrich's sarcasm.

"You also know that Zukov ordered me to make sure a neutral carrier went out with it in order to protect my cover as Apollo Security Chief. Anyway, I could never have gotten into that lab and come out with the rock without triggering the alarm which I myself devised—"

"So what kind of neutral carrier do we have on the ice now?" Landau insisted, his eyes fluttering in rapid semaphore. "Do you have any idea what will happen if he blows the rock out there? Disaster, Dietrich, disaster for millions. And when the Americans check back, they will know about our ship and our trawlers in Smith Sound, and in the end the whole mess will land on the steps of the Kremlin."

Dietrich folded his arms and leaned against the wall. He took off his glasses and peered at them intently, not wanting to look at Landau, who projected an image of total disarray, who was already looking for a hole like a mouse anticipating the cat.

"I have not been taken completely by surprise in all this, Landau," he finally said in a preoccupied tone, holding his glasses up to the light. "We do have our Russian teams moving down."

"What good are they? You think Thorsen will let them get anywhere near him without pulling the pin on that rock?"

"And I have taken other steps—"

"You mean that—that clergyman? A man who really is the least capable on ice and certainly not fully committed to killing Thorsen?"

"I thought you programmed him on that. You are not sure now?"

Landau lifted his hand in a gesture of warding off any argument. "Oh, I can assure you, Otto, that Mr. Sebastian shows all the signs of a mind controlled to assassinate Thorsen. The penetration of his brain during sleep, together with the use of the neuro-mass ray—"

"But you sound as if you are still doubtful."

51

"I told you I never worked on a religious man before."
Landau found a cigarette and put it between his thin lips,
trying to control the shaking of his fingers. "It is a complicated mind at best. I do not know how far my own
controls can push across the religious barriers. Besides, he
can be too easily counterprogrammed if his religious ide-
ology plays too big a part in his life."

"What would it take to counterprogram him out of
killing Thorsen?"

Landau shrugged. "I expect it would have to be someone like himself, who knows the religious mind, the se-
mantics, and who can use that language to jam the circuits of his present inputs and bring recall to his religious
values."

"And who might you be suggesting will do that up
there on the ice?" Dietrich asked sharply. Landau glanced
at him, sensing irritation. Those languid gray eyes were
beginning to show a coating of hardness, indicating the
storm that was building there. "Thorsen, perhaps? How
about Ah-Ming?"

Landau caught the note of sarcasm. "Look, Otto, I
do not mean to say there is any possibility at this time."

"His one link to counterprogramming is his Bible, as
you said," Dietrich went on. "And we took care of that.
What about your semantic perception test?"

"He failed on almost every card."

"Which means he can't get recall on his religious con-
ceptualizations. Am I correct?"

"I can't play God in this, Otto—"

"Well, hell, you better start playing God in the same
way I have to right now," Dietrich retorted. "I don't need
a case for the impossibilities, nor do you!"

Landau found a paper match, lit it, and tried to light
his flapping cigarette. The match went out. He threw the
cigarette on the floor in exasperation, turning his back on
Bosman, who was watching him.

"I am merely stating that I am concerned with the
existing percentages, Dietrich, that beg us to consider
those impossibilities—"

"And I have worked those meager percentages too,

even before you got into this operation," Dietrich answered, his voice gone back to the even, ever-patient tone used in dealing with a child. "And I have anticipated Sebastian's possible failure too. . . . Bosman, show him what you've got."

Bosman moved back and revealed a box with a large, square TV screen on the table. Landau peered at it intently. On the screen were two points of light, very small. One was high up on the screen; the other was down in the lower left corner. Both flashed on and off intermittently.

"That pinpoint of light up there," Bosman explained, "is Professor Thorsen. He has a small electronic impulse unit no bigger than a postage stamp planted in his thermal underwear. It gives off high-frequency electronic impulses every six seconds. The other light, there a little lower down on the left, is hooked into our man Sebastian—"

"It's not moving," Landau cut in sharply, turning toward Dietrich. "Are they down? I thought you said you were putting Sebastian down ahead of Thorsen."

"The storm has blown them off course," Dietrich commented mildly. "We can't raise them on the radio in this weather. It's unfortunate, but all we can hope is that he will make up the ground. With Ah-Ming, he should have no problem." Landau did not look very happy about it, but Dietrich said to Bosman, "Go on, Bosman."

Bosman took another sip of his Coke and lit a cigarette while the room sat in its cocoon of electronic gadgetry, humming a steady tune of high-frequency bleeps. "As Sebastian gets closer to Thorsen, those pinpoints of light will begin flashing more rapidly. When they get within ten feet of each other, the lights will converge. At that point we hit the red button here and trigger an electronic charge. All twenty-five charges will go off at once. Most of that steel will fly forward through a small jet tube, thus saving the scattering effect totally. Those chunks of steel will be flying at Thorsen at about sixty miles an hour. The shock will kill him outright. At the same time, we also get our man Sebastian. In short, there is nothing left to have to clean up."

"But the explosion," Landau said with skepticism.

53

"Won't that jar the capsule carrying the rock? Thorsen is bound to have it close at hand."

"The explosion," Dietrich interjected, "is below the seismographic sensitivity of the capsule. The detonation material in those capsules is made of gelatin, so it has a low flash propellant. A problem would arise only if Thorsen were holding the capsule in his hands and those pieces of steel penetrated it—but I doubt if he would be that cautious."

"And the weight problem on Sebastian with all that steel on him?"

"We are talking about eight pounds in that parka. He'll feel a little uncomfortable, but he'll have no cause to check it in the short time he's up there."

Landau nodded at the screen, indicating approval, although his squirrel-like face continued to carry a look of dubiousness. "It is hoped that Thorsen does not change his underwear then?"

Bosman grunted a kind of laugh. "We are counting on a man sixty-three years of age, bent on destruction, to forego that—but even if he does, his other suit is wired with the same device."

Landau turned to look at Dietrich. "You provided him with the Arctic gear he needed, Dietrich?"

"Only the thermal underwear. The kind we use in space is the best, and he knows it. When he ordered out two suits for himself a week or so ago, we made certain the sensors were put in."

"You never told me this, Dietrich. Why?"

"Your job was to program him, to control his brain; our job was and is to control his movements. And if we could not do that, then to prepare for the eventualities."

Landau thought for a minute, then turned to look at the screen again. "Why did you insist on this man Sebastian being programmed to shoot Thorsen if you had this sound sensor explosive?"

"Two systems work better than one, Landau. Our main concern was to get a vehicle we were sure would carry the payload to Thorsen. If Sebastian shoots Thorsen or not is really not that critical, but we have to be sure he

54

closes with Thorsen on the ice. Then we can be positive about the rest."

"Suppose Sebastian tries to take Thorsen from a distance beyond which the explosive device will work?"

"We are gambling on the fact that Sebastian is convinced he can only do the job effectively within the range that the gun works best."

"You are sure the explosive device will work?"

"Houston Apollo Center has used the electronic sensor with one hundred percent effectiveness in their docking maneuvers in space. We simply use the same device for our own ends. Our experiments proved highly successful at sixty miles."

"And how will you know for sure it worked?"

"The disappearance of both lights on the screen, naturally. Thorsen's sensor is sewed into his underwear over the breast bone—"

"Can't he feel it?"

"No. It's really a flat piece of soft plastic over a bed of about three hundred microscopic wire transistor cables. About the size of a knee patch, maybe, and feels like cotton. . . . Anyway, those charges will hit him just about dead center. The same for Sebastian."

Landau tried another cigarette, and this time Bosman reached up and held the match for him. Landau peered at him before accepting the flame, not too sure of the gesture, and then took it, puffing up a billow of blue smoke around his head.

"You knew all the time this man Sebastian would go all the way?"

Dietrich gave that spasm of a smile, knowing he had Landau catching the scent of success. "His letters to Thorsen some months back in Houston indicated to us that he might prove to be the key—that is, if the eventuality arose that Thorsen did, in fact, get to polar ice."

"Sounds to me as if you knew all along Thorsen would do that," Landau replied morosely.

"I have learned to anticipate," Dietrich replied mildly.

"But how could you be sure Sebastian would go?"

"We checked out his exploits in Palestine, Cuba, and

Berlin, and they indicated to us that here was a man of unusual evangelistic fervor. He's a rare one to come out of a strongly separatist religious culture, in the sense of getting involved with the grit of the Cold War. But we knew we had a man with that deeply fanatical spiritual instinct, a conviction of the all-important value of the individual in the sight of God. And in Thorsen's case, he becomes too big a soul for the cause of Christianity to let slip through. Beyond that, of course, Sebastian failed once in trying to prove God's power to Thorsen; now he is aching to redeem himself."

"But he is moving to commit a contradictory act of redemption on behalf of Thorsen; that is what worries me," Landau commented.

"Whichever instinct takes over finally," Dietrich explained, "it will still drive him to overtake Thorsen. That is what we are counting on, and that is why we had you program him to kill Thorsen. Either instinct wins for us."

"And after you finish them off, both of them, what then? You still have that rock out there on the ice."

"Our Russian team will be close at hand."

"And the American military? And the Chinese?"

"I have called off the American forces at Thule for now. My authority as Chief of Security supersedes the military in this operation. And by the way, that authority took me nine years to earn," Dietrich added as an aside. "Nine years of playing the role of a trusted, capable security chief for the moon shots—you can tell that to Zukov while you are at it—and right now those nine years are about to pay off for the biggest energy find in the universe. As for the Chinese, they have not moved off Spitsbergen as yet. If they do, we will have a proper delaying party for them by our Russian team up there."

"You think the military coordinator of Moon Rock is going to sit on his hands watching those Russians move down on Thorsen?" Landau asked skeptically, taking the cigarette out of his mouth and spitting out a piece of loose tobacco.

"He has no choice. To go over my head to ask for different orders is to put his own head on the block. American espionage bureaucracy is as stupid as their government's. Admiral Fish is no hero on that score."

"And what about Thorsen's party of college kids out there with him? Won't they take the rock once Thorsen is dead?"

"I doubt if they even know the power of that piece of silicon. Our information says that Thorsen recruited those six college kids just to verify Cook's route to the Pole."

"Nobody has verified or discounted that yet?"

"No point in doing so. Cook's claim was written off the history books as a fake. Thorsen alone keeps the flame alive; he tried once five years ago to prove it but got himself marooned on an ice floe and had to be rescued by air."

"Surely those kids know he has the rock on him."

"Sure, but you can be certain Thorsen wouldn't have told them what he is about to do with it. They would hardly stick with him if he did."

Landau was not convinced, but he let it go. He watched the two pinpoints of light on the screen again. The Sebastian flasher remained stationary along with Thorsen's.

"And if Sebastian fails to get to Thorsen?" Landau decided to risk the big question. "What then?"

Dietrich did not reply immediately, and Bosman half turned toward him as if he knew it was the critical question too. "Well, then it will be up to our Russian brothers," Dietrich finally said in a subdued tone, which meant he didn't like that option either.

Landau knew, if it came to that, that the risk of Thorsen's blowing the rock would become very real. And though committed to the Soviet Cold War struggle himself and knowing the value of that moon rock to Russian nuclear domination, he still did not like to think of a million tons of ice being liquefied in one blast. But he sensed too that Dietrich had to put it all on the line about getting both Thorsen and the rock. And looking at the screen, he knew Dietrich had something here that could turn it around; in that, he had to admire this German Jew as much as he despised his cocksureness.

As if Dietrich knew he had done and said everything

57

he could to satisfy Landau—and, he hoped, Colonel Zukov of the KGB—he turned toward the door, pulling his parka hood up over his head.

"Don't leave that monitor, Bosman," Dietrich said. "And keep your eye on that weather front over Canada. If it changes course and starts moving its full force over the Arctic Ocean, let me know immediately."

He was gone then, the bite of Arctic wind blowing into the room as he opened and closed the door. Landau shivered and puffed on his cigarette. He blew his nose again, wincing at the burning of the raw and chafed skin, longing for the warmer, dryer climate of Mexico where he was used to working. Bosman sucked on the last of his Coke and sat down to stare at the pinpoints of light on the screen. It was 2:35 P.M. Glancing up at the big wall map, Landau saw the blue marker indicating Thorsen's last position this side of the Big Lead, probably plotted from air reconnaissance earlier. But the light on the screen in front of him showed that Thorsen was across already and well on his way north. How could that old man keep moving in this weather? He turned to look out the Quonset window. It would be impossible to see ten feet out on the ice by 3:00 P.M. The wind shook the glass in the window frame and sounded like the rattle of bones on the tin Quonset frame. He noticed it was snowing more heavily too. An amateur like Sebastian would never catch Thorsen, Ah-Ming or no Ah-Ming. And that was beginning to send ripples of worry in the back of Landau's brain.

What if the weather should lock Sebastian and the Eskimo into total immobility on that ice? And what if Thorsen did not give into the storm and kept moving? Surely the old man would bow to the elements too? But if he didn't, it could mean that Sebastian would miss him for sure. If so, they would have then reached the critical point in the operation.

Landau shivered again. He had programmed Thorsen well, too well, almost rewriting his brain to become obsessed with the idea of running with the rock. As Dietrich had said, it was too good, so much so that Thorsen had been pushed over the line to self-destruction. Landau had created a whirlwind of a man, even at sixty-three, trusting too much to Dietrich's confidence in being able to get Thorsen before he got too far out of reach. It was a crazy plan to begin with—but if they pulled it off now, it would be the biggest piece of good fortune the Soviets had ever had in an espionage maneuver.

When he looked up at the minute star of light tied to that man Sebastian, he almost had to laugh. Had they come down so far in trying to master the world that they had to use flotsam like that to accomplish it? Oh, for the good old days, when they grappled with the best brains and muscle in the spy business. Now they had to use the church?

Finally, unable to tolerate the room with its shrill cacophony of high-frequency sounds, all of which seemed to carry a mocking grace note to all that had been planned here, he mumbled good night to Bosman and stepped out into a swirl of snow and wind that sucked out his breath and tore through his body with painful rapier thrusts of ice.

3

It was a total whiteout below as the helicopter hesitated in its jerky descent to the ice. Sebastian, looking down from the open cargo hatch and hanging on to the line overhead for dear life, could not tell where sky left off and ice began. The storm was already clamping hard on the remaining haze of daylight, squeezing it relentlessly to oblivion. The wind was stronger too, pushing the copter around in gyrating movements.

"I'm going to put you over on the ladder!" one of the crewmen, a sergeant, shouted into his ear. "We can't take a chance on setting her down in this wind! We could get blown over!"

"Are you sure of our position?" Sebastian shouted back.

"We're as close as we can figure it!"

"That's not good enough, sergeant! Dietrich said to make sure we hit it on the nose."

"Sir, there's no way to hit it on the nose in this wind and with that whiteout below us! We'll be lucky to get you down and your cargo with you! You better hurry, you're going to need what light is left to pitch camp!"

He was right, of course. Sebastian figured he would have to take his chances on their position. He waited while the nylon rope ladder was thrown over. The copter settled a few more feet until the ladder went slack, indicating that it had touched the ice somewhere below them by ten or twelve feet. Ah-Ming was up and tossing bundles of cargo out the door, watching each piece drop into the heavy snowdrifts being whipped by the gusty wind. Sebastian felt the cold slice through his parka, cut into his face with stinging needles. He found his face mask and put it on hurriedly, then pulled the strings of his parka hood tightly. He felt somewhat protected, but not much.

After the cargo was down, the dogs were next. The pilot settled the machine lower, trying to hold it against the wind gusts. The dogs yelped in excitement, anxious to get out of the uncertain, swaying machine. Ah-Ming scrambled down the ladder. Once he was on the ice below, caught in the blur of the slanting snow and ice, the dogs felt no fear in making the short ten-foot jump into the snow. They bounded over and hit the snowdrifts below, coming up to nip at each other and lift their snouts into the wind, eager for battle with the elements they knew best. Big Bay was last, and he looked down uncertainly at the other dogs, knowing he was not accepted by them.

Just then the copter jerked to the left, and when Sebastian looked down he could not see Ah-Ming or the dogs. "You better get over now, sir!" the sergeant yelled at him. "We can't hold her any longer without getting zapped on that ice!"

Sebastian glanced at Big Bay, who was finding it hard to keep his legs on the pitching deck. The copter dropped suddenly. Sebastian sensed that the pilot was trying to give him the shortest possible jump. He turned and picked up Big Bay in his arms, straining with the weight of the husky, looked down toward what he hoped was a soft landing, and dropped him. The dog hit a puff of drift a long way down, it seemed, but got up apparently unhurt. Sebastian ignored the ladder, knowing it would take too long, and half jumped and half dove out the cargo door. He hit the snow and ice in a skidding slide, the gun in his left pocket digging hard into his thigh. He rolled over quickly and watched the copter jerk upward again, its red signal flasher disappearing quickly in the swirl of flying snow.

61

He was alone. He heard only the wind and the steady staccato beat of the ice pellets on his parka, cutting into the exposed flesh on his face. He could not see more than five feet in either direction and had no idea in which direction Ah-Ming would be. He tried to get up. Big Bay licked his cheek, as if to tell him that it was all right. Finally he stood up, lifting one arm as a shield, trying to get the angle of the wind he remembered when Ah-Ming went over. He moved uncertainly against the mixture of ice and snow, leaning his body into the gusts that tore at him with a vengeance.

He stopped, knowing he couldn't be sure he was going right, and turned his back to the wind, trying to see around him. He tried yelling as loudly as he could, hoping Ah-Ming or the other dogs would hear him. But it was useless. Only the high shrill of the wind and the steady beat of the ice crystals on his parka answered him.

It couldn't end here, he thought, before he had even begun! Why wasn't Ah-Ming looking for him? But why should he? He had his money anyway, whether Sebastian did what he was supposed to or not. His god of the ice wasn't about to let another challenge him. . . .

Then he heard Big Bay barking and turned to see the dog behind him. Was the dog trying to tell him to follow? Well, what other choice had he? So clumsily, already tightening up with the cold, he turned back into the wind, holding his mittened hand up against his face to ward off the fusilade of biting snow and ice. He kept walking, sometimes stumbling on ice, sometimes on deep snow, following the shaft of brownish-red hindquarters, knowing he could be moving away from Ah-Ming rather than toward him.

Then, just when he was about to try another direction, he saw the dogs even before he heard them. He yelled his relief, and Big Bay wagged his tail, maybe trying to tell him it wasn't really that hard to do, if you had a dog's instinct. He saw Ah-Ming working in front of the yellow vinyl tent he had managed to get up in the wind, but the Eskimo did not even turn around; he went on

62

pegging the tent down into the ice and snow as if he knew all the time that Sebastian would be coming. Sebastian realized that the Eskimo had been right to stay put; if he had tried to find him, they both could have been lost.

He didn't say anything to the Eskimo, respecting the silence and the cold. He cuffed Big Bay affectionately around the ears for his part in leading him home. The other dogs growled and snapped at Big Bay for the special attention he was getting, and Sebastian knew that it wouldn't be long before they jumped the dog because of his preferred position, so he led the dog away from the pack, and while the dog lay in the snow and watched, he worked to get the cargo boxes and sleds near the tent. Then he carried into the tent the supplies he felt they would need for the night.

When the tent was pegged down to Ah-Ming's satisfaction, he went over and led the two dog teams toward it. There he tied them to harness pegs which he drove into the snow. The dogs continued to howl at the wind until Ah-Ming opened the cans of pemmican and tossed the blubber to them. The dogs devoured it with a snarl, fighting each other for any droppings. Sebastian waited for the Eskimo to toss a portion to Big Bay, but he simply put the cans back into the pouch and went over to fuss with the sleds. Finally Sebastian found the pemmican himself and fed Big Bay, while the other dogs strained to get more, some of them wanting a piece of Big Bay at the same time.

A few minutes later Ah-Ming crawled inside the tent, after making sure the cargo boxes were piled on the sleds and the canvas tarp was secure over them. Sebastian crawled in behind him and pulled off his parka hood. It was not warm in the tent, but to be away from the cutting wind was a relief. He found the small primus stove in one of the boxes, poured some of the fuel into it, and lit it. The bright yellow flame gave the tent a glow of warmth and snugness.

"Why do the dogs keep howling?" he commented, pulling off his mittens and holding them close to the hissing primus.

63

Ah-Ming was untying his sleeping bag with those sure movements of his and did not answer for a long time. When he got the bag spread out on the caribou hides covering the floor, he said, "Bear around."

"Bear? Polar bear?"

Ah-Ming did not answer.

"The dogs want to chase it?"

Ah-Ming pulled off his parka hood and found a cigar inside his coat, bit off the end, not looking at Sebastian, and stuffed it into that gap in his front teeth.

"Bear old female," he said indifferently, in a tone that said he was saying only as much as he had to for the money he was getting. "Bad teeth . . . no hunt seal no more . . . so she hunt what comes."

"You mean us?" Sebastian said, wanting conversation more than anything to dispel the cold and the feeling of isolation that pressed in with the sound of the ever-searching wind begging fruitlessly for companionship on the walls of the tent.

Ah-Ming did not reply. He lay there on his back, staring up at the ceiling, chewing on the cigar that bobbed and weaved in his mouth, like a marker buoy. Finally Sebastian found two tuna and bacon bars in the box of supplies and dropped them into a deep-bottomed pot and placed it on the lid over the primus flame. He took his canteen, unscrewed the cap, and moved to pour water into the pot. Nothing came. He shook it. No sound. He put his finger down into the neck and felt the hard ice. He placed the canteen next to the primus stove to thaw, but he knew it would take a long time. And already the tuna and bacon bars were starting to burn.

Finally Ah-Ming sat up, unzipped the tent flap, and reached outside. He pulled his hands in quickly and moved to drop the snow into the pot. He got three handfuls of snow, the last one carrying the yellow streaks of dog urine mixed with it. He didn't seem to notice, or maybe he didn't care. Sebastian swallowed but said nothing. Soon the tent was carrying the rich aroma of the soup, and Sebastian, too hungry to worry about the chemical mixture, dipped two tin cups into the soup and put one on the floor near Ah-Ming. He was sure Ah-Ming, trying to look indifferent, was watching him through the corner of his eye. Finally Sebastian lifted his cup and sipped. The rich taste of bacon and tuna was sweet to his palate.

He said, "Seasoned just right." Ah-Ming's eyes flicked toward him, not sure of the remark, not sure Sebastian had actually partaken. When Sebastian took another good swallow, the Eskimo sat up, reached over, and took his portion without a word. He found a can of pemmican, opened it with his fingers, dipped one piece of the oily seal blubber into the cup of soup, and plopped it into his mouth.

"You eat," he said, extending the can toward Sebastian. The smell of it was enough to curb whatever appetite he had, but when he glanced at the Eskimo's impassive face, he saw the watchfulness in those red-rimmed eyes, the black thumbtack pupils as fixed as fish eyes on Sebastian's hands wrapped around his tin cup. "You eat, or you lose push. Seal blubber keep you warm. Eat."

Sebastian finally reached over, took the open can, and looked down at the grayish-white mess within. He got a piece of the slippery blubber from the can and dipped it into his soup, trying not to notice the muscles of his stomach beginning to knot up. He flipped the blubber into his mouth, sensing the sogginess and slipperiness of it, catching the taste of fish and something even more strange to the palate before he swallowed it. His throat began to contract against the tightening of his stomach, but he did not move. He took another quick sip of the soup from his cup and then another, unmindful of the burn in his mouth. All the time Ah-Ming watched him, his face showing nothing except patience, as he waited for Sebastian to bolt for the outside and empty himself.

"Not bad," Sebastian said into his cup of soup, but not with much bravado. He handed the can back to the Eskimo, who took two more pieces, dipped each one into his soup, and rolled them around in his mouth for effect before swallowing. Sebastian finished the soup, helping

65

himself to another cup to try to kill the taste in his mouth. Ah-Ming finally turned back to his sleeping bag, belching loudly, closing the lid on the can and putting it back into the cellophane bag. Sebastian found a chocolate bar and ate all of it, glad for the pungent sweetness in his mouth, mindful now of the sweat that was sticky on his forehead and wet around his neck where the fur parka dug in.

Ah-Ming tossed his empty tin cup toward Sebastian, took off his parka, and crawled into his sleeping bag. In a few minutes he was snoring lightly.

Sebastian found some hard raisin cookies in the rations and chewed on them, watching the primus flame. He was conscious now of another sound above the wind, something he had been hearing for some time but was unable to identify. Sometimes it was like a freight train rumbling in the distance and fading out. Other times it seemed closer, a kind of cracking, snapping sound that ended in a long, low rumble. Then, as he turned to take a piece of paper toweling to clean out the cups and the pot, he heard the jarring, almost explosive rip of something above the wind. Ah-Ming's snoring stopped, and, though his eyes did not open, Sebastian was sure he was listening and had heard it too. It had to be the ice. The ice was breaking up out there, not too far away. The rumbling sounds were from the ice moving underneath. He would have liked to check with Ah-Ming to be sure, but the Eskimo was breathing evenly again. He wasn't snoring, though. Maybe his brain was only half under in sleep.

Sebastian cleaned up and put everything back in the box, trying not to think of the breaking ice around them. Now and then the dogs let out a howl against the wind, reminding him of the bear too. It was almost five o'clock. The sun would be up by five the next morning; maybe not in this weather. He didn't feel sleepy. He finally took off his parka, glad to be free of its weight, laying it alongside his sleeping bag. He let the primus burn a little longer while he snuggled down into his sleeping bag. It was cold. Forever, eternally cold. But the stove helped some. He lay there listening to the rumbling around him, staring up at the yellow ceiling of the tent, still tasting the pemmican in his mouth, feeling cramps in his lower stomach. How many miles of this had he in front of him before he could be free of this wind, of the jarring, splitting sounds of ice tearing loose somewhere out in this hell of a night?

Unable to sleep, he turned off the primus stove and found his flashlight. He took the paperback *Cook's Route to the Pole*, going back to Cook's experience again, and began reading by the flashlight. He shivered; the tent had begun to cool off more, now the primus was out. But he continued reading, sometimes pausing to listen to those freight-train sounds or straining to catch Ah-Ming's breathing that would indicate the Eskimo thought nothing of the night as he slept on. But Sebastian didn't hear that breathing now. Once he shot the flashlight glow toward Ah-Ming. He saw the head, the push-broom crop of black hair sticking out of the sleeping bag. The eyes were closed, but Sebastian could not see the rise and fall of the sleeping bag that would indicate sleep.

He continued reading by flashlight, seeing words, some of it getting through, wondering if Cook himself or even Peary ever lay like this, listening, wondering, unsure of what was going on in the mysterious Arctic night. He read on, skipping pages at times, seizing those words which offered more interest. Finally, knowing he needed rest, he switched off the flashlight and shoved his shoulders back down into the sleeping bag, straining for warmth. Now it was dark in the tent, thick, awesome, amplifying the sounds in the night ten times over in portent of disaster.

He was like a child, trying to sleep against the terrors of the unexpected caprices of a mounting storm. The cooking smells lingered, mixing with his own sweat. Above that was the familiar odor of the Eskimo: fish, wood smoke, and cigars. The insistent wind rattled the tent, sometimes rising to a banshee wail. And always that darkness making him feel as if he were falling a long way down. . . .

He reminded himself that he was a man of God. He

had been in equally bad places before—although maybe this carried one more dimension of eeriness that he could not explain. He tried to get his mind fixed on God to recall the promises that had kept bigger men than he throughout history. But all that filled his mind was the sound, the blackness, the terrible heaving and grunting of the ice around him. It had to be hell, he thought, this surely had to be it, where darkness and the ghostly voices of death blotted out the name of God and left the soul quivering like a child's—to be conscious only of self, isolated from any living thing, from sun and light and God—and he felt the shaft of fear grip him sharply and intensify his stomach cramps and the sweat was fresh on his face again, giving off that sweet smell that comes strictly from fear. So he lay there, knowing he had to, trying to shut out the torment of the night around him, because he was sure Ah-Ming would be listening to his restless turning in the bag, waiting perhaps for him to turn on his flashlight and ask about the ice, and somehow he managed to drift off. . . .

He awoke with a start.

The blackness held heavy before his eyes; the wind was still there. But something else was happening, and he sat up quickly, groping for his flashlight. He was conscious at the same time of a hasty movement in the tent, and when he heard the zipper of the front flap being ripped open in a sudden sound of urgency, he turned his light that way. Ah-Ming was there, pulling on his parka quickly, almost jerking it on. With the other hand, he was throwing things out the tent flap.

Sebastian kicked himself out of the sleeping bag, not knowing yet what was happening, trying to phrase a question. But as he pulled on his heavy outer parka, he felt the sudden motion under his feet, lifting him, then dropping him again. At the same time, his flashlight showed a bulge underneath the caribou hides, and the snapping, rumbling sound was growing louder in the tent. *God, the ice was breaking up beneath them!*

There was no time to ask Ah-Ming, no time to think

about it. He grabbed what was within reach and dived for the door, even as he felt the tent coming down over him, the ice flying in broken chunks around him. Outside, he swung his light around. Ah-Ming was slashing the dogs free from their harness pegs with his long knife, and they jumped away, howling in fright. Sebastian got up and helped Ah-Ming push the one sled loaded with supplies back away from the tent that was now sinking into the black water between the gleaming jaws of the crevasse of open ice. He pushed the sled with all he had, knowing that the line of the crack in the ice could be following them, could at any minute spring open and pull them in. . . .

"Push!" Ah-Ming yelled above the wind, and Sebastian leaned into it, finding the weight of the loaded sled almost too much without the dogs. The other sled was still sitting behind them somewhere, also loaded with supplies.

Finally Ah-Ming paused and straightened up to look back. Sebastian swung his light behind them. There was nothing there; tent and sled were gone, swallowed up in the dark murkiness of the frigid waters of the Arctic Ocean. The ice kept rumbling underneath, then subsided somewhat. The light showed open water extending back in a black strip between the ice break beyond the beam and at least ten feet wide.

"Put other tent here," Ah-Ming shouted above the wind.

"We're right on the line of that ice break," Sebastian replied. But he wasn't really sure, mainly wanting reassurance from the Eskimo.

Ah-Ming said nothing as he untied the ropes holding the canvas tarp on the sled. He found the spare tent, and Sebastian helped him roll it out, knowing he had to trust the Eskimo's judgment. By the light of the flashlight they managed to get the tent up and pegged down. Ah-Ming then went after the dogs, which had clustered a few yards away, watching, whining, still not sure themselves. Big Bay stayed by Sebastian's feet as Ah-Ming tied the dogs again.

Sebastian then crawled into the tent, lit the primus

stove, and tried to take inventory. They had lost one set of caribou hides for the tent floor but had managed to save their sleeping bags, the stove, and three five-gallon cans of ethanol fuel. But the sled they lost had carried the radio.

Sebastian was glad for the yellow flame of the primus in the tent, helping to cut the cold. His watch showed nearly 11:00 P.M. He knew he would not sleep the rest of the night. Ah-Ming, however, came inside and climbed into his sleeping bag without taking off his parka. He lay there quietly on his back, his head lost in the hood of his parka.

"Have a cigar." Sebastian tried to play it light. "You earned it."

The Eskimo still did not respond. Then, in a voice carrying some awe and wonder, he said, "Ano angry now. Ano tell us death follows us."

Sebastian wasn't sure who Ano was, but he sensed it had to do with the spirit of the ice, the supernatural being that the Eskimo believed in.

"Ice breaks up all the time," he said, trying to bring the Eskimo back from a state of what seemed to be fatalistic despair.

"Ano take my wife, two children," the Eskimo said, almost as if he were talking to himself, not even conscious of Sebastian. "He mad then. I use snowmobile from Thule; Ano say only dogs on ice. Wife foolish Eskimo broad, swallow everything at Thule: snowmobile, Bible. No longer Eskimo . . . no longer believe in Ano . . . so Ano take her and two children through ice. Now he comes for me." He paused, and his head turned slowly toward Sebastian until those black pupils fixed on him. "You. You go back or Ano take you too. Ano owns ice. You make Ano mad like my wife, foolish Eskimo broad."

Then, without waiting for a reply, he turned over and put his back to Sebastian as if he had delivered the proclamation as given by Ano and there was no point in talking further.

Sebastian decided to let it go. The night was already

full of the bizarre, the mysterious, the dangerous. The wind continued to batter the tent, and the sound of the thumping of moving ice rode over it now and then to let him know calamity was never far out of reach. He got into his sleeping bag with his parka on, wanting to be ready to dash out if the ice broke under the tent again. He thought of the loss of the radio, what it meant, not only to maybe knowing where Thorsen was but also to their survival here. Without communication to Eureka, he had no way of reporting his needs. With supplies cut in half, and with Ah-Ming committed to dying under Ano, the margins for making it were flimsy at best. It almost seemed that his only chance was to find Thorsen, do his job, and use what supplies Thorsen had while waiting for Dietrich to rescue him. In any case, it was imperative he intercept Thorsen now; he couldn't last more than about three days on what was left.

Finally he turned off the primus, sensing that every minute of fuel spent was that much more of a problem later. He lay back in his sleeping bag, trying to sort it out, trying to work out the best way to keep Ah-Ming from yielding to the inevitable. But all that came to him was the death rattle of the wind on the tent, and the cold that seemed to get more intense.

It was after four o'clock when he awoke. He remembered opening his eyes several times during the long hours he lay there, cramped and cold and alert to the sounds of the rumbling ice. He could not hear Ah-Ming's snoring either. Once he turned his flashlight toward him, but there was no movement, just that mound of lumpy fur buried in the sleeping bag.

But now there was light. He got up, hearing the wind that had not let up in the night at all. The dogs were yelping again too. He poked his head through the open tent flap. The cold bit his nose and cheeks and made him suck his breath in against it. The glimpse he had was of a world frozen in white, being whipped by slanting snow driven by the fury of the gale. Visibility was poor, and he

71

had to look hard to find the dogs, some of which had curled into balls of fur to ward off the cold and the snow.

There would be no travel today. He could only hope Thorsen was forced to hole up as well.

He pulled back into the tent, found the primus, and lit it. The flame lit the tent, but it did not move Ah-Ming at all. Sebastian got his mess-tin cooking pot and reached outside the tent flap to scoop in fresh snow, making sure there was no dog urine in it. Soon he had oatmeal and raisins simmering on the primus, and he felt the first lift of spirit that cut some into his deepening sense of impending failure. He heated more snow and had a cup of freeze-dried coffee, the warmth of it shaking some of the paralyzing cold that had stiffened his muscles to almost total immobility. He managed to whip up a small batch of dried eggs along with it, being careful how much he spooned into the pan.

But none of the appetizing odors prodded Ah-Ming out of his sleeping bag. Sebastian tried conversation; he even whistled as he worked, a sound that was peculiarly discordant against the whine of the wind outside. When Ah-Ming still did not respond, Sebastian went out and fed the dogs himself, gasping against the murderous cold that the wind threw at him. He fed Big Bay separately. The big brown husky seemed playful and tried to run off with the cellophane wrapper in which the pemmican can was wrapped. Then he grabbed the corner of the canvas tarp covering the boxes on the sled and would have pulled it off if Sebastian had not cuffed him behind the ear.

He was back in the tent again, glad for the warmth inside, feeling the rawness of the cold down his windpipe subside. His parka was caked with snow, so he took it off and hung it from the tent pole overhead. It continued to drip drops of water down on his sleeping bag, so he moved the bag around to put himself near Ah-Ming's head.

The Eskimo continued to lie there, with his eyes closed but giving no sign of the easy breathing of sleep.

"Can't go shopping today," Sebastian said loudly. "Nothing to do but watch TV. . . . There's an ice break a few feet from the door." He thought for sure that would get the Eskimo up, but there was not even a ripple of movement.

So there was nothing to do. He tried not to think of what would happen if Ah-Ming decided to go into a "willful freeze," as one of his instructors at Eureka had described it. "If you lie all day in your sleeping bag, your body will adjust itself to the decreasing blood flow and temperature and after a while you'll go into a total doze, slipping farther and farther down into it until everything stops."

What would he do? Ah-Ming was his one chance to stay alive out here. With no radio, all Sebastian could hope for was a reconnaissance plane happening over him —but the chances were poor. And the weather? It could blow like this for a week. He would be dead by then.

All he could do was wait. If he had to, he'd drag Ah-Ming out of his sleeping bag. Right now, though, he felt sleepy himself. The food was warm in his stomach. The primus was building up a little more heat in the tent. He had to spend all day here anyway. So he slipped down into his sleeping bag and allowed the warm, gentle sleep to come. Though something kept warning him to stay awake, he was tired of being on the alert. It was good to sleep. . . .

General Buckner was not much interested in his breakfast. He was deep in his job as military coordinator of Moon Rock, and he was beginning to get testy about anything that appeared out of line.

"I didn't know Dietrich had authority to call off the military," he said to Fish, rather petulantly.

"As Chief of Apollo Security, he can," Fish replied, chewing on his scrambled eggs but not with too much relish, because he was trying to figure that one out himself. "Anyway, he must have a design of his own for getting Thorsen and doesn't want our military complicating it."

"And the Russians? What about that complication?

It's a lucky break in a way that we have a weather problem on the ice; at least that keeps them anchored for a while."

"Let's hope it stalls Thorsen as well," Fish commented.

Just then Lieutenant Bob Hestig stepped through the doorway of Fish's private quarters, hesitating before moving in all the way.

"You got something, Lieutenant?" Fish said, half turning toward him in his chair.

Hestig came in with a clipboard on which were fastened a number of yellow radiograms. "I just wanted to report that we've been picking up a strange microsound distortion bouncing into our radar screen."

"A blip?" Fish asked, looking up at him with interest.

"No, sir. It's more like a sound wave, very sophisticated, very strong, too strong for our regular high-frequency sound detectors."

Fish sipped his coffee, frowning. "When did you notice it?"

"More seriously around three in the afternoon yesterday."

"What's so unusual about it?"

Hestig hesitated, glancing at his clipboard of papers. "Well, we recorded the sounds on tape and fed it through the computer. What we got back is that we have the sound associated with the antimissile missile guidance system."

"You could have a radio distort or a short-out bouncing a hot signal in the atmosphere."

"Sir, the computer—"

"Bob, what is an antimissile missile sound track doing out there on the polar ice?" Fish asked, smiling at Hestig, who licked his lips as if to say he knew how far-fetched it seemed but the facts remained.

"I am not unacquainted with that hardware," General Buckner said. "That is a signal that helps guide the ground in winging an antimissile rocket toward an oncoming missile in midair. Could the Russians be using it out there on the ice?"

74

"It's also been used in a more sophisticated manner by Apollo Houston as a guidance system in docking maneuvers in space," Hestig added, trying to lend credence to his discovery. "We managed to home on it enough to get the general area of source. It's coming out of a spot just about forty miles north of the Big Lead and a little west of it. The Russians are far over to the northeast, a good hundred and fifty miles away."

"Did you check Dietrich on it?" Fish asked, still not thinking it particularly relevant.

"I did, sir. He said he doesn't know of any signal like that coming in."

"And he's got more powerful equipment than we do," Fish added. "You got any ideas about it, Bob?"

"Well, sir, it could be that Dietrich has put another man on the ice equipped with a sound sensor so they can track his movements in relationship to Thorsen—"

"That would necessitate Thorsen's having the same kind of device," Buckner interjected.

"Was there any report of a similar signal any earlier?" Fish asked.

"The radar watch logged in a sound ripple on their sets three days ago," Hestig replied. "Since then we've tracked two distinct sound waves cutting into our screens. They are on infrequent signals, about six seconds apart. The computer separates them as two signals some distance apart."

"Dietrich has to know about it then," Buckner insisted.

"Two different signals could mean Thorsen has a sensor on him," Fish went on. "Only one sound wave three days ago meant that the radar was picking up Thorsen's going up Nansen Sound, maybe. Now it could be that there is another vehicle carrying a second." Nobody said anything for a minute; then Fish added, "It could be that Dietrich is operating on a top-secret priority in his attempt to go at Thorsen this way, trying to bring his own target in on Thorsen by the use of a tracking beam."

"I beg your pardon, sir," Hestig came in again. "If you'll permit me, that's a very expensive and complicated piece of monitoring beacon to use for an operation like this."

"Well," Fish countered with a smile, "this is a desperate case we are working on, you know."

"But, sir, if he merely wanted to track on a sensor device, there is a more efficient one, proven for that kind of job, the radio beacon super-sensor tracking beam."

"Just what is so sophisticated about what Dietrich is using?" Buckner wanted to know.

"It has to be laser components, General," Hestig replied.

"Laser?" Buckner exclaimed, glancing at Fish quickly.

"Yes, sir," Hestig went on. "Laser impulse was put into the antimissile missile guidance system two years ago; it is also used in the space guidance program on an experimental basis. It's really not that proven yet."

"So why is Dietrich, if he is using it, employing it for this kind of tracking?" Fish asked, pouring himself more coffee from the Silex.

"Well, only if it is a kamikaze operation—"

"A what?" Buckner cut in with a frown.

"Suicide vehicle, General," Fish explained, and gave off a heavy sigh. "The same as the antimissile gimmick . . . only this time a man carries the payload to Thorsen. When the guidance system registers closure, they hit the juice."

"You mean Dietrich got a volunteer to—"

"Why not, General? A one-man human bomb is nothing compared to what happens if Thorsen blows the rock, right?"

Buckner continued to stare at him. "All right, but why is Dietrich not sharing this kind of information with you, the coordinator of ice movements on Thorsen, and with me, the military coordinator?"

"He's a big man saddled with a big responsibility," Fish remarked offhandedly. "Maybe he figures Washington clearance would slow things down."

"Nobody is authorized to use laser filters without

76

clearing with all responsible parties involved," Buckner went on.

"You want me to phone Washington, General, and argue your point?" Fish was not looking at Buckner; he was concentrating on the coffee grounds in the bottom of his cup.

"All right, but doesn't it strike you as a bit odd that Dietrich orders off our military reconnaissance flights and ice teams at the same time that we pick up this signal? Apart from that, Admiral, who is going to be on top of Thorsen when and if that—that suicide vehicle, as you call it, does blow him up? The Russians, of course, while our people are nowhere near."

"Dietrich is practically next to the President himself when it comes to security," Fish argued. "I have to have a pretty good case going for me if I am to hint even remotely that Dietrich is derelict in his observance of rule zilch on page zonk of the Military and Civilian Procedures Manual Governing the Use of Laser. Especially if I managed to get Washington to muck up Dietrich's plan when the man may be trying for a kill out there that we can't effect ourselves."

"You have every right to question an operational procedure—"

"You're wrong, General, I don't have the right to question any operational procedure of a superior. But *you* have every right to do exactly that, as military coordinator, do you not?"

Buckner did not respond.

Fish ran his right hand through his thin brown hair in a gesture of futility. "Well," he went on in a more controlled tone, "I guess the least we can do is to get our Civilian Air Rescue to do some observing up there when the weather breaks. Bob, can you fix any specific position for those sensor signals?"

"We can try to narrow it down on our monitoring radio beam satellite, Admiral, but it won't be right on the nose."

"Okay, get me what you can. When you have it as

77

defined as you can get it, let me know. Meanwhile, get Dietrich back for me. I'll tell him we have a strong signal off the ice and we need an update on what he's doing."

"Supposing he won't cut you in on it?" Buckner asked bluntly.

Fish sighed. "Then as military coordinator, General, the ball is in your court, right?"

Buckner lifted one eyebrow, realizing that Fish was going to pin him down to taking the initiative in going over Dietrich's head, if they had to. He gave a small smile of acknowledgment of Fish's maneuver. "Then I will re-alert our military ice teams to get back on the ice," he said.

Fish nodded. "As you wish, General, but I would keep them at a safe distance. If Dietrich finds out you are mucking up his plans in any way, both of us may be stuck here in Thule for a very long time."

"I'm partial to a fish diet anyway." Buckner was trying to play it lightly.

Fish smiled, but his mind was not with it. He knew something was not right in what was happening on the ice, though he would not confess as much to Buckner. A laser guidance system was desperate, much too desperate for Dietrich to initiate on his own. Why would a man with nine years of playing it safe as one of the top security chiefs in the system suddenly get that reckless? Buckner had only vague suspicions. But for Fish, unless Dietrich could explain it, there was something definitely out of balance. For one thing, Buckner was right, of course; it didn't make sense for Dietrich to order off the American military teams at the precise time he put a kamikaze on the ice. That did, in fact, leave it open for the Russians . . . and even if they reactivated the Thule ice teams to go out, it would take days to get back within distance of Thorsen. The Big Lead was reported as much as a mile or two wide now, and not freezing over with the rise in temperature, and if this blow kept up, or if a fog moved in, as was often the case following the first spring storm on the ice, there would be no way to fly them in over the Lead either.

78

"Have the PBY ice rescue aircraft stand by for a flight, if and when this blow dies," he said to Hestig as they walked down the hall together. "I want to verify that kamikaze joker's presence on the ice if I can. He must have a radio, the crazy gooney bird. I hope he gets bogged down long enough for us to get operational on the ice, yet I hope he can do his job quickly enough before the Russians close any more, too. . . . You better get Dietrich right away. I don't like any of this either, any more than General Buckner does. Put the PBY on classified transmission, so nobody can decode."

"That include Dietrich?"

"Especially Dietrich, for now; I don't want him to know we are tampering with his orders. And you better try contacting that Interpol agent to find out her position. . . . Hell, I don't know what a woman is going to do about it anyway. But maybe she can get there in time to get the rock after the kamikaze takes Thorsen. She's not more than sixty miles north of Thorsen, and that will diminish as Thorsen keeps moving."

"She's been on the move, Admiral," Hestig said quickly.

Fish looked at him. "How do you know?"

"Well, she radios on her special frequency every day, same time, exactly at ten hundred hours. It used to be simply a routine check, garbled in code. Now it's definitely a change in territory. She was at eighty-six degrees north; this morning she was at eighty-five."

"Wise chick at that; she transmits at a time she knows Thorsen is probably busy moving his sled and won't be listening in. Well, next time she transmits, tell her not to close with Thorsen until we are sure the job is done. Got that?"

"Yes, sir."

"She's probably as green to ice conditions and travel as a duck climbing a tree. She could stumble slap-dab into Thorsen and not realize it. Sometimes I wonder," Fish went on in a heavy tone, "about the choices of people Interpol goes with." He turned into his operations shack and paused to add, "All messages come to me first, Bob;

79

even if Buckner asks, tell him to see me. I'll take Dietrich on my own frequency when you get him."

"Right, sir," Hestig said and moved on down the hall. Fish closed the door and leaned his back against it, frowning into the room. The wind-velocity monitor on the wall still showed it was gusting outside up to forty-five miles an hour, down some from the sixty-miles-an-hour bursts during the night. But the temperature gauge now showed thirty below, a rise of ten degrees since four that morning. If it kept going up, fog was inevitable on the ice. And that sometimes lasted for days. Thorsen could run by everybody in that soup and make it to the Pole before anyone knew where he was. Except maybe Dietrich, who had the monitor on him. But it was going to be tough to close with him, if visibility got marginal.

He could only hope that the human bomb up there on the ice had sense enough to know how to play it.

4

Sebastian awoke to silence. He blinked up at the roof of the tent, trying to orient himself in time and place. The sounds he had gone to sleep with, rumbling ice and rattling wind, were gone. He sat up quickly, knowing it must be late; they had to get moving.

He glanced toward Ah-Ming's sleeping bag. It was empty. He could hear the dogs giving that guttural kind of yelping that was mostly from the throat, expressing their hunger. Sebastian figured Ah-Ming was outside getting the pemmican ready for them.

He pulled on his boots, stood up, and reached for his parka, still hanging from the ceiling and still damp. As he pulled it on, he glanced down to see an empty fuel can by Ah-Ming's sleeping bag. Funny. The can had plenty of fuel in it last night, and the primus hadn't used very much. It wasn't like Ah-Ming to leave anything lying around like that. As he moved for the door, he stopped, realizing something was different about himself too. The parka . . . why was it so much lighter? He reached into his left pocket. The gun was gone.

He dashed out the tent door, catching the scene of drifted snow and huge hummocks of ice poking skyward in skyscraper dimensions. The air was still and warmer. But overhead it was misty, almost blotting out the low sun, which showed only as a feeble light bulb behind the screen. Fog. It was coming down in

81

wispy cotton shapes even as he stood there, his eyes moving around frantically for a sign of Ah-Ming. Nothing. The dogs strained at their harness pegs, wanting to be fed, wanting to be run. Big Bay nibbled at his right-hand mitten, trying to pull it off, to run with it. Sebastian cuffed him in the snout, impatient now, wondering if he should think the worst about Ah-Ming, yet afraid to.

Then he saw the tracks moving southeast away from the camp. He followed them, recognizing that the steps were jerky, staggering. At one place he saw where Ah-Ming must have fallen, the shape of his small body still visible in a snowdrift. The Eskimo had to be drunk; he must have drunk the ethanol fuel during the night, trying to build up courage to ward off Ano. And now what? Running for his life, maybe trying to get back to Eureka, anything to get off the ice he was sure was going to destroy him? A drunken Eskimo on the ice, Sebastian thought. He felt the jab of knowing that unless he got to Ah-Ming fast, his own chances of survival were limited, to say the least.

He pulled his parka hood over his head, went back to the tent, and got the snowshoes. The dogs kept up their racket as he did so, sensing that he was going off in pursuit, wanting to join the chase.

Big Bay stayed on Sebastian's heels as he moved off awkwardly on the snowshoes, trying to follow the staggered line of Ah-Ming's tracks in the snow. The parka felt heavy again, and he realized that it was taking on a coat of ice from the dampness still clinging to it. But it wasn't as cold. He was glad of that. Little things like that helped stave off his own sense of wild urgency to find Ah-Ming. But the dog counterbalanced it. He could see a good fifty yards ahead of him, but he knew it wasn't going to be long before visibility was practically zero.

He must have gone a quarter mile, he figured, and climbed up a small incline of snow and ice that had been a huge berg at one time. He was panting heavily when he got to the top. Big Bay was beginning to yelp for some reason—maybe because he had the fresh scent of Ah-Ming? As Sebastian got to the top of the ice mound, he noticed first that the ice ridge was a continual line of humps in a half circle. Below him, about ten feet, was the flat surface of the main sea ice. The circle of ice was a kind of a bowl, strung out in that freak kind of eruption that was so characteristic of the Arctic.

Then he saw the bear. It was standing on a pinnacle of ice like his own, maybe thirty yards away, looking down into the bowl. It was big, its yellowish-white coat almost camouflaging it completely against the background of ice. Its reptilian head lifted now and then to sniff the air, but its eyes remained intent on whatever was below.

Sebastian looked down too. The flat surface of main ice was probably a hundred yards in diameter. But as his eyes traveled rapidly around the circumference, he saw the broken hole. It stood out as a jagged piece of broken glass, a piece of irregular blackness against the outer lip of white snow. On the lip of the break lay Ah-Ming, not moving, sprawled flat on his back. Even at this distance, Sebastian could see the spreading dark mark of water seeping out from under him. He must have fallen through the ice, but somehow he had managed to get out without the ice giving to his weight. Sebastian continued to watch. Ah-Ming did not move; he could be frozen to death. Beyond him a few feet Sebastian saw the shape of the long barrel and butt of the gun cast into a mold in the snow.

The bear appeared to be getting ready to go down, apparently assured that here was game for the taking. There wasn't much time. Sebastian knew there was no way he could rush down into that bowl and drag Ah-Ming off before the bear got to him. He kicked his snowshoes off, finding them too cumbersome, as Big Bay began to growl and yelp, wanting to get at the bear, held only by Sebastian's grip on the hair at his neck.

Sebastian got up and started back, dragging Big Bay with him. One dog would be no help against the bear. He had to have all of them to keep the animal busy if he expected to do anything about Ah-Ming. He got back to camp, slipping and sliding in his run over the snow and ice. He slashed the harness stays free, and the twenty dogs took off in a rush across the ice toward the bear scent, Big Bay leading them.

When he reached the ice hummock overlooking the bowl, the dogs were already circling the bear, which paid little attention to them. Its mind was on the body at the open ice hole, and when two of the dogs jumped in to nip at its hairy flanks, the bear flipped them into the air with one whipping, murderous swing of a front paw. The dogs landed twenty feet away in the snow, rolled over, and charged again. Sebastian waited, catching the glint of the bear's yellow-white teeth as it snarled. If this was the old female Ah-Ming had mentioned before, it still showed all the murderous tools needed for tearing a dog or a man apart. So whatever move he made now, it had to be right, at a time when the bear was most distracted. . . .

The dogs started circling again as the bear moved off its perch and down the side of the bowl, to reach Ah-Ming before the dogs could get too pesky. At the same time, Big Bay jumped for the bear's neck, getting the advantage from a higher level. Five of the other dogs jumped with him. The bear skidded to the bottom of the bowl, righted itself, and went at the dogs seriously, its paws flashing out, hurling dogs to the right and left. All Sebastian could hear was the awful snapping, growling, and howling of the dogs, some in pain, some in the savageness of their attacks. The bear was certainly giving its full attention to them.

Sebastian decided it was time to move. He slid headlong down the ten-foot slope to the bottom of the bowl, righted himself quickly, and began running across the ice toward Ah-Ming. He sensed, rather than saw, the bear turning toward him, catching the new movement across its vision. The bear was thirty yards away from the hole, having to fight off the dogs to move at all. Sebastian figured he was maybe a few yards closer from this side. But even as he put his legs to pumping across that treacherous ice and snow, he knew the bear could be on him in seconds. He concentrated on making sure he made his steps count, trying not to slip, praying only that if he got to the gun, the breech and trigger mechanism would not be frozen. In the last six yards, he half slid to Ah-Ming, all the time conscious of the bear coming at him, ignoring the dogs, out only to save its prey. It was as if Sebastian were seeing his own moves as a slow-motion film, while the bear's movements seemed to be on fast forward wind as it lumbered across the ice, a couple of tons of mean, angry, snapping, murderous animal with a record of survival on the ice because of its capability for handling occasions such as this.

Sebastian had the gun up. Almost simultaneously he noticed the gloss of ice coating the breech, threw off his mitten to get a grip on the trigger, and rolled over to aim, knowing that a nine-millimeter weapon was hardly going to stop a charging bear of that mountainous size. As he pulled the trigger, there seemed to be an eternity of time before anything happened . . . and then the gun began bucking in his hands. He saw the bullets splatter across the front of the animal, digging explosive red furrows. But the bear wasn't going to stop. It kept on coming, looming higher and higher across that narrow open break in the ice, the dogs left behind in the chase, some of them limping from their wounds, others backing off from the sound of the gun. . . .

Then the gun was empty. Sebastian could only lie there next to Ah-Ming, waiting, hoping it would be quick. He had a split-second thought about the irony of going this way, alone, frozen, here in the endless white wilderness waste that man ignored and left only to a few animals like the bear. Of all the scrapes he had been in, this was not the one he would have chosen to end it. But then, his was not to choose. . . .

Now the bear was so close that Sebastian could see the saliva dripping from its teeth, the red tongue, the wildly rolling black eyes. As he closed his eyes against the first crunching blow, he felt something sag under the ice beneath him. At the same time, there was that familiar splintering sound. He opened his eyes in time to see the bear going stiff-legged into the open lead of water where Ah-Ming had broken through. The ice, breaking under the bear's weight, flew up in a cascade of a thousand nondescript parts, showering Sebastian. The bear, taken by surprise at the sudden collapse of the ice at the open lead, floundered in the water, letting out an angry roar at being denied its rightful due. Sebastian knew the bear was at home in such water and would not remain there long, but it gave him time to roll over and hunt for another magazine clip for the gun from Ah-Ming's hastily assembled pack. He found one, slammed it into place, turned quickly to let the bear have it . . . and instead he was confronted with emptiness. The open lead, where the bear had fallen, was only a froth of foam and bubbles, turning red. He watched it a long time until the bubbles stopped and just the crimson hue of the water remained, turning to a brittle glaze as the ice began to form again.

Now all he felt was sadness. "It was your world," he said to the red froth in the water, his lips hardly moving in the cold. His voice cracked. "I didn't want it this way. . . ."

Then he felt pain in his right hand and looked where it still gripped the trigger guard. He tried removing it but winced. His hand was stuck, frozen to the metal. Somewhere in the back of his mind, maybe put there by someone in Eureka, was the information that the skin freezes in just one minute of exposure to polar air. How long had he been lying there with his bare hand on that gun? There wasn't time to be academic about it, so with all his strength he yanked the hand off, yelling as he did so, the pain shooting up from his hand through his shoulder. He held it, bleeding and scraped, with his other hand, trying to warm it. He found his mitten in the snow and finally jammed his bruised, burning hand into it. The hand continued to throb even as he turned his attention to Ah-Ming.

He bent his head over the Eskimo's chest and heard the faint beat of life there like a distant drum fading over the horizon. Then the dogs started to whine again, telling him they were still hungry, having lost the bear they had counted on. Sebastian grabbed Ah-Ming by the collar of his fur parka and lifted him up. Staggering uncertainly under the load, he managed to get the short Eskimo up over his left shoulder. He fell three times trying to get back up the slope he had come down, the Eskimo tumbling away from him each time like a frozen board. He finally found a shallower ascent, got to the top, and hunted for his tracks. The fog was thicker, so dense that he could hardly see three feet in front of him. If it weren't for the dogs, who seemed to know the direction of the camp, he would not have found the tent.

Once back, he lit the primus stove, turning it up all the way to get the heat into the tent quickly. He pulled off Ah-Ming's outer clothes; they were frozen to the inner parka. The outer parka was nothing more than a clump of ice itself. The Eskimo should have been dead by now. Two minutes of exposure to polar water was about it; and how long had he lain out there on that ice? Maybe—if it didn't poison him—the ethanol in his system would save his life.

Once he got Ah-Ming into the sleeping bag, he went out and fed the dogs, going to each one and examining its wounds. Three of them would never make it. He got the gun and shot them, wincing as he did it, and then dragged them safely out of reach of the other dogs and covered them with snow. He would have to remember where he put them, because, much as he resisted the idea, he might have to eat them in the end. He noticed Big Bay had a big gash in his left ear, but the blood was congealing, so he would make it all right.

Sebastian returned to the tent. Ah-Ming lay very still in the sleeping bag. Only his head poked out, showing the white patches of frostbite. Sebastian examined his feet and found three toes on the left foot and two on the right already swelling rapidly. Both his hands were stiff and white. If Ah-Ming did live, he was going to lose a few toes and maybe all his fingers. . . .

Sebastian held both the Eskimo's hands in his own, trying to impart the body warmth that would cut the paralysis of the frostbite. Now and then he rubbed gently, trying to bring back the circulation. The tent was getting warmer, too. In the back of his mind, as he worked, was the need to be on the move: he was conscious of Thorsen, the moon rock, the urgency of his mission. All that, though, seemed remote; he had to keep reminding himself that he might have to go on alone. As ludicrous as it seemed, for he knew he had very little chance to negotiate the ice on his own, he had to make the attempt anyway. As long as the fog held this thickly, Thorsen couldn't do much traveling either. When it cleared, though, he had to be ready. He didn't know what he intended to do with Ah-Ming, leave him or carry him. But he knew he had to start moving, if for no other reason than that so little food was left to keep them alive.

Sometime later in the day, Ah-Ming opened his eyes just a crack. A low groan came out of him, sliding off into a feeble gasp. The pain of the frostbite must be digging into him hard. Then his eyes opened wider and he looked over at Sebastian, who was trying to organize things in the tent.

"*Oppernadleet*," he said, with a croak in his voice.

"What?" Sebastian asked, continuing to look for the food bars.

"Where—where we are?"

"Right back at the ranch, Ah-Ming."

The Eskimo did not respond. A groan came from him again, either in realization that he was still on the ice or else from the ethanol hangover which was now undoubtedly burning his insides.

"Ano put me through ice," the Eskimo said again, barely above a whisper. "Death come again soon."

88

"Yes, but you beat him once already," Sebastian countered. "You crawled out on him, something few men could have done. And the bear, which you didn't see, was cheated out of the final round. That animal died of a bullet, Ah-Ming, so if Ano had it in mind to do you and me in, it only proves he has a weak spot too. Now I think the fog is going to lift some, so maybe after a bit we can start moving. But if you want to stay here and wait for Ano and let gangrene set in in those fingers and toes and die a death not becoming an Innuit, it's up to you."

The Eskimo said nothing. Sebastian went outside to get a few more things from the sled, including the first-aid kit. He noticed the fog was lifting, but a curtain of heavy, mushy, white, soupy air still remained overhead. The sun was fading, creating a soft, reddish glare that blotted out the distinctions between ground and sky. Navigating in that was going to be hopeless, if not downright foolish, but he would have to try it. . . .

When he returned to the tent, Ah-Ming said, "You crazy holy man."

Sebastian paid no heed and dug into the first-aid kit.

"You think you beat Ano . . . but he wins . . . in the end. . . . You no cheat Ano. You no find T'orsen anyway; too late."

Sebastian found the antibiotic salve and put it aside. He rubbed his burning hand with snow from beneath the hides on the tent floor, waited a few minutes, and then applied the antibiotic to the raw skin. He was going to have trouble with that hand, he was sure. He moved to apply the ointment to Ah-Ming's fingers and toes, but the Eskimo refused.

"Let heat work. Salve only keep heat from doing job."

Sebastian put the salve back into the kit and got his cooking pot and went outside to scoop snow into it.

When he came back in, Ah-Ming said, "You dumb like Eskimo broad." His words were thick, a sign he was still suffering from the ethanol hangover. There was pain glazing his eyes too. "You should leave Innuit to die on ice. Ano wills it."

"Not yet, Ah-Ming," Sebastian said, putting the pan on the primus. "We'll find Thorsen first."

"Only one Eskimo sled left! Ah-Ming no use feet, no can walk, must ride—"

"Well, we've got eighteen dogs out there and enough harness to hitch them all," Sebastian replied, dropping three tuna bars into the cooking pot and putting it on the primus, watching the snow melt over the heat. "They'll pull you, as you said, to hell and back and hardly know it."

The Eskimo grunted in disapproval. "We go to hell, then, but we no come back."

"You just point me in the right direction to find Thorsen," Sebastian went on, "and keep me out of the open leads and crevasses. When we find Thorsen, Ano is beaten."

Ah-Ming tried to laugh, but it was smothered in his pain. He probably knew what their chances were, if Sebastian didn't, and he was as much as saying they weren't good.

For the next few hours, Sebastian tried to feed the Eskimo tuna soup. Most of it came back up. "You keep it down, Ah-Ming," Sebastian coaxed him. "By now that ethanol is fading out. You should have a big appetite. You eat and earn your money now. We've got to get moving, and you're going to help me find Thorsen. If you want to die, you're going to have to do it riding the sled."

The Eskimo looked up at him through the narrow slits of his eyes. He said nothing. Finally he took the cup of soup in his frostbitten right hand and drank it down. Sebastian handed him the pemmican. Ah-Ming put down three chunks of seal blubber and then rolled over to go to sleep.

Sebastian waited until 1:00 P.M. and then looked outside the tent again. Visibility was back to about fifty yards, but the sun was not coming through any

90

more. Though it was thicker and glowering overhead, he knew he could make some time in the few hours left before dark. He uncovered the dogs he had shot and loaded them on the sled. He got the supplies out of the tent and wrapped Ah-Ming carefully in the remaining caribou hides. He put an extra pair of woolen liner mittens on the swollen hands, an extra pair of socks on the feet. Then he carried Ah-Ming out to the sled and placed him on it, covering him with the extra fur parka. Finally he took down the tent and loaded it too. But there wasn't room to get it on, so he unloaded two of the dead dogs, kicking them aside into a snowdrift. The dogs began whining then, trying to tell him maybe that they didn't understand why he insisted on pushing them with such a load in this half-light and fog. They didn't want to chance running into thin ice they couldn't see in the fog, but Sebastian whipped them into line and hitched the harness. Maybe it was silly to attempt to go this late, but all at once he felt the urgency to be on the move.

The traveling was bad from the beginning. They were moving in fairly good snow, but the mounds of rafter ice were almost impossible to get through. According to Ah-Ming they should stay on a direction northwest because the ice drifted southeast. They would have to make up time even to get ahead of where they landed two days before, since the drift had already dropped them a good ten miles south of their first position. Ah-Ming kept shouting all this from his lying position in the sled, the cigar flapping in his mouth like a dry twig in a windstorm.

Sebastian's only hope was to gain the original position Dietrich had intended to drop him. Once on that "hummock of ice," maybe he could yet spot Thorsen with the binoculars.

But the going was tough. The ice ridges were getting taller, uglier. The dogs began looking over their shoulders at him as he drove them on. The fog, at the same time, took on a thick, milky cast, and visibility

91

was not more than twenty yards or so. The whole landscape around them, as he could see now, was nothing more than a continual line of upheaval, with jagged ice rafters poking bony fingers of ice skyward, like corpses frozen in a pose of accusation against this awful universe of death.

Finally they ran up against an impassable ice ridge that loomed ten feet over them and ran on a line either side beyond their limited vision. Sebastian got the ax out of the sled and began chopping at the ice while the dogs sat in the snow and whined and snarled at each other. He went on chopping against the stone-like yellow ice that yielded no more than an inch after what seemed an eternity of hacking at it. The sweat rolled down his cheeks and froze there, but he continued chopping, driven by that inner awareness that they could be locked forever into a boxed canyon of ice. Cook had said that in his log. He had found a way out by running twenty miles around one ridge, but Sebastian could not do that; there wasn't enough time or food left to allow them a twenty-mile end run around anything. He had to keep chopping, to kick a hole in that wall, to get through and maybe find that escarpment before night. . . .

It was getting darker, and the fog had all but swallowed the sled and Ah-Ming, only ten feet behind him, when he managed a passageway big enough for them all to get through. He slid down into the snow, too weary even to walk. It seemed to be getting colder, too. Maybe the fog would lift. They would camp here overnight and make a fresh jump for it at dawn.

He got up slowly and went back to the sled. Ah-Ming said nothing to him but just lay back in the bundle of furs, eyes closed, the cigar hanging limp in his mouth.

"We'll camp here," Sebastian said, and began throwing the supplies off the sled in movements that were almost painful with fatigue.

"No," said Ah-Ming suddenly.

"What?"

92

"No camp under ice ridge. Bear come down on you . . . or snow come in night, pile up under ridge, bury you. Move away from ridge."

Sebastian didn't argue. He threw the supplies back on the sled, snapped the dogs to attention, and moved them out into the murky fog and poor light, feeling as if he were being swallowed up in a tunnel of asphyxiating vapor.

"Here," Ah-Ming said, and Sebastian stopped the sled. He unhooked the dogs first this time and pegged them down. He put up the tent in slow, painful movements, his chest hurting with the effort. When the tent was up and the supply boxes lugged inside, he fell down on the caribou hides, too tired to take his parka off. But he got up anyway, went outside, and lifted Ah-Ming out of the sled, feeling his legs cave under the weight. He half fell with the Eskimo in the tent, but there was no sound from Ah-Ming. When Sebastian finally got him down on the floor, the Eskimo said, "You got to push like—"

"I know, like a good Eskimo broad," Sebastian interrupted, panting heavily as he stretched himself out alongside Ah-Ming. "How far do you think we got in that three hours?" he asked wearily, wanting something to help him believe he was going right.

The Eskimo did not answer immediately. Then he said, "Maybe two miles."

Sebastian lifted his head to look into the face a few feet away. The eyes were open, still showing the redness from the ethanol, the two black pupils glazed with pain from the frostbite.

"Two—two miles?" Sebastian rolled over onto his back and closed his eyes. In that moment he felt he could not get up again. Two miles! All that sweat and strain with the dogs, pushing the weight of Ah-Ming, cutting through and around ice ridges, running over open ice at times—*two miles!*

But he hadn't time to think about it. He couldn't allow himself to get dragged down by it. He got up and lit the primus, turned it up full to get the heat in the tent, but then remembered he had only two five-gallon tins of fuel left. He turned it down. He counted what was in the supply boxes. Eight tuna bars, five of bacon, one package of a dozen beef bouillon cubes, six beef bars, a half dozen rice bars, a half pound of oatmeal, a half pound of dried eggs, and a small box of raisins. He counted again. When he added up the pemmican, there were maybe four cans he could afford to keep; the other dozen would have to go to the dogs. And they would finish most of that tonight. . . .

The tent was warmer now, so he took off his parka, glad to be rid of its weight. Ah-Ming was watching him, he knew, through those slitted eyes. The Eskimo would be thinking about food too, balancing how much they had against what they would need.

Sebastian put in two tuna bars, resisting the temptation to toss in another. The soup heated quickly with melted snow. It smelled good. The tent soon took on an atmosphere of coziness, warmth, fellowship. Sebastian dipped out a tin cupful for Ah-Ming and handed it to the Eskimo, who took it and sipped it slowly, finally drinking it all.

"I can give you a little more," Sebastian said, because he knew the Eskimo's stomach would be crying for bulk.

"Enough," Ah-Ming said simply. "Feed dogs now."

Sebastian got up and went outside to the pemmican supplies. He tossed eight cans of blubber at the animals, who devoured it with the usual snaps and snarls. They continued to wait for more, but Sebastian decided to hold four cans back. He thought of the dead dogs he still had on the sled.

He went back inside, saying nothing to Ah-Ming. The Eskimo probably knew anyway. He found a half-eaten candy bar in his food pack and munched on it slowly, trying not to think of the big questions hanging over him. Did they know where they were, or did Ah-Ming? How long could they go on with so little food and fuel? Was there even a slim chance of finding Thorsen? If not, would it be better to consider it an impossibility, as the Eskimo suggested, and try to head back to land? Could they even make the sixty miles to land and then go another hundred down Nansen Sound to Eureka? The loss of the radio had tipped the whole operation off center; wouldn't Dietrich surely get a plane over them as soon as it cleared, anticipating that they had a problem?

He sat on the sleeping bag by the primus, listening to the ice tear apart not too far away, hearing the rumbling shock waves reach out to them.

"When you find T'orsen, you kill him?" Ah-Ming suddenly asked, his voice heavy with sleep and pain, his eyes closed.

Sebastian didn't reply immediately. He had almost forgotten what he was supposed to be thinking about on that level, so absorbed was he with the events of the past few hours.

"Yes," he said finally. He still felt a sense of confusion when he said it; wasn't he saying it right?

"Holy man no kill," Ah-Ming replied in a mumble.

Sebastian thought about it. "When a dog goes mad you kill him before he kills someone, right?"

Ah-Ming lifted his head an inch and looked directly at Sebastian. "T'orsen is mad dog?"

"Didn't Dietrich tell you about it at Eureka?" Sebastian asked.

"Dietrich say find T'orsen for you, no more."

Sebastian swallowed the last of the candy bar and told Ah-Ming what it was all about with Thorsen.

When he finished, Ah-Ming closed his eyes again and lay still as if asleep. "You no holy man if you kill," he said then. "If T'orsen mad, Ano take care of him . . . ice take care of him. You read Bible like dumb Eskimo wife?"

Sebastian hesitated without knowing why, unable to follow what should be a natural conversation. "Yes, of course."

"Dumb Eskimo wife say Jesus say love enemy, so she no hunt musk-ox or seal; no kill, only fish, so she fish and cut hole in ice . . . ice break, and she go through

95

with two children of Innuit." He paused as if recalling it all, the light of the primus flame casting a dim glow on his face, sharpening those small black thumbtack eyes. "She dumb. You kill enemy—T'orsen—you kill man. Eskimo wife not even kill seal to eat; dumb Eskimo broad read Bible like that."

Sebastian remained silent. He opened his mouth a couple of times to respond, but nothing came. That same peculiar fog hung over him, preventing him from finding the words. Ah-Ming's eyes remained slitted a long time, watching him, waiting. Behind his words, so void of expression, was that note of wonder, the inevitable tone of question, maybe to ease his own grief. And maybe he was confused, not able to understand, trying to find a pattern that would fit his own world of pain, perplexity, and emptiness.

Finally, when Sebastian looked at him, his eyes had closed and he was breathing heavier, his face in a sagging pose of sleep. Sebastian turned out the primus stove and crawled into his sleeping bag, glad for the darkness of the tent. But he heard the ice crumbling long into the night as he tried desperately to bring his mind to focus on God, on what he had possessed somewhere in what seemed to be such a long time ago. *God, what has happened to me?*

But there was no answer in the darkness of the tent.

Dietrich had been in the communications center most of the day, watching the storm gust up to sixty miles an hour. During that time the two pinpoints of light on the screen had not altered much. But during the day of March 11, forty-eight hours after he had put Sebastian and Ah-Ming on the ice, Thorsen's blip had definitely begun to move upward. Sebastian's did not change.

All morning and into the afternoon they watched the screen. Thorsen's blip moved steadily upward; Sebastian's crept almost imperceptibly up the glass face, but it was far too slow.

"That old fool won't stop for fog," Landau commented dismally, referring to Thorsen.

"What time is it?" Dietrich asked from his crouched position behind Bosman, his eyes on the screen.

"Going on six P.M.," Bosman said.

"How long has it been since Sebastian's blip last moved?"

"About three hours. They must be camped to wait out the fog."

"Have you gotten any acknowledgment to our radio signals from our party?" Dietrich asked for the third time in the past hour.

"None," Bosman replied.

"He must have lost his radio," Landau said. "And who knows how much of everything else?"

"It appears now that Thorsen is opening up quite a lead on him," Dietrich said, mostly to himself. "We could try to get a plane over Sebastian and drop him a radio. When is this fog supposed to lift?"

"Weather plots it about two days," Bosman replied.

"By then Thorsen will have opened an impossible lead on Sebastian," Landau said, with a heavy tone of pessimism.

"We'll have to keep our bets on him anyway," Dietrich replied conclusively. "Ah-Ming knows that ice."

"But you also said Thorsen won't let anybody approach him from the rear; he expects the military to come that way."

"Sebastian'll have to chance the pursuit," Dietrich argued. "He's all we've got to do what has to be done right now."

Landau said nothing to that, lapsing into an uneasy silence, sniffing loudly. "Admiral Fish is getting hot about our not helping him figure out the laser sound waves. What are you going to tell him?"

"As I said, nothing."

"They must have a sharp electronics man in Thule to pick it up at all," Bosman commented. "If he's that

97

smart, he'll know sooner or later that we've got the latest guidance sensors on a laser."

"Let's hope we will have finished our job by then," Dietrich replied.

"If Thorsen continues to pull away from our man, what then?" Landau went on. "What are you going to do?" Dietrich looked up at him, not comprehending. "I mean, Otto, are you going to let the Thule people maybe pick him up with all that explosive on him? Once he talks, your cover has blown and that puts the Kremlin in the hole, having to answer."

"That's the least of our worries right now," Dietrich replied with some impatience. "Bosman, you better alert our Russian teams on the ice to go on Phase Three, just in case."

"You've got that Interpol agent up there, too," Bosman offered. "We've been monitoring her frequency. The messages to Thule say she's on the move to try to intercept Thorsen."

Dietrich thought a moment, staring at the monitor screen, as if trying to see the girl up there somewhere. "You better warn her off," he said then. "If she gets in there ahead of Sebastian, we've a complicated scene at best. Tell her to hold where she is until we give her further advice."

"She maybe has the best chance of taking Thorsen now," Landau insisted. "She's less than fifty miles from him. Our Russian teams, even on Phase Three, in this kind of weather, won't make it that far west for at least three days."

"You want her to get the rock then?" Dietrich countered, showing irritation. "I haven't come all this way, planned all this, just to have the rock fall into the wrong hands."

"I am more interested in somebody getting it than allowing it to stay with Thorsen!" Landau snapped back.

"And I am only interested in the Soviet Socialist Republic's getting it, comrade!" Dietrich's voice carried a tone of warning, and the pupils of his gray eyes began to dilate as they fixed on Landau.

Landau sniffed and wiped at his nose with his handkerchief. Nobody said anything, as they watched the screen and the two stars of light.

"Shall I transmit to her on general or priority classification?" Bosman asked. "Do you want Thule to hear?"

"No. Go on priority—"

"She'll check back on an order to hold. What then?" Landau interjected. "You can't keep on giving Admiral Fish reason to believe we don't know what we're doing."

"Landau." Dietrich straightened slowly from his bent position, taking off his horn-rimmed glasses. His eyes showed red streaks of fatigue, and there was a drawn look to his face. "I must warn you to stop playing the KGB game with me here. As long as I am in charge of this operation, you will keep your second-guessing out of it. Is that understood?"

"I am responsible to protect the name of the Soviet Socialist Republic, the Kremlin—"

"You are responsible to advise me only on what I can expect from the people out there you have supposedly programmed to do your bidding! Anything else is none of your affair! If you cannot abide by that, you shall be put under arrest and confined to your quarters! Do I make myself quite clear, Mr. Landau?"

Landau blinked a rapid commentary with his eyes. "As you wish," he said stiffly.

Dietrich sighed, made to put his glasses back on, but folded them instead and stuffed them into his shirt pocket. "I am tired," he said, his voice regaining its even tone. "Perhaps we all are. . . . Bosman, you stay on that monitor until four. Landau, you go on from four to eight. I will be here then. If any change occurs between now and then, notify me. Is that understood?"

Bosman nodded. Landau blew his nose, saying nothing. Dietrich left without further word. Landau watched the screen a long time and then went for coffee. He did not sleep. He stayed in the galley until four. Then he went in and relieved Bosman, who had already dozed off in front of the screen. He awoke with a start, glancing furtively at Landau.

"Sleep well, Bosman," Landau said to him and sat down in the chair vacated by the fat man. Bosman stood for a few minutes, watching to make sure Landau had knowledge enough of the knobs on the set and especially how to use them. When Landau had demonstrated his abilities, Bosman turned and walked out, rubbing his swollen eyes, glad for the reprieve.

Landau sat a long time watching the screen, rethinking everything. He had to see beyond what Dietrich saw here. He had to anticipate how Zukov would react. He knew he could not allow that man Sebastian to wander all over the ice and maybe get picked up by the American military. There was too much at stake. If they did find those charges on him, and Sebastian did talk—which he would—Admiral Fish was going to put it all together. It would be disastrous if the Kremlin got implicated in this, especially if, in fact, Thorsen managed to blow that rock, and the old man could run right through them all now at the rate he was going.

No, Landau decided, he would wait here, and when he was sure Thorsen was opening a hopeless lead over Sebastian, he would hit the button. That would take care of the damning evidence. It could be done on this watch even before eight o'clock, or, if he had to wait, he could hit it any time, even with Dietrich and Bosman there. Dietrich would not dare punish him. They were equals on the KGB roster. And Landau knew Zukov would commend him for the action.

He turned up the sound control on the panel. The five-second bleeps sounded in synchronization with the flash of lights; to Landau it was like catching their slow heartbeats. It would be getting close to light up there now. By daylight the lights would change. Thorsen would be on the move again. Sebastian? Well, maybe his star would never move. He was either dead or totally immobilized. It would be interesting to see if his signal moved at all by eight in the morning. If it didn't . . . Landau looked at the red destruct button next to him. Maybe it would come sooner than he thought.

100

5

Sebastian awoke to fingers of light poking under the walls of the tent, turning the ceiling to a light glow. He sat up and looked toward Ah-Ming's sleeping bag, saw the familiar mound of his parka hood sticking out of the top. He sat up and pulled himself out of his own sleeping bag. The first shaft of the cold hit him so hard he grunted. He winced as his right hand took the weight of his body, and he glanced at it quickly. It had throbbed most of the night, pounding at his brain under the light cotton of sleep. Now it looked red and puffy in the palm where the skin had been torn off by the gun metal, and the redness was beginning to creep back over his wrist. Even his fingers were swollen and would not bend easily.

But there wasn't time to worry about his hand now. He got up and went about the usual ritual of preparing breakfast. When he went outside to get snow for his cooking pot, he noticed that the sky was still grayish and overcast, though visibility on the ice was better. The huge ice ridge that he had hacked at the day before was ahead of him, but more to his left now, indicating the drift of the ice during the night. He could still go out that way, but he would have to come back to the right again and hope to get on a proper course toward intercepting Thorsen.

He made the oatmeal, careful to weigh out the

portions in the fast-dwindling bag. By then Ah-Ming had stirred in his sleeping bag, but the Eskimo was making no attempt to sit up. Finally Sebastian went over to him, unzipped the sleeping bag, and pulled out Ah-Ming's hand carefully. It didn't look at all good. The fingers had swelled up even more and were purple-red in color. But what concerned Sebastian most was the grayness of Ah-Ming's face coming through the smoky-red hue of his normal skin color. The ethanol was not dying so easily in him. Sebastian was afraid that the poison might have damaged the Eskimo's kidneys.

As Sebastian leaned over him, the Eskimo opened his eyes, revealing dark pupils laced with the glaze of pain and fatigue. "*Ingluc-tu!*" he said, his voice sliding uncertainly, hoarsely, and his smile was a bit lopsided but game. "*Tigi-su conitu!* The Big Nail is near!"

Sebastian grunted. "About four hundred miles, that's all," he said in a bantering tone.

"*Ka-aga,* then!" Ah-Ming replied and pushed himself up on his elbows. Sebastian eased him back down, propping another sleeping bag under his back.

"Eat first," Sebastian said.

"Eat quick, move quick," Ah-Ming countered brusquely. Sebastian did not comment, sensing that the Eskimo was thinking of the necessity of finding Thorsen too. He ate some of the oatmeal and served up a portion for the Eskimo. Ah-Ming took a few spoonfuls, then pushed it away. "Pemmican," he said, and Sebastian found the open can from the night before and gave it to him. The Eskimo ate a few pieces and handed the can back.

As Sebastian finished the last of the oatmeal and washed it down with hot tea and a piece of the remaining chocolate, he wondered if the Eskimo could stand the ride in the sled with the temperature beginning to slide down again. It was nearly seven in the morning. He could wait here, maybe, for the sun to break through, hoping it would help cut the cold. But he knew better. If the cloud cover lifted for the sun, the temperature could go even lower. The best thing to do would be to travel while the warmer air still hung over them.

He fed the dogs the last of the animal pemmican; he knew it wasn't enough just by the way they kept looking at him, expecting more. Sebastian debated whether to dip into the four remaining tins he kept out for emergency for himself and Ah-Ming, but figured he'd cut up the dead dog later if he had to and feed it to them. He was about to turn back to the tent when he spotted Big Bay a few feet away, watching him. He had not fed him anything of the remaining pemmican, because the other dogs fussed too much. But now the dog was licking his chops, whining softly. Sebastian debated what to do about Big Bay. He was not pulling his weight in any way. Should he then be fed, taking away from the rations of the working dogs? The other dogs seemed to sense his hesitancy and looked up at him, watching, trying to get some hint about how he was going to treat them in relationship to the freeloader among them. But Sebastian, for some reason, felt Big Bay was a good omen for him. The dog had helped him with the bear. He felt a spirit of loyalty there that might be the only thing he could keep going with later on. So he went back inside the tent, got a can from the emergency pack, and gave it to the dog, using the whip on the others who tried to jump from their tether lines to fight Big Bay for it.

Back inside the tent, he gathered the supplies together, took them out, and lashed them to the sled. He saw the dead dog still lying in the canvas tarp. The cold had kept it well preserved. He didn't like the idea of having to cut up the animal to feed the dogs—or, who knew, maybe he and Ah-Ming would be sharing in it before long—but he knew it could come to that now.

He returned to Ah-Ming, got him out of his sleeping bag, and tried to get mukluks onto his swollen feet. The Eskimo grunted once as Sebastian tried to force the boot on.

"Wrap foot in mitten liner," Ah-Ming said simply.

"Crack that foot and you get infection, gangrene—"

"Wrap foot!" the Eskimo barked at him. His voice snapped, almost demanding.

Sebastian wrapped the small feet, pulling the woolen mitten liners over the woolen socks.

"We no go today," Ah-Ming went on. "Tent warm, good for frozen feet."

"We hold up, we die," Sebastian replied.

"You move in fog, you die too quick," Ah-Ming snapped back again.

"Hokay, hokay," Sebastian said lightly, but the Eskimo didn't respond. There was only a small frown between his eyes, evidence of the pain running through him.

"They'll send a plane over us today," Sebastian said then. "Dietrich must know our radio is gone. Better we be out on the open ice where they can see us."

"Plane take long time to find us now," Ah-Ming said indifferently. "Sky stay heavy outside, plane no see ice. Best you let Ano come, make death easy."

"There is no easy way to die," Sebastian replied shortly. "The worst thing anyway is to let it come a nibble at a time."

Ah-Ming did not respond to that either. Sebastian finished his work on the Eskimo's feet, finally tying a wrapping of wolverine fur around them for good measure. He picked him up and carried him out to the sled. Ah-Ming did not protest. Sebastian went back and struck the tent quickly, sensing there might be snow in the air. The wind was picking up again. He got the dogs into harness by using the whip.

"Huk! Huk!" he yelled at the dogs, and they moved out, heading for the gap that he had chopped in the ice barrier the night before.

It took almost an hour to get the sled up through the narrow pass in the wall, even with the supplies unloaded. Ah-Ming insisted on getting out as well, to ease the load on the dogs, and he lay there on the ice, watching, his feet resting on a small wooden box holding tins of food to keep them off the ice. Sebastian drove the dogs up the six-foot sharp abutment to the five-foot-wide enclave in the ice wall. Time and again they failed and fell back down with a lot of yelping and whining. Finally Ah-Ming scooted on his knees over to Sebastian and, before Sebastian could protest, was throwing his shoulder into the sled with him. The dogs pulled gamely this time, glad for the extra help, and finally they pulled up and through the narrow passage, the sled leaping over with them. Sebastian jumped quickly, trying to grab the end handles on the sled, to hold it from plummeting down the other side and overrunning the dogs. He missed. When he scrambled over the ridge, the dogs were caught in a wild scramble twenty feet below him—dogs, harness, and sled all jumbled together. The dogs were giving some terrible cries, the sled having hit them a mean wallop.

Sebastian went back first to pick up Ah-Ming and carry him to the other side. He noticed the woolen mitten liners and fur around Ah-Ming's feet were wet, already taking on a coating of ice. He put the Eskimo on a small hummock of ice and then turned the sled upright. Sebastian returned for the supplies, making two trips. When he examined the dogs, he noticed one of the lead huskies dragging a broken back leg. He led the dog away from the others and shot it. Ah-Ming did not look at him from his prone position on the ice ledge, keeping his eyes on his wrapped feet, but when Sebastian moved to leave the dead dog behind, Ah-Ming said, "Put dog in sled." Sebastian jammed his gun into his parka holster and dragged the dead dog to the sled and loaded it onto the canvas tarpaulin with the other corpse. He reharnessed the dogs, lifted Ah-Ming back into the sled, and started out.

This was the Arctic death by nibbles, and he knew it. The dogs first, one by one; what next? If the cold didn't do it, which would be a merciful way to go, starvation would.

He forced himself to concentrate on what was ahead. The world around him was filled with those same jabbing fingers of blue and green ice. In every direction there was nothing but a horizon of white or the cutting edges of that blue-green steel. The sky overhead boiled in its flurry of gray until he felt the first snowflake hit his cheek with the frozen harshness of a ghost's kiss. They were moving at a pretty good clip, gliding over a crusted snow that had melted some during the higher temperatures and now took on a new coating of ice that did well for the steel runners of the sled. But snow, if it came heavily enough, could bog them down again. He knew he would have to get as far as he could today, hoping he might chance on Thorsen. The possibilities, though, were slim. By now the more experienced scientist would be well ahead of him. In that case, he could only hope for a plane to come over; he **had** to keep hope alive that Dietrich would be trying to find him.

"That way!" Ah-Ming called out to him again, giving him course changes, watching the ice ahead, directing with an instinct born in him. After a couple of hours of running and pushing on the sled, Sebastian wanted to stop to ease the pain in his right hand, to release his grip on the sled handles. But he knew a stop would only cut into his will to keep going. . . .

The snow was coming in light, fitful spurts around noon when they began to come up on a slow rise in the ice mounds. Sebastian was sure they were approaching the ice hummock Dietrich had told him about, the place where through binoculars he could probably spot Thorsen. They crossed through a difficult line of rafter ice that slowed the dogs and dragged on the sled and finally moved into an open plain of ice and snow that extended a long way out in a flat tableland. At that point, in the lee of an ice ridge, Sebastian called a halt. He felt a weakness in his legs, and his breath came in stabbing shafts of pain in his chest, while his right hand felt fiery hot inside his mitten.

"Why you stop?" Ah-Ming asked, not looking around at him.

"Lunch," Sebastian said and dropped down onto a small ledge of ice, feeling the exhaustion slide down through his shoulders and out his legs. The cold was a mean presence within him too, taking firm hold around his feet, running a constant stream of chill up through his legs and spine, ending at the back of his head, where it pounded at his eyeballs. The end of his nose, despite the face mask, felt raw, and his lips were hard chunks of bare skin that he dared not even lick lest they turn to ice.

"You eat, dogs want eat," Ah-Ming said flatly, his voice almost lost in the rising gusts of wind. "Eat this, dogs no smell, keep moving."

Ah-Ming extended a piece of white tallow back over his shoulder toward Sebastian, the kind Sebastian had seen at Eureka being used as a candle when the power needed to be conserved.

"Wax?" he asked, getting up slowly, painfully, and moving over to the Eskimo.

"Fish oil," Ah-Ming corrected. "Chew slow . . . swallow slow . . . put heat in stomach."

Sebastian took a bite of it and caught the sharp taste of fish, right enough. It had the consistency of wax, but it was rubbery, like gum. There was another taste in it too that made his throat constrict, but he didn't dare ask Ah-Ming what it might be. He took two bites, then stuck the rest in his parka pocket, picked up the whip, and slashed it over the backs of the dogs. They moved out at a fast clip again, straight into the northwesterly wind and the snow.

It was getting on to two o'clock in the afternoon and the snow was fitful, sometimes coming in a driving torrent and at other times fading off into a miserable sleet. They had been running well, and Sebastian was looking for a way to cut directly north, heading for what he saw was a gradual incline, probably going up high enough for him to get some kind of view. At the

107

same time, Ah-Ming told him to swing left. The dogs obeyed, taking off for the challenge of what appeared to be some kind of ice island. Sebastian knew the wind was in his face, but the numbness of his skin kept him from feeling it any more. He was anxious for one thing: to get up on that escarpment of ice. . . .

But just as he was sure it would not be a difficult passage, Ah-Ming yelled, "Stop!" Sebastian halted the dogs quickly. He saw immediately what the Eskimo had seen a few seconds earlier. A black strip of water lay like an ugly smudge of ink against the snow and ice, widening even as he watched. There was the usual rumble of breaking ice above the sound of the wind. The floe they were on was tearing apart from the main ice island ahead. If they were going to cross, this was not the place. Already the open lead of water was better than six feet and widening.

"That way!" Ah-Ming yelled, and Sebastian whipped the dogs into a run to the left, running parallel to the open lead, hunting for a crossover. As he moved along, his heart sank. The black water was opening wider as he moved back the way he had come. He did not wait for the Eskimo to tell him to turn around. He pushed the sled into its turn, ignoring the stabbing pain in his hand. The dogs, sensing his urgency, threw all they had into it, and they rushed back along the open lead. They kept going along the edge of the floe, Sebastian ignoring the rumbling and cracking sounds under his feet, bent only on finding that part not yet separated from the ice island.

"There!" Ah-Ming shouted. Sebastian stopped to look at a thin glaze of ice covering the lead that was twenty feet across. It was new ice, recently formed, air bubbles still showing under its light gray afterbirth.

"Too thin!" Sebastian shouted at Ah-Ming.

"You wait, you no go!" The Eskimo shouted back. He got up, throwing off the fur hides covering him, and tried to get over the side of the sled to the ice.

"Stay on!" Sebastian yelled at him. But he knew

108

what the Eskimo was doing. They had to lighten the weight of the sled if it was going to have a chance of crossing on that flimsy piece of ice. Sebastian grabbed the furs out of the sled and threw them over Ah-Ming, who lay on the ice, watching the lead. Then Sebastian went over to it, poked at it with his boot, put his weight on it. The ice gave under him, bending more than breaking.

"Good!" Ah-Ming called to him.

Sebastian shook his head as he returned to the sled. "She'll hardly take the weight of the sled," he said. He tried not to think of what would happen if the dogs broke through, the sled dragging them under, and he himself going into that frigid water. How long then?

He also knew, by looking down the length of the lead as far as he could see, that this was the only chance. The floe was pulling away relentlessly, and if he was going to avoid being marooned here, he had to chance it. He made a move to toss the supplies off the sled, to lighten it further, but a resounding thump under his feet checked him. It was now or never.

He whipped the dogs forward, and they moved reluctantly toward the gray ice, glancing at him over their shoulders, wanting to be sure he knew what he was asking. The lead dogs wanted to hold up, but Sebastian knew that would be costly, so he whipped them, shouting, "Huk! Huk!" Even then the dogs slowed and would have stopped, but suddenly Big Bay galloped ahead of them as if he knew what his master wanted. The lead dogs, not wanting to be last to their bitter rival, picked up their pace, rolling at a good clip for the ice, yelping as they went, maybe trying to warn each other about the danger they were running into.

Sebastian watched the thin gray ice come up in his vision, trying to see if it still held firm. It looked the same, deceptively strong, realistically fragile. Off to the right about ten yards, the lead was opening wider. Soon the break would be complete. . . .

Big Bay galloped across the lead first, slipping and

sliding on the ice, bounding over to the other side. The pulling dogs, sensing what he had done, quickened their pace, and Sebastian gave a big push to the sled as they hit the ice.

He felt the ice giving under him as the sled's weight hit, but he did not look down. He kept his eyes on the opposite side, where Big Bay waited, watching. The speed at which they hit provided a momentum that carried the sled in a glide across the smooth new ice. There was a rumbling underneath, a snapping sound, even as Sebastian hooked his feet onto the long bars of the runner, going with the ride. The dogs scrambled to stay ahead of the sled, which picked up speed faster than they could keep the tension on their harnesses. Dogs and sled were all sliding straight across in a blur of uncontrollable speed. Then the ice broke, and the two lead dogs went in, just a few feet from the other side. Their heads went under as they fought to get free of their harnesses.

Sebastian, ignoring the crumbling ice around him, slid headlong across the few feet to the dogs, his knife slashing at their harness. He grabbed one husky by the long hair of his neck and threw him up over the side of the broken ice. He did the same with the other, as the rest of the dogs turned in fright and pulled the sled in a sheer desperate attempt at survival. Sebastian, at the same time, rolled over in two or three quick moves, trying to get away from the lip of the broken ice before it cracked under his weight. But it was the sled, suddenly yanked forward by the frantic dogs, that saved him; the rear end of the runner, with its hooked flange of steel where his foot rode, caught in the right pocket of his parka, and the sled jerked him for five feet along the ice, away from the broken slash, until it stopped hard against the opposite bank. He got up quickly, took three quick strides to the firm footing, and urged the dogs on until they were well up from the threat of the broken ice and the now-collapsing bridge over which they had come.

Sebastian simply stood there, his breath coming

110

hard and painfully. The two wet dogs shook off the water and ice on their backs, no worse for their ordeal. Their long hair was a natural protection against the elements. Sebastian also took time to acknowledge Big Bay, who nuzzled his mittened hand, wanting some recognition.

"Good dog," Sebastian said to him, his voice sounding feeble. Exhaustion was now pressing heavily down on his brain.

He turned from the dog, a little confused about what to do next, and as he looked back over the widening lead of water, he saw Ah-Ming out on the ice, still lying where Sebastian had left him. Ah-Ming looked like a piece of excess baggage left behind, a pile of litter cast aside. He lay flat on his back, not even looking toward Sebastian, staring up at the heavy sky, probably yielding himself to Ano for the last visit he knew was coming. In that moment, Sebastian hesitated. In the back of his mind was the urgency to move on, to keep going, to fulfill what had to be the larger picture: Thorsen. His mind told him there weren't enough supplies for dogs and *two* men to take them on the necessary journey ahead. That was what Ah-Ming was trying to tell him too, as he lay out there unmoving, resigned to his fate.

There was another irritating spark jabbing him: Could he make it without the Eskimo? But that gave way finally to something else, something intuitive. Did something deep inside the frozen chambers of his mind and heart rise up to tell him it was all wrong that that mound of nondescript humanity over there was resigned to death while he stood here determined to fight for life? Was there something about the Eskimo's fatalism that gnawed at him, that pricked at his conditioned spiritual life that had always refused to yield to contrary forces in the universe? He didn't really know. . . .

As he stood there debating, he heard the crunching sound of the ice again that continued in a foray of sound. He looked toward the left, and not more than fifty yards away he saw the ice floe come together with the main ice island he was standing on. Maybe it was one last em-

111

brace before parting altogether, but for that moment there was a bridge, a solid one, back over to the floe and Ah-Ming.

Sebastian did not hesitate. He whipped the dogs out into a loping run, down across the closed lead, and out onto the floe again. If he worked fast, he could be back over that bridge again before it parted.

As he came up to Ah-Ming, the Eskimo lifted his head off the ice to peer at him in disbelief. Sebastian picked him up and dropped him into the sled, threw the furs in after him, then gave the whip to the dogs again, pushed the sled around, and started back for that solid bridge.

He wasn't even halfway there when the familiar rumble started under his feet, followed by a splintering crack. The floe had broken loose again, only this time it shifted in a violent break away from the ice island. The bridge dissolved and gave way to the ugly black strip of open lead. Sebastian stopped the dogs. He could only watch as the floe pulled away from the ice island, opening a lead that grew wider and wider. Sebastian urged the dogs on, hoping he could find one bridge still intact on the back trail from where he had come earlier. But it was the same there. There were only open leads of water around the half square mile of ice he was on. And as he looked southeast, the direction of the drift of the floe, he saw no large ice packs on which the floe could hook again. There was nothing but open black water filled with tiny floes that had broken up with the movement of the ice. As far as he could see in that direction, there was nothing but water. Only to his extreme left, eastward and northeast, a long way off, could he see the familiar skyscrapers of the main ice pack. But there was no way that the ice floe could hit that, not with its present direction. It was going to keep drifting southeastward, maybe to hook finally with the main ice pack on the Greenland shoreline. But, more likely, before it ever got that far, the floe would break up into smaller and smaller chunks and finally dissolve totally.

"Hee-heee-hee!" Ah-Ming's laughter sounded weird, almost mocking, the humor of the fatalist. Sebastian waited for him to say something. He didn't. The laughter said it all. Finally Sebastian picked up the Eskimo and put him down on the ice. Then he unloaded the supplies, put up the tent, unhooked the dogs, and tethered them. He didn't feel like thinking about ice or open leads or water right then. He wanted the tent, the warmth, some food and sleep. If he was going to die, he wanted it to come around a turned-up primus flame and a reasonably satisfied stomach.

Once when he looked down at Ah-Ming to see if the mocking grin was still there, he noticed only a deadpan face, the slits of eyes studying him, the Eskimo still unable to understand the stupidity of his action. There had to be something else too, Sebastian sensed; was the Eskimo maybe thinking that, as long as he had to die anyway, he didn't want to do it with someone who had committed a totally senseless and incomprehensible act in a world that did not accept such gestures? Sebastian didn't know what was going on in Ah-Ming's mind, behind that stoic face with the small, digging frown between the dark eyes. The laughter had said much, but he was unable to interpret it fully, because he did not know this world or recognize the parameters of life and death that kept it in cycle.

So he picked up the Eskimo in his arms again, noticing that the bundled feet were coated with ice, and moved inside the tent. He turned up the primus, rolled out his sleeping bag, and fell on it, his parka still on. He tried to stay awake, to be alert to the dangers of the floe breaking up, but slowly the cotton came down on his brain, and he slid into it, unmindful of the rumbling ice beneath him or the rattle of ice drizzle on the tent roof.

Later that night, at 2300 hours (11:00 P.M.), Admiral Fish was called into Bob Hestig's world of computers, radarscopes, and tracking beam signals. Fish was not in a good mood. He had not managed to get anything out of Dietrich about the laser sound waves. All he got was: WE ARE ON COVER OPERATION AND DO NOT WISH TO DISCUSS ON OPEN CHANNEL. YOU ARE TO STAND DOWN ON COMMUNICATIONS TO US. DO NOT ACTIVATE ANY MILITARY UNITS ON THE ICE. Fish had asked directly if Dietrich had a suicide vehicle on the ice, but Dietrich did not even comment one way or the other.

Now Fish came into Hestig's area after having tried to get a few hours of sleep. He had not managed very well. He could not reconcile Dietrich's attitude in the events now taking place, and he was still debating as to whether to put through a verification request to Washington on Dietrich's use of laser guidance hardware. To do so, however, was to cast suspicion on a trusted top-level security officer. Unless he had something more to go on, the ripples coming back from Washington would swell to tidal-wave proportions by the time they got to him. Even General Buckner demurred from making that kind of move on his own.

"Anything new, Bob?" Fish asked Hestig, who was busy poring over a thick manual of code classifications. The lieutenant looked at Fish in surprise, apparently not expecting his superior to be back in the code room at this hour.

"It may not be much of anything, sir," he said. "I picked up a coded message some time back and only now was able to break it. It has the Eureka call letters on it." He handed Fish the penciled message: CANNOT ACCEPT ORDERS TO HALT. AM PROCEEDING THORSEN INTERCEPT AT 84 DEGREES, 50 MINUTES NORTH. LITTLE BO PEEP.

"So who is this—this Little Bo Peep?" Fish asked, rubbing his hand over his two-day-old stubble of beard.

"I believe it's the code name for that Interpol agent, Admiral."

Fish nodded, continuing to study the message. "Looks like Dietrich gave her the order to hold off intercepting Thorsen, too. That figures, I suppose. He wants to get his kamikaze in there first. When did she last transmit to us?"

"At ten this morning, sir. She said then she was shut-

114

ting down and would contact us after final experiments."

"Experiments?"

"She uses that language over the air to give Thorsen the idea, in case he's listening, that she's with the Norwegian ice team measuring ice drift. But what she's saying is she'll contact us when she gets to Thorsen."

Fish frowned. "Why didn't Dietrich talk to her in code we could monitor so we'd know what's going on? Why is he getting so clandestine in his operations all of a sudden?" Hestig did not respond. "How did you crack this code anyway?"

"It's international military classification," Hestig said. "I noticed the Sigma signature when it came in. I worked on a few of those when I was breaking code for the military chief of staff in Washington a year or so ago. So I took the gamble, sir, and sure enough I found the key in our Thule classification of international military."

Fish nodded, still feeling perplexed. "So that gal up there—Little Bo Peep?—has actually told Dietrich to go to hell. Why? She must know that no outside agency like Interpol, cutting into Moon Rock, has the authority to disobey an order from the chief of the operation. What does *she* know that we don't? I better try to get a flight to Eureka. How's the weather?"

"No ceiling yet, sir," Hestig replied. "Maybe in a couple of days."

"Great," Fish growled, beginning to pace the floor, the message in his meaty fist. "Is Dietrich's line open?"

"It's been on a blackout for the last six hours, sir. Could be the weather."

"Very convenient," Fish muttered. Then, "I'm going to have to try for verification on Dietrich's use of laser, Bob."

"Washington, sir?"

"Why not? They don't seem to have any reluctance to send us priority messages at all hours of the day and night as to what we are doing."

Hestig hesitated. "Verification on Dietrich's laser only, then, sir?"

Fish looked at him out of red-rimmed eyes. "No, I

115

want verification on the kamikaze move, too. Dietrich is supposed to file that kind of action with the big boys. I want to know if he has."

"It's late in Washington, too, sir," Hestig advised. "Do you want me to put a priority classification out? That means somebody has to get out of bed to take it."

"It's time they lost a little sleep," Fish snapped. "Get on it, Bob."

It took an hour before Hestig cleared the channel and got a response to the verification request. Fish was on his fifth cup of coffee, which added up to at least twelve for the day. His stomach burned from the acid, and his head throbbed.

"I've got Sullivan on the other end," Hestig said. "He's the clearance chief for the CIA."

"What about the big man, Morton?"

"Not available at this time, Admiral."

"That's just great! We got a world disaster in the making and he's not available!"

"Sullivan says Morton's with NASA officials now, has been all day."

"All right, all right. Tell him we need verification of Dietrich's use of laser guidance vehicles on the ice and also of his possible commitment of a suicide vehicle."

"Right, sir," Hestig said and began transmitting in the code sequence that only the CIA in Washington could respond to. After a few minutes, he turned and handed Fish the penciled message: STAND BY ON CHECK OF LASER AND DESTRUCT VEHICLE DIETRICH. SULLIVAN.

Fish grunted and looked up at the clock. "Who knows how long that will take to get through channels? I'm going into the lounge and try to get a few winks, Bob. Let me know when."

He had only been dozing a short time, it seemed, when he jerked awake to see Hestig bending over him. "Washington, sir." He got up from the lounge chair with a grunt, taking the cup of hot coffee Hestig handed to him, and squinted up at the clock on the wall. It was five minutes after two.

116

"Morning or afternoon, Bob?"

"Morning, sir."

Fish glanced up at him. "That has to be a time record on a simple verification message out of Washington," he said, and walked out into the communications plot room, Hestig on his heels. The message was there, done up as usual in Hestig's neat pencil·

VERIFICATION REQUEST ON DIETRICH-LASER-KAMIKAZE. NO COMMUNICATION DIETRICH. ATTEMPTING CONTACT AGENT FOXTROT INSIDE EUREKA. URGENT YOU USE ALL MEASURES PREVENT KAMIKAZE CLOSING WITH THORSEN. REPEAT. PREVENT KAMIKAZE MISSION THORSEN. WILL ARRIVE THULE TEN HUNDRED HOURS MARCH 13. MORTON.

Fish let out a low whistle. "Get Buckner," he said to Hestig, who got on the intercom to call the general. A few minutes later Buckner came in, looking disheveled, as if he too had not been sleeping. Fish filled him in on the Washington message.

"Looks as if it's beginning to boil over," Fish added.

"Do you think this Agent Foxtrot is one of the CIA's or NASA's, checking on Dietrich?" Buckner asked, reading the message again.

"Everybody watches everybody else in the space program, General," Fish replied dryly. "And certainly on this operation. There's even somebody keeping an eye on you and me in this place, did you know that?"

Buckner looked up at him as if he didn't comprehend. "No, I didn't."

"The point now is that our suggestion of a kamikaze moving on Thorsen has caught Washington by surprise," Fish went on. "That means Dietrich has not informed them either. And that is odd, very odd. Well, General, you'll have to get a copter up under that cloud cover as soon as it's light and try to find that kamikaze, right?"

"We don't even know officially yet if he is a kamikaze," Buckner said dubiously. "Can't you get him on the radio and call him off?"

"We have had no radio signals off the bearing where

the sound sensor is coming from," Fish said. "He probably lost his radio . . . or maybe Dietrich ordered him to stay off the air."

"What are you suggesting I do if I should spot him?" Buckner asked.

"Well, try to set down on him and tell him it's all called off," Fish said a little uncertainly.

"Is he going to accept that without verification from Dietrich?"

"I don't know. If he doesn't, I guess you know what to do, right, General?"

Buckner thought about that a long minute before responding. "We started out to try to shoot Thorsen. Now we have a second fish in the barrel."

"That's the way these things crumble, General." Fish tried a smile on him.

"Okay, but setting down on the ice in this wind. . . . What if I can't?"

"Talk to him over a PA. What I'm saying is try every means to back him off short of zapping him. I expect you'll have to do what the conditions call for. In any case, our assignment is to prevent the kamikaze from closing with Thorsen, so you better get your military teams moving again too, in case you miss."

"They're stalled this side of the Big Lead."

"Then unstall them," Fish said shortly.

"Why doesn't Washington just let the kamikaze go ahead and do the job?" Buckner argued. "What reason would they have to ask for a prevent or even destroy?"

"General, when Washington told me to do something, I've never asked them to play patty-cake instead, have you?"

"Well, it's still a pretty big chew without verification of cause, especially when we don't know what Dietrich has in mind."

"So I guess it will have to be my chew, right, General?" Fish replied, looking straight at him. "Bob, where were the Russians at last sighting?"

"We had them at eighty miles west of eighty-five degrees and thirty-six minutes north. That's about where

Little Bo Peep is right now. But we haven't had a recon over them in thirty-six hours."

"So you can bet they are a lot closer," Fish said. "General, we've been wondering how the Russians could know where Thorsen is all the time. Well, maybe the source is kind of narrowing down, wouldn't you think?"

"Are you going to pin everything on that Interpol girl up there?" Buckner asked skeptically.

"Well, she's closer than anybody else now. Our estimated guess on that kamikaze—if he is that—puts him south of Thorsen, a good twenty-four hours off the track, maybe more. To answer your question, General, yes, she's all we've got right now, and Washington is apparently putting it all on the line with her too. But we better get our recon planes up today and get a fix on the Russians and certainly on Thorsen. If we can, have one of our planes make a pass over Little Bo Peep and drop a message to her on Thorsen's course. Better not try to use the radio."

"Yes, sir," Hestig said.

"I'm going to try Dietrich one more time," Fish said, moving for the door. "Keep me in touch, Lieutenant."

He went out then, and only Buckner remained in the room with Hestig. The general kept reading the message in his hand, still not sure. Finally he said, "Lieutenant, you better give me that kamikaze's last and nearest position."

"It's only approximate, sir."

"That will have to do." Buckner paused, rubbing his right hand over his mouth. "Poor fool. He won't know who to believe or trust now . . . not a very good way to die, in any case."

Otto Dietrich came into the communications shack at Eureka a little past four that morning, summoned by Landau. Landau, who had been watching Sebastian's tracking beam all day and seeing it slide farther off the closure with Thorsen, had held off hitting the destruct button. But since around six earlier the previous evening, it was obvious, even as Bosman indicated, that the Sebastian track was moving slowly southeast. Landau knew then it would have to be done. He also had the latest top-priority message out of Washington, only minutes old, asking for clarification of laser filters and whether a suicide vehicle had been launched. Landau figured to put it up to Dietrich, hoping he would give the order for the destruct. But if he didn't, Landau was fully prepared to do it himself.

When Dietrich came through the door, opening the room to a frigid blast of Arctic air, Landau handed him the Washington message at first. Dietrich pulled off his parka hood, then his mittens, and took the message, reading it slowly.

"You will have to tell them something," Landau insisted loudly, his eyes fluttering. "And you can be sure Fish must know. He's probably the one who asked Washington for a verification on lasers and the matter of the possibility of a suicide vehicle. You should have told them you were doing it."

"They would have refused to allow it," Dietrich said flatly. "And that would mean having Washington men crawling all over this place."

"Why wouldn't they allow it?"

"Because they would consider it too dangerous to the rock to try to set off a charge so close to Thorsen, that's why. By the time I got through assuring them, or maybe failing to do so, where would Thorsen be then?"

"Well, where is he now in relationship to your man?" Landau fired back. "Anyway, Washington is not going to sit around knowing the Russians are getting closer."

"It will take them too long now to make the move to change the course we are on," Dietrich snapped, growing impatient with Landau again.

"You think they will be pleased that you used a—a clergyman who is not even aware that he is loaded with explosives?"

"Landau, I don't give a damn right now what they think," Dietrich retaliated, his eyes snapping. "I am committed to the action in front of me."

120

"Your man is hopelessly out of it!" Landau was almost yelling. "You are only going to let him fall into the hands of the Thule military, and when he talks—"

"I already have a copter ready to go up at first light and pick him up," Dietrich cut in abruptly. "We are going to drop him north of Thorsen's route and try again."

"It's too late for that now!" Landau screamed. Bosman looked up at him quickly. "The weather is not even fit for birds to fly in! You won't find him for days up there!"

"Landau!" Dietrich barked, his voice commanding silence. Landau paused. "I warned you once to stay out of this! I am operating on a priority clearance here from Washington! Now you are either going to abide by my actions here and keep quiet about it or—"

"You have been derelict in all this, Dietrich, to the undoing of the Soviet!" Landau went on, his voice rising raucously. "I will not be a part of this, nor will I allow you to implicate us all in this hopeless attempt!" In one quick move, he turned and slammed both palms down on the red destruct button on the panel beside Bosman. Dietrich did not move. Bosman only stared at him. "So it is done!" Landau bellowed in triumph. "And you will have me to thank in the end, Dietrich, even for saving your neck with Zukov! Now watch your bright star on that screen die, Dietrich, and know that your own star dies with it!" He turned and looked at the screen, then, and his crooked smile began to fade slowly. "It does not go out!" he said in disbelief. "It—it doesn't work! All this time you knew it would not work! All this time you deceived us."

"Of course it does not work, Comrade," Dietrich said quietly, his voice on a flat tone of indifference. "Do you think I would let that red button hang out for anybody to come along and play with? It is only activated when a key is turned in the mechanism underneath the connecting circuits. And I, Landau, am the only one who has that key."

"I don't believe you!" Landau almost screamed

121

back at him, and his skeletal body shook with rage under the heavy brown sweater that hung on him like a blanket, and the redness in his neck ran up to engulf his face in an eruption of bulging blood vessels. "I have never believed you, Dietrich! Not even from the beginning in Houston! You are not one of us! You spent too much time with the decadent bourgeois in Houston! Everything you've done here has been amateurish. Zukov will know—"

"Get hold of yourself, Comrade!" Dietrich broke in sharply. "I am warning you for the last time! You will conduct yourself as becoming a soldier of the Soviet Socialist Republic! Is that understood?"

Landau paused, staring at him, breathing heavily in the aftermath of his own outburst, but not so sure he could continue to push Dietrich without serious repercussions. "I am a soldier, a loyal one," he said in his own defense, but his voice had gone back to a tone of appeal. He found his handkerchief in his pocket and blew his nose hard.

"Then I suggest you get some sleep, Comrade," Dietrich advised in his even, controlled tone, almost weary now, as if he knew this exchange was a waste. "Go on, you've been hanging around here far too long."

Landau looked aimlessly around the room for an ally. Then he shrugged, pulled on his parka, and went out without further word.

Dietrich said nothing to Bosman for a long time. Finally Bosman said, "That Interpol agent up there still won't reply or comply with your order to hold off. Do you want me to try again?"

"No," Dietrich replied in a meditative tone. "Let her go in. I may not be able to find Sebastian in this cloud cover anyway. If she goes in and takes care of Thorsen, our Russian teams will be right on her. It looks now as if they are no more than twenty-five miles west of that intersecting point she is on. Be sure you keep them out of the picture until we are sure."

"Will she radio if she is successful with Thorsen?" Bosman asked.

"You can bet on it."

"Does she know the Russians are close by?"

"Maybe. But she can't hold out against thirty of our people by herself either. And Thule has been stalled too long to get up there fast enough. Is Thorsen still on the move?"

"He's slowed down quite a bit. In fact, he didn't do much all day."

Dietrich weighed that in silence, studying the screen closely. "And Sebastian hasn't done much either?"

"He was moving slowly southeast all night, for some reason. Now he's stationary."

"Southeast?" Dietrich asked quizzically. He thought a moment, then added, "Could be he's marooned on an ice floe."

"In the meantime, there have been quite a few classified messages out of Washington during the night asking for an update. Do you want to answer them?"

"Shut down all incoming and outgoing transmissions to them and to Thule," Dietrich said. "Put out a power-failure limitation."

"Yes, sir. They may send somebody in from Thule or Washington to check. What shall we do when they arrive?"

"You better move your monitoring screen to the place we suggested as soon as you can," Dietrich replied. "But if they should drop in before you can do that, remember that you are simply using a tracking beam to keep Thorsen and our rescue in sight. Don't mention anything about a suicide vehicle. Cover your destruct lever there too. Anything else?"

"No, sir."

"Very well. I am going for breakfast. When the helicopter captain says he's ready, call me."

Bosman hunched up against the cold that swirled into the room and went back to studying the screen. He sensed the first real sign of a crack in Dietrich's composure. Landau's raking of him had shaken him more than he would admit.

He glanced at the few Washington Class A, top-

123

priority messages that had come since the one Landau had taken. They all repeated the same thing, the need for verification of the laser and the suicide vehicle. Bosman wondered if he should call Dietrich's attention to the urgency of these messages, all of them signed by Morton, the coordinator of Space-CIA Operations. It was unusual for the big man to make a direct approach like this. But then, Dietrich would not pay any heed to them. He was determined to make the suicide package work, and nothing would stand in his way. So Bosman dropped the messages into the metal container by his foot and lit them with a match. Then he put a shutdown on all communications coming in as Dietrich instructed, laying on power failure as the reason.

Now it was all reduced to that screen with its little white stars and Dietrich's ability to make his moves fast enough to change the complexion of things on the ice before Washington or even Thule jumped in here. It was going to be close, very close.

Landau did not go to his quarters as Dietrich suggested. Still seething inside and convinced he had to do something about the growing danger that Sebastian posed, he went to the helicopter pad where the crew was busy making preparations for Dietrich's flight. It was light now, and the clouds were still hanging heavy, but there seemed to be an indication of a break later on in the morning.

Landau looked to the left, where another copter was sitting about twenty yards away. Two crew members were preparing to turn the rotors over to keep it lubricated, as was the custom to prevent freezing. Landau knew that it was the patrol helicopter used to make brief forays up and down Nansen Sound every few hours to do routine checking on any possible unlisted exploring parties.

Landau finally went over to the sergeant who was knocking ice off the copter pad with an ax. "We are ordered up, Sergeant," he said crisply.

"Sir?" the sergeant said, turning to look up at him. "We are going as back-up copter to Dietrich's, over there. Dietrich has ordered us up over the ice area in search of our ice team. You know about that ice team?"

"Yes, sir," the sergeant responded. He hesitated. "But I got no standby orders—"

"Sergeant, we have no time to follow protocol!" Landau hissed at him. "If you want to tangle with Dietrich in the mood he's in, you better be ready to put your military career on the line! Do you understand me?"

The sergeant turned and looked at his two crewmen, who had stopped to listen. They looked a little dubious, but both of them shrugged, and the sergeant said, "Okay, Mr. Landau. We were heading out for patrol over Nansen anyway. We could use a little change of scenery."

"Good!" Landau chirped. "You have armament on board?"

"If you mean do we have weaponry, yes, sir!"

"Good! I want to ride up front with you, Sergeant! I will handle the radio, all right?"

"Anything you say, sir!"

"Have you navigation charts on board?"

"Yes, sir, all we need is the bearing."

"That I have, Sergeant! So let us be off now, before Dietrich has us all in the cooker!"

"We going to get Thorsen, Mr. Landau?" the sergeant yelled in expectation as they made preparations to lift off.

"Could be, Sergeant! Could be!"

6

He awoke to darkness in the tent. He lay there a long time listening, knowing something had brought him out of sleep. He sat up, trying to piece together time and place and events. Then he heard it: a thump, some way off, but quite different from any other sound. He got out of the sleeping bag, his jaws immediately beginning to rattle with the cold. His watch showed it to be 4:20. He pulled on his heavy clothes and parka. The parka was wet, and he hated to go outside only to have it ice up again. But he had to check right then.

He took his flashlight, stepping over the sleeping form of Ah-Ming. But as the light swung across the Eskimo's face, he saw that the eyes were open, watching him.

"You hear that thump?" Sebastian said to him.

Ah-Ming did not respond immediately. Then he said, "Ice hook on to other ice." His voice sounded weak, almost uncertain.

Sebastian turned and went outside, pulling on his face mask against the cold. The dogs were sleeping yet in their balls of fur, not rising to his flashlight playing over them, knowing it was too early. Sebastian walked southeast on the floe, keeping the light ahead, looking back to make sure his footsteps showed on the fresh snow leading back to the tent. He had walked maybe ten minutes when he realized, by shining the light ahead, that the ice floe had in fact hooked on to the other ice.

There were no signs of black water where it had been the night before. The view in front of him, as far as the light would go, showed a continual ongoing of the flat bed of ice, until he saw the first shapes of the huge rafters beyond. That was the main polar ice pack! That same line was east and north of him when he camped last night. Had the ice floe shifted around with new currents during the night? If so, while he had slept, the floe could have moved northward, maybe carrying him farther than he probably would have gotten with the dogs in the same period of time! Maybe?

Excited by that possibility, he ran back to the tent, anxious to get breakfast out of the way and be on the move. He lit the primus, saying to Ah-Ming, "We hooked on to the main ice pack. Could we have drifted northeast last night?"

The Eskimo said nothing. Sebastian noticed that his face was pinched, a sign that he was feeling even more pain in his hands and feet. He went ahead and made the small breakfast, using up the last of the oatmeal. But Ah-Ming would take none of it, not even the pemmican.

"You don't eat, you die." Sebastian tried, prodding him. Ah-Ming again said nothing. Finally Sebastian went outside. It was after six, and the sun was turning the cloud cover to an explosive red. Today, maybe, it would lift, and a plane would be over him. He would have to get Ah-Ming out right away and take his chances on going after Thorsen himself.

When he went inside again, he took off his mitten to examine his right hand. The redness was up over his wrist and creeping up his arm. The antibiotic salve had done some work on the palm of his hand, but the infection was still in his fingers. He couldn't be sure how long he would be able to use it.

He decided to feed the dogs the pemmican from the remaining cans in his emergency pack. It was hardly enough, and they broke out in vicious fighting to get what little there was. Later tonight they would have to chew on the dead dog, unless a plane came over with a drop. As for himself, he was down to the tuna and bacon bars. His body even now did not respond too quickly to the meager breakfast of oatmeal and tea. He was tempted to finish the remaining chocolate bar then, but he realized that the point of extremity was not here yet. By tonight, maybe. Right now he would have to make do.

He hitched up the dogs again, after fighting their surliness, put Ah-Ming into the sled, and covered him with the furs. The sun was climbing on him now, boring holes in the cloud cover, putting the entire landscape into a strawberrylike hue. He knew that every day would bring the sun up higher and give him longer hours of light. But at the same time, it was getting colder; he noticed it was down already to 41 below. He looked at Ah-Ming. The Eskimo had his eyes closed, and there was a rattle in his breathing. Sebastian got out his compass and watched the needle spin crazily, being so close to the magnetic pole. In fact, the needle pointed south, as if it were telling him he was more north of south than south of north!

He tried to get a fix from the direction of the rising sun until Ah-Ming said, "That way . . . east," and he lifted one arm in the general direction of a huge pinnacle of ice taking on the full bloom of the red rays. Sebastian didn't argue and gave the whip to the dogs. The going was rather easy on fresh snow. It was not deep enough to bog down the sled, and now and then the runners hit an open patch of ice and it was smooth sailing.

By ten o'clock in the morning he had come into the main area of ice ridges that formed the main body of polar ice. Here the going was slower, but the dogs didn't balk at the ridges so much. They found their openings and moved on quickly, as if sensing they might be coming to the end of a journey. By then the sun was out in longer periods as the cloud cover broke up in patches, showing the promising blue above. The ceiling, though, was still not lifting that high, and now and then a snow squall poured out of them. But surely a plane could get under that long enough to spot him?

He was, as best as he could figure, going at a north-northeast heading now, moving purely by the sun's position or Ah-Ming's command. But now he was conscious only of the dogs making good time. His hand hurt with a fury, his feet were slabs of ice in his boots, but as long as the runners of the sled hissed their sound of progress in the snow, he had a rising sense of hope.

It was coming up to noon when he heard the sound of a plane's engines. Or maybe it was something else, more stuttering in its engine beat. He had heard that sound before. It had to be a helicopter! He halted the dogs and moved out from the line of ice ridges he was following, looking up into the patches of broken clouds, straining for sight of the machine. He made sure now, too, that he was out in the open, his form well silhouetted against the fresh new snow. The engine sound went over him, but the copter did not penetrate the cloud cover. He yelled as loudly as he could until his throat hurt. The sound of the rotors died off in the distance. They were looking for a hole down, he was sure, but not knowing exactly where he was, they would probably break open in the distance, too far away from him.

He went back to the sled and started the dogs out again, trying to shake off his feeling of futility. He was hungry, hungrier than he had ever been before. He wanted to stop then, but he also knew that he had to make what time he could.

He had just swung around a huge ice ridge and was pushing across a field of them when the copter engine sounded again. This time as Sebastian looked up, he could see the machine through a thin vaporous cloud break. He ran out from the ridgeline again, waving his arms and yelling. The copter dipped down through the clouds, ran down away from him for a few miles, and swung sharply back toward him. It passed over him, a big green copter with double rotaries and extra fuel tanks. Now he watched, his hopes rising, waiting. He saw that the cargo door was open, and he was sure that on the next pass they would dump over a crate of food for him, surely with a radio in it as well. But as he watched the copter

129

come back, lower now, he saw someone standing in the open cargo hatch, but he was also pointing something straight down at him. Almost at the same time, he instinctively jumped sideways and rolled over three times on the ice. He heard the *thunk thunk thunk* into the ice where he had been standing.

"It's me!" he yelled aimlessly, out of a rising sense of anger. "Not Thorsen, you ninnies!" The copter had gone down the line of ice ridges, dipped back around, and started toward him again, close over the ice. "Hey!" Sebastian yelled again, waving his arms. He could even see orange markings on the fuselage that said U.S. AIR FORCE—EUREKA.

Sebastian sensed, however, that this was no friendly visit, for reasons known only to them, so he ran back to the sled and what protection he could find near the ice ridges. This forced the copter to swing out away from the ridges and shoot at him against the glare of the sun on ice. He whipped the dogs into a run, as the *thunk thunk thunk* sounded again, and chunks of ice from the ice wall over his head showered down on him. He did not look at the copter now, keeping his eyes on the ice ridges, looking for something that might offer protection.

"Ahead!" It was Ah-Ming's voice, the first sound he had uttered all day. The Eskimo, apparently jarred out of his semiconscious state by the new sounds around him, was becoming aware of the danger too. He was pointing at a huge berg straight ahead that had an outcropping of ice sticking out and a curving inward. If they got behind that, it would offer something of a shield.

The copter had disappeared into a cloud bank that was hardly a hundred feet off the ice in places, some places lower than that. Sebastian got to the protective iceberg just as the copter appeared again, about half a mile behind him. He grabbed Ah-Ming from the sled and dove with him behind the ice barrier as the bullets again splattered over them and into the ice shield. He heard the dogs let out a yelping almost in concert. Now

130

the bullets were sounding *thwack thwack thwack* as they hit the iceberg and tried to find Ah-Ming and him. The smell of exhaust fumes was pungent and gagging as the copter made pass after pass over them, and the heat from the rotors was a strange kind of contrast to the cold. Sebastian looked up once to see the copter stagger in the air, maybe trying to settle down on the ice. But the clouds were back, and a sudden snow squall came in on a stiff breeze. The copter went into the clouds and moved overhead in tight circles, the rotors rattling in an angry grumble at being cheated by the elements.

Finally, after what seemed a long time, the engine faded away altogether. Slowly Sebastian rose from behind the ice shield, looking down where the dogs were. Some of them were lying still in the snow. He reached down and lifted Ah-Ming up. The Eskimo grunted as his swollen feet touched the ice.

Sebastian put the Eskimo down on a ledge of ice while he went to check the dogs. The mounting anger was beginning to build in him as he counted: six dogs dead, four others too badly wounded to go on. Sebastian simply stood there and swallowed his feelings about the carnage instigated here for no justifiable reason. Why was Eureka chasing him down? He had expected Dietrich to be looking for him, but why shoot at him?

He got his gun and shot the wounded dogs, dragging them off from the others. He had only six dogs for pulling now. Big Bay would have to go into harness too, despite the front foot that still caused him to limp. But could seven dogs pull two hundred pounds of sled, supplies, and Ah-Ming?

He walked over to Ah-Ming, not even sure he wanted to try to come up with any answers. It was too cold. He was hungry and frozen. Now would be a good time to quit, if ever there was a time. The copter he was looking for to resupply him was not in the offing. On top of that, he was being hunted, and when the sun broke out, they would have no trouble finishing the job.

"You mad now?" the Eskimo wondered. Sebastian

131

looked at him as he reclined against the iceberg wall a few feet above Sebastian.

"What do you know about it?" Sebastian asked wearily, kicking at the snow with his boot.

The Eskimo continued to look at him through those slitted eyes, his full-lipped mouth remaining in an expressionless line, the brush of black hair sticking out of his parka hood. The hair coated with hoarfrost made him look older.

"Time for Innuit have drink," he said, trying to bring his voice up above a whisper.

Sebastian did not respond. He turned and looked across the flat, rolling plain of ice. Back of him about seventy-five miles or so was Greenland. To go that way was to ask for sure death. Northward and eastward, nothing showed but those looming, cutting teeth of icebergs and rafter ice, their rapier fingers jabbing insults skyward. The endless stretches of frozen white and the empty caverns of crystal architecture, like beckoning tombs, made him feel a first serious stab of loneliness and hopelessness. The Eskimo must be feeling it too. Few men, even with the best equipment and supplies, could survive on this ice. He had read that in the book on Cook, and he had had it in his brain since Eureka. So what of himself and Ah-Ming, with so little to hang on to?

He knew he would have to keep moving. To move was probably a futile gesture at best, but if he camped here, he would never get up again. And the copter, coming back sooner or later, seeing his tent, would end it all, with no explanations.

"Ano," the Eskimo said again, as if he sensed Sebastian's thoughts.

"Yes, well, Ano does not come with U.S. Air Force painted on its side, right, Ah-Ming?" Sebastian said brusquely. He thought he saw the Eskimo's lips jerk in an attempted smile as Sebastian picked him up and put him back into the sled, trying to be careful with his feet.

"Copter come back," Ah-Ming said, warning him.

Sebastian felt the snow coming again; the cloud

132

cover seemed thicker. "Not for a while," he said to Ah-Ming. He hooked up the seven remaining dogs, putting Big Bay, the strongest of them, in the lead. The other dogs snarled at him for his commanding position, but the whip brought them under control. "Huk! Huk!" Sebastian yelled at them, and they moved out, straining in their harness. Sebastian knew they wouldn't pull long without full rations. But for now they moved as he pushed the sled to help them, going over the humps of ice, then into the crusted snow line again, which helped even more. He tried to keep to the rafter ice as much as possible, never knowing when the copter would jump down on him unexpectedly. And when he thought there wouldn't be any more visits, he caught sight of a copter directly ahead, moving in and out of the cloud cover. It wasn't the same one. This one was yellow, and he could not read the markings on it. It passed across his vision, moving away from him. He waited to be sure it was out of sight, and then he pushed on again, keeping his eyes up, watching the clouds closely.

He didn't know how far he'd gotten, when the sun finally went below the horizon. It was 3:40 in the afternoon. The days were getting longer. But that only meant more daylight for the helicopters to keep up their search for him.

When he finally stopped near an ice ridgeline, Ah-Ming said, "Build snow house now."

"What?" Sebastian said, leaning on the handles of the sled, so tired he could hardly stand. His face was numb from the cold; his hand was a throbbing pulse running up into his shoulder.

"Build igloo," Ah-Ming repeated, his voice heavy. The rattle was back in his throat.

"What for?"

"When copter come in morning, maybe, they no see you in snow house. In tent, they shoot, no chance."

"Yah, well . . ." Sebastian didn't want to argue about it; he was too bone weary. "How—how do you build one of those?"

133

Ah-Ming told him to get the long knife made of iron out of the sled, and began instructing him on how to cut the blocks out of the snow wall. Slowly and painfully, Sebastian did as he was told, surprised at how the ice yielded to the blade. He managed to cut the blocks according to Ah-Ming's specifications and laid them on top of each other. He knew inwardly that Ah-Ming wanted a proper house to die in, the way an Eskimo died, more than protection from the returning copter. But Sebastian did not resist. He went at the job doggedly, bent on committing at least one act of kindness in this frozen wilderness, to have at least one good thing to show for all this.

When he finally got the blocks stacked on top of each other and made the front crawl-in tunnel, he got Ah-Ming off the sled and guided him inside.

"Cover sled with snow," Ah-Ming said from inside, his voice barely audible.

Sebastian went back to the sled, unloaded the supplies, and shoved them inside the snow house. Then he tossed loose snow over the sled with his hands until there was hardly any of it showing. The dogs meanwhile looked up at him with expectation, so he cut up two of the dead dogs, all the time wincing at his clumsy butchering, and tossed them the meat. They devoured it without hesitation.

Sebastian crawled into the igloo and spread the two or three remaining caribou hides on the ice floor. He rolled out Ah-Ming's sleeping bag and helped him into it, taking off his outer parka as the Eskimo requested. Then Sebastian lit the primus, and the heat from the stove soon began to melt the snow blocks in the ceiling so that they welded smoothly together and showed a gleaming, waxy gloss. The igloo was warmer than the tent, and the stove took less time to heat it. Sebastian cut up several tuna and bacon bars into the pot of melted snow. He figured enough for another day, maybe two. But he tried not to think of that now; he only savored the pleasure of the smells in the snow house, the warmth. Maybe he would not leave the igloo either. It was cozy and warm.

134

He had no desire to face the cold again or those ice ridges or that murderous helicopter. He wanted to eat and sleep. Even Ah-Ming took a generous portion of pemmican and some of the soup. Sebastian fed him, because both the Eskimo's hands were puffed up and an angry bluish color and the skin seemed ready to break open. The smell of the flesh slowly turning gangrenous was strong in the tent too. Still, the Eskimo found a cigar in his parka and stuck it in the hole in his lower jawline, giving him an air of jauntiness that contrasted strangely with the stark ravages of the pain slashing his face. He managed to lean over to the primus flame and light his cigar, puffing on it weakly. The smell of smoke in the warm igloo was a welcome reprieve from the odors of death; it was as if the Eskimo lit up purposely, knowing the problem at hand. But he did not smoke long. He began coughing, and his lungs sounded tight. Finally he let the cigar go out, and it dropped finally on the floor of the igloo without his noticing.

Sebastian finished his meal without looking at the Eskimo, who, he knew, was trying to die with the least amount of fuss. Finding some penicillin pills in the first-aid kit, he managed to get four of them into Ah-Ming. Maybe it was too late for that too, but he had to keep trying.

He examined his own right hand in the light of the primus. It wasn't any better either. It was hot to the touch and had a lot of pus oozing out of the palm and fingers. He spread antibiotic ointment on it again, wrapped it in some gauze, and lay back on his sleeping bag to stare up at the gleaming ice ceiling. Sleep, though, would not come easily. He read some from the paperback on Cook's travels, now and then turning to look at Ah-Ming, who had begun babbling in his own tongue. Once Sebastian checked Ah-Ming's cheeks and found the skin hot. He gave him more of the penicillin pills, forcing snow water between the slack lips.

Finally, knowing he was short on fuel, he turned out the primus. It was darker in the igloo than in the tent,

135

and he wondered how he could get out fast enough if the ice broke up under him here. That tunnel to the outside was hardly big enough for one man to move through. And trying to knock the ice fort down now that the cracks had frozen over was going to be no easy task.

He put that thought aside finally and lay in his sleeping bag, thinking of the helicopter and why they would shoot at him. His own people? He had been in the same spot once before, in Berlin; it had mystified him then, but in that kind of Cold War politics, he had more or less expected the bizarre. But out here?

In the darkness, with the unanswerables hanging over him, with Ah-Ming babbling with fever, with his own survival uncertain, he groped for God. But all that commanded his brain was Thorsen. As always, since he had begun, the need to find Thorsen and complete the job he had been sent on was uppermost. Even when he knew he was probably too far behind the scientist even to bother with it, still he would lie there trying to calculate where he might be in relationship to him. Or what he would have to do tomorrow to make up time, or how he should do it with seven weary, hungry dogs and a dying Eskimo.

But always, even with that, came the fear that clutched at his stomach. It was not the fear of dying. It was that other thing, the sense of being cut off from everything that was truly himself. To feel isolated from God was worst of all. The one resource he had always counted on in moments like this was gone from him. And so he lay there baffled by it all, close to panic at the thought that even God might have abandoned him. Was it judgment for his motives in chasing Thorsen? Was it judgment because he wasn't sure of his motives? With that heavy curtain of darkness pressing in on him in the hollow confines of the igloo, he cried out, "God!" and his voice came back to him in the hollowness of the snow house, sounding like a child's voice in the night. "This poor Eskimo is dying," he went on, "and I can't say one meaningful thing to him about life and death, hope and promise. . . . Only Thorsen is there; always it is Thorsen,

136

kill Thorsen. . . . God, it is better that I die now!"

His voice rang off the ice blocks and died in the darkness, giving way to the rumbling of the ice again. Maybe now he knew why he had to find Thorsen. Maybe he had to find Thorsen and do what he must to get that part of his brain back that was lost. He sat up with the suddenness of the thought, peering into the darkness, feeling that he wanted to start out afresh now, to make up time. . . .

But then Ah-Ming began muttering again, and he sank back into his sleeping bag, feeling his body throb with pain and exhaustion. In the morning then, at first light, he would put all he had into it. For now, it was sleep laying hold of him quickly and dragging him under. . . .

He came awake to the sound of the helicopter's rotors swishing overhead. He glanced at his watch in the darkness of the igloo. It was 6:30 A.M. He had slept longer than he had intended. He sat up, listening, waiting for the sound of the copter coming back. It didn't. Ah-Ming was right. If he had been in the tent, they would have hit him before he could have gotten out of his sleeping bag. He rose, pulled on his parka, and went through the snow hole, sticking his head out cautiously. It was not snowing. The air remained still, sharply cold as usual, and the cloud cover was present but seemed to have lifted some. The sun was slashing through the clouds more boldly, and Sebastian sensed that today it could lift altogether. That would give the helicopter plenty of room to look around.

He returned to the igloo and checked Ah-Ming. He was not as warm, but the Eskimo did not open his eyes to Sebastian's touch. He was breathing more heavily, and now and then a few unintelligible words came from his swollen lips. Sebastian knew there was no way the Eskimo could travel. He was caught in a mean dilemma. He could not leave Ah-Ming here, to die alone. And yet what point was there in remaining, since all he could look forward to was death by starvation?

He put together a breakfast of tea and a couple of

137

bacon bars which he ate without cooking. He got four more penicillin pills and broke them up into a quarter cup of water. He took a spoon and half forced the medicine between the Eskimo's lips. Then he went outside and climbed the ice ridge directly behind the snow house. He used the binoculars to scan his back trail. There was no movement there. He searched in a 360-degree circle, but all he saw were spires of ice and endless tracks of snow.

He reentered the igloo and leaned over Ah-Ming, debating what to do. Finally, he knew he would have to try it alone, hoping that God would smile on him. He put the open cans of bacon and tuna, a can of water, and the penicillin next to the Eskimo. He lit the primus stove again, after filling it with the remaining fuel in the one can. He had one five-gallon can left to carry him. He gathered the few remaining provisions and stuffed them into a backpack that he had taken off the sled. Then, still feeling guilty about leaving Ah-Ming alone, he went out and found the snowshoes on the sled and put them on. Next he pulled the sled over to the ice ridge and leaned it up against its side, pushing it up as far as he could so that its nose stuck up a good four feet above the peak of the ridge. Finally he took the orange marker flag which he was supposed to use to mark his position for hunting aircraft and tied it to the top of the sled.

Satisfied, he got down again. The dogs were waiting, looking at him expectantly. He cut them loose from their tethering lines, took one last look at the igloo, and made sure the entrance tunnel was sealed well enough to prevent any wolves or polar bears from poking their noses in. Then he turned and started out, the dogs following uncertainly, looking back toward the snow house and the sled, not understanding why they weren't being hooked up today as usual. Big Bay bounded out in front, looking back over his shoulder as if to say that this was a much better way to travel.

He walked clumsily on the snowshoes at first, but after a while he began to get the feel of them, and his movements became more rhythmical, the only sound that

138

of the webbed snowshoes lifting and dropping onto the crusted snow. The sun broke through more frequently as he walked, and he took his reckoning as best he could. He recited what he had memorized out of the book about Cook last night:

"To get direction, multiply the time of day on a twenty-four-hour clock by the number fifteen and you arrive at the approximate heading of the sun; add the necessary number of degrees to arrive at true north and keep on that heading."

He didn't have a course bearing, but he did the other computation to get the heading of the sun. The way he figured it, he was walking straight north, so he angled more to the east, hoping that he was cutting a diagonal line up the polar sea on a course that might take him across Thorsen. As much as he knew that he was acting in the dark, it was all he had. He would simply keep going until he dropped, or until that copter caught him in the open and finished him.

As he thought of the copter, he became irritated, so much so that he began to feel that his biggest triumph here would be to beat them at their own game. In fact, the more he thought about it, the more he was sure that the copter represented interests designed to keep him from finding Thorsen. He began to think of how to outwit them, make them sweat all the way in their attempts to knock him off. As the clouds got brighter and patches of blue let the sun splash the snow, he knew he could get another calling card any time. Meanwhile, the dogs kept with him, nipping at each other at times, now and then chasing off ahead of him, following some uncertain scent.

He was conscious of walking through a range of icebergs and screw ice, some towering over him like mountains. He was feeling weaker, his breath was short, and his heart throbbed unevenly in his chest. He stopped once to lean against a huge ice cliff and noticed that his eyes were blurring. The sun on the snow was beginning to bounce back a mean reflection at him. He thought of

139

the sunglasses he was sure had been on the list of supplies back at Eureka. He was almost sure he hadn't seen them, but he took off his pack and hunted through it. Probably they, too, had gone down with the other sled. He knew he could not go on very long without them lest he go blind. Maybe he would have to camp by day and travel by night. Nobody in his right mind would do that on polar ice, but then, was he really in his right mind?

As he put his meager supplies back into his pack, he noticed the dogs beginning to sniff the air and yelp in a throaty way that was typical of them when they were excited. He turned and watched Big Bay put his nose to the snow a little distance away and then run around in circles.

Sebastian shouldered his pack again and walked over to where Big Bay and the others were sniffing. He knelt down and put his hand in the indentations in the snow. There could be no question about it; they were caused by sled runners—and not too long ago, if they still held their shape like that. Thorsen? Who else could have come through here heading north? Maybe Eureka or Thule ice teams in pursuit? In any case, he had made contact with possible survival.

He bent down over the marks in the snow and ran his fingers lightly in the ice-molded ruts. Maybe a day old? If it had snowed steadily in the past twenty-four hours, he would not have found those ruts. The slight thaw on the ice and then the quick freeze at night had left the evidence for him. He pondered the miracle of it, still not sure how he could have stumbled onto this trail so quickly. It could only be as he had surmised earlier about the ice floe—its drift had swung around to northeast while he had slept and pushed him to the main ice pack, closing the gap between himself and Thorsen. Gripped with a new sense of excitement, he turned and began slogging along faster on the trail, the dogs chasing way out ahead after the scent of man still lingering in those tracks.

He was so intent on following the trail that he didn't

140

see the copter come sliding down on him from the left. The dogs were a hundred yards ahead of him, and Sebastian saw them stop and peer toward the sky. He paused warily, not moving, turning to sweep the jagged horizon with his squinting eyes. The copter was the yellow one this time, not the green, not as big. He scooted clumsily for the ice wall to his left where there was an overhanging porch of ice, solid on one side, and pressed himself in as far as he could. The copter passed over him, vomiting the usual gases of spent fuel and hot grease, went into a tight circle, and came back to hover above him, a little to the left. They were undoubtedly watching the dogs farther along, looking for signs of Ah-Ming and himself. The copter came down lower, turning slowly. Sebastian peeked out at the open cargo hatch; there was a man peering down, and he did not have a gun this time. He was looking at the snowshoe marks that probably ended below him, just about where Sebastian hid under the porch of ice. But Sebastian noticed too that his snowshoe marks blended in with the trail marks of the dogs and men in the party that had gone before him.

It seemed a long time that he waited there, pressed up against that cold ice block. His hand reached in for the gun inside his parka coat. Would he use it if he had to? Somebody yelled something. The sound of another human voice was almost enough to make Sebastian jump out of hiding, throw up his hands, and hope they would be merciful enough to give him the benefit of the doubt about whatever he was supposed to have done worthy of death.

Then the rotors accelerated sharply. The copter lifted and moved away. He stayed there hiding, waiting, feeling strange emotions that ranged from being glad they had gone to being sad that he could not reach out to his own kind when he needed that touch so desperately.

After a while it was quiet again, and Big Bay came to him there, scrunched up under the ice canopy. The dog whined and nudged at his mitten. Sebastian patted

141

him on the head, then got up and moved out on the trail, looking around for signs of the copter. There was no sound of rotors. Maybe they had caught the trail frozen there and decided to go on ahead to see what they could find. In that case, it could be Thorsen ahead.

He moved along another hundred yards and stopped in the lee of another skyscraper of ice. He waited, not wanting to get too exposed on the ice, just in case they came back. Besides, his eyes burned and watered. Everything in the distance was a blur. Even up close, his mittened hands appeared fuzzy. He sat there with his eyes closed as the dogs lay down a few yards away from him, tongues hanging out, breathing hard from their running. After a while, he opened his eyes again and noticed the sun had gone behind a cloud, easing the glare. But he had to move again, because if a heavy snow squall hit, the trail he was following would disappear. At least the copter would not take him by surprise again. He got up stiffly, ignoring the dogs' whining in their hunger. He felt the heavy pall of weariness drag on him; the pain in his body was a thumping pulse. His right hand felt almost useless as it pounded, reminding him of the spreading infection up his arm. His eyes continued to water and burn, and he stumbled more often in the snowshoes. He pushed on, even though the trail in front of him was beginning to blur now too.

It began to snow again, the slashing ice crystals hard on the exposed skin of his face; then it turned into more solid flakes, drifting easily on him like flecks of cotton. It was the heavy stuff. An hour of this, and the trail would disappear.

He didn't know how long he had been going, or how long he had been shuffling along with the trail covered. It was late in the afternoon. The light was fading. He staggered up a mound of ice, hoping to get some kind of view around him through the binoculars. He wiped at his eyes with his mittened gloves, then lifted the glasses. He swung around in his search, the snow clouding up the lenses but allowing him enough vision to search the frozen landscape.

142

He came back to make one more sweep of the mounds of ice in front of him, stretching out across that flat plain of emptiness and frozen ice. He was almost too cold to continue and was about to drop the binoculars when he caught sight of something, something different, in the ice mounds. He wiped at the lenses of the binoculars, adjusted the focus, and went back to squinting through them at that same image . . . no, nothing . . . and then he saw it. It had to be an igloo! He stared at it, until his eyes burned and watered, but he was sure he saw the little lines in the snow house where the ice blocks had been placed on top of each other. He scanned the area, looking for dogs, a sign of equipment . . . none. Maybe an empty snow house? Maybe where Thorsen had camped a day ahead of him? Then he caught sight of another snow house, maybe thirty yards from it, closer this way . . . and then as he looked, with the wind coming at him from the northeast, the dogs began to yelp again in excitement. He turned to look at them; they were standing on their hind legs, lifting their snouts into the air, definitely catching a scent of something. Then he knew; he too smelled the acrid, pungent, familiar odor. Seal meat being cooked over a fire! That smoke had to be drifting out of an igloo opening. He continued to study the area, looking for signs of movement, people . . . there were none.

He lowered the glasses and slid back down the ice mound. The dogs were chasing in circles now, trying to get on the track of those smells. Sebastian waited and then reached into his pocket, took out the gun, and examined it, wanting to be sure. He found a magazine of ammo in his pack, jammed it into place with his good left hand, tried getting his mittened finger around the trigger. It was painful, but he managed. Well, when it was time, he'd make it work; the point was to start making his move. The sun was gone. He had maybe a half hour of light to go by. Maybe that was the best way. There probably would be less of a guard up when he walked in, half staggering, to their camp. He knew he posed no threat, not the way he must look, a four-day growth of scraggly beard on his cheeks, eyes red and watery, white hoarfrost hanging from his chin. For a moment, he felt a strange pang of regret for what he was about to do. He would rather meet the scientist and share food over his primus. He felt a great need for a touch of human companionship in this Godforsaken place, to feel a vital link with humanity once more, to know that there was yet some human order left. . . .

As the dogs began to yelp, catching the scent of cooking food and beginning to chase in circles, hunting for the trail to it, he put the gun back into his parka holster. There was no time to indulge the needs of his inner self. He had his job to do, what he had come all this way for. To delay for any reason was but to complicate it. He felt hunger coming as a strong urge even as he moved around the ice rafter and started over the other mounds toward the igloo camp a couple of hundred yards away. The dogs were already racing ahead of him, but it didn't matter if they announced his presence. Thorsen would come out to see before he did anything. Once he was sure it was just one lonely, scraggly piece of humanity, the pressure would be off. So be it! The rest would be easy. . . .

"We didn't get him," Admiral Fish said with some disgruntlement to Henry H. Morton, who stood in the middle of the plot room, his arms folded, a long-stemmed, big-bowled briar pipe in his mouth, puffing up a cloud of questions. It was four on the afternoon of March 13. It had started snowing heavily outside, and the wind gusts were back up to thirty-five miles an hour. It was because of the weather that Morton was late getting into Thule.

"Did you see him at all?" Morton asked. He was a tall, heavy-set man with a streak of gray in his long black hair and a sprinkle of the same winter in his bushy mustache. His face was seamed with jagged lines that looked like cracks in a brown crockery jug. He had intense blue eyes that fixed on any object—floor, desk, radio console, light bulb—and never left it while he continued a given line of conversation. Right now he was staring at the half-filled cup of coffee in Fish's hand, the coffee having long since grown cold.

"We think we spotted his trail," Fish said, "but that cloud cover over the ice is murder."

"He's out there with dogs and a sled," Morton argued. "He can't be swallowed up that easily." Nobody responded to him, so he added, "You'll have to get back over him."

"Mr. Morton, I've had planes up all day, and I lost one trying to skim the ice looking for Thorsen," Fish replied, keeping it polite but feeling a bit gritty in being pushed to the wall. "Ceiling drops to under fifty feet in some spots up there."

"Did you see Thorsen?"

"No, sir."

"You have any idea where he is now?"

"We have projected him close to eighty-four degrees, fifty minutes north, judging by his pace and the bearing we last received."

"And the Russians?"

"They are now about thirty miles west of that heading."

"And you say you believe the Chinese are moving in?"

"All I'm saying is that our radar got a blip moving up from Spitsbergen a few hours ago and lost it at that point. I can only speculate that it is the Chinese, we figure about twenty-five miles southeast of Thorsen's heading."

"And where did you spot the kamikaze last time out?"

"Yesterday we judged him at about fifteen miles south of what we projected as Thorsen's position. But as I said, until we are sure where Thorsen is—"

"And how about Little Bo Peep?"

Fish shrugged. "We don't know for sure. She had to shut her radio down lest Thorsen monitor her signals and be on the alert. But she can't be far off his position either."

"Are you getting through to Dietrich?"

"We were until early this morning. Then we were notified of a power blackout and haven't had anything since."

"So it is with us," Morton muttered into his pipe bowl. "How close are our military teams to Thorsen?"

Fish turned to Buckner, who up to this time had been content to stay out of the exchange. "We are on the other side of the Big Lead, about thirty miles directly south of Thorsen's last reported position," Buckner said.

"Which could mean you are farther back if Thorsen has kept moving all this time. Are you moving now?"

"In daylight—"

"I mean *both* day and night, General."

"No, sir." Buckner shot a quick glance at Fish. "To move at night in that kind of ice among open leads, crevasses—"

"Use magnesium torches and move your men around the clock," Morton said shortly, squinting at Fish's cup. Then he lifted his eyes and stared at Bob Hestig's identification badge over his left shirt pocket. "Gentlemen, we've got to make a sure kill on that kamikaze, is that understood?"

"Well, we figured if we spotted him we might be able to set down and talk with him," Fish offered. "Of course, we know he may be a fanatic—"

"Exactly," Morton cut back. "A fanatic. A mind geared to outwit you, Admiral, correct?"

"Well, sir—"

"Admiral," Morton went on, "two weeks ago an Eskimo bolted out of Thorsen's party down in Smith Sound and staggered into Egluk about three days ago. You know that Egluk is a Canadian weather and ice monitoring station about a hundred and twenty miles south of here. Yesterday morning we got a message from the Royal Canadian Mounted Police, who provision Egluk, that the Eskimo kept saying Thorsen is carrying big medicine around his neck. We didn't think much about that until we got your suggestion of a kamikaze moving

146

toward Thorsen, and then we began to wonder what any kind of charge full of shrapnel would do to that capsule."

"What is the capsule like, sir?" Buckner asked.

"Square and made of highly resistant plastic. The top of it is thick glass. The rock is long and flattish, rather than bulky, so Thorsen could carry it around his neck without too much discomfort."

"But it would not be able to resist shrapnel penetration," Fish said thoughtfully. "Are you sure you can believe that Eskimo, Mr. Morton?"

"No," Morton replied. "But would you take a chance on not believing him?"

"Dietrich is the one who ought to know about that," Fish went on. "He controls the kamikaze."

"If Dietrich was prepared to risk the suicide vehicle, he is undoubtedly prepared to play the long shot." Morton concluded abruptly. "Anyway, how do we contact him?"

"Well, you said you had Agent Foxtrot in there."

"We have to wait for his transmission time," Morton said. "He did transmit to us last night after a forty-eight-hour silence that there was a suicide vehicle out. He can only transmit when he's sure he won't get picked up by Dietrich's radio beams. He will probably get through no sooner than midnight tonight."

"You can tell him to get to Dietrich," Fish said.

"If we could be sure Dietrich would believe him, yes. But to do so means that Foxtrot has to break his cover. But nine times out of ten Dietrich won't stop now, no matter what the appeal."

"I still doubt that Thorsen would carry so heavy an item around his neck," Fish said skeptically.

"On the other hand, if you had a bomb that big in your possession, would you let it ride like a piece of cargo on a skittering snow sled?" Morton countered. He turned to move over to the huge map on the wall. "And there is the other consideration now, gentlemen. If we can get the kamikaze before he gets to Thorsen, Thorsen stays alive. The Russians and Chinese know that as long as Thorsen is alive and holds the rock, they can't chance trying to take him, lest he blow it up on them."

"But if the kamikaze makes it, it's all over anyway, right?" Fish asked of no one in particular.

"Which is the lesser of two evils?" Buckner asked, a bit perplexed.

"We must count on the girl," Morton said, puffing smoke rings up at the map. "Keep Thorsen alive and keep him running straight into her."

"That's a long shot too," Fish said dubiously.

"And the Russians and Chinese will be right on top of her," Buckner chimed in again. "Even if she gets the rock, they surely won't let her get away with it."

"All the more reason for your military to get up there," Morton advised.

"That's a three-way shoot-out then," Fish said at Morton's broad back.

"Confined action," Morton corrected. "We can handle a small brushfire shoot-out, Admiral, better than we can afford to have the rock blowing up on us or falling into either Russian or Chinese hands. That's the way it stands."

"We'll have to be ready to get that girl out once she radios she's got Thorsen and the rock," Fish put in, frowning at the map, seeing the totally ludicrous percentages in which to work.

"We can have a copter over her ready to drop down on signal," Buckner offered. "But that depends on weather."

"Weather or no weather, gentlemen," Morton said with finality, "this will have to be a maximum effort all the way. And would you say, Admiral, that by tomorrow morning at the latest the Interpol girl should have cut into Thorsen's line of march and completed the job, if she is going to succeed?"

"Yes, sir, she will have to by then, or Thorsen is going to see Russians and Chinese around him, and that could make him nervous, too nervous. . . ."

"Why not mount a commando unit and hit Eureka

and blow the kamikaze from that end?" Buckner asked. The general didn't like the idea of trying to pull all this together out on the ice with the weather deteriorating again.

"Good idea," Morton said lightly. "But how do you propose to make Eureka in time now? Fly?"

Buckner shook his head, knowing that the wind and snow outside prevented that. "Maybe tomorrow," he said lamely.

"And it will be all over tomorrow," Morton countered, still staring at the map.

"And what if the girl fails?" Fish dared to ask, trying to see ahead.

Morton did not respond for a long time. Only the sound of the air whistling through his pipe as he puffed on it hung over them, mixing with the bleep of high-frequency sounds from the electronic hardware.

"Then we have a disaster," he said simply. Again nobody said anything. Fish knew that all the variables were too marginal to be sure. Even Morton knew that. If they did get the kamikaze, if they didn't; if the girl did get Thorsen, if she didn't; if the Russians got there first, or the Chinese—it went around and around in his tired brain, never stopping, because there was never any sure answer, at least not yet.

Finally he said, "Mr. Morton, how long have you known that Dietrich was playing the double agent in Houston?"

Morton shrugged and removed his pipe from his mouth to stare intently into the bowl. "For nine years, Admiral, we have had our doubts but never anything to go on."

Fish looked at Buckner, whose face took on an expression of surprise working to a pinched reflection of anger.

"Then why did you wait for this countdown to move?" Fish asked.

"Admiral, analyses of that nature are not in keeping with the present crisis. Suffice it to say that our

149

business is to cool it until the mouse comes out of the hole, looking to hobble the cat."

"Well, this mouse Dietrich is not exactly in the cat's paw yet, either," Buckner interjected in a bellicose tone. "And he's going to follow through on his suicide package, come weather, Washington, Thule, or the Chinese."

"Well said," Morton replied agreeably. "But then I happen to believe, along with the President of the United States and a lot of other big boys around the world who are interested in how this is going to come out, that you and Admiral Fish will get our kamikaze before Dietrich puts a bell around the cat's neck, right?"

Morton was trying to smile on them now, and the creases in his face softened some. Fish felt for him then; he didn't like him any better, but he sensed that on Morton rested the entire success or failure of Moon Rock.

"Then we better get at it," Fish said abruptly. "General, we'll need a commando force ready and loaded on a copter prepared to hit Eureka if the wind dies even a little—"

"Sir?" Hestig spoke up for the first time. Morton turned with Fish to look at him, but Hestig was looking at Fish. "You should know that the laser sound waves on the kamikaze indicate that he's on the move and has been for some time. I would project his bearing now at close to eighty-four degrees, maybe thirty minutes north. He's not far behind Thorsen, at that."

Fish glanced at Morton and then said, "Thanks, Bob."

"Keep me posted," Morton called after them.

Landau moved into the communications shack at Eureka, feeling miserable about his aborted effort to knock off Sebastian when he had him on the ice. He had no relish for facing Dietrich either, but when he looked around the room he could not see him anywhere. In fact, even Bosman and the monitoring screen were gone. Finally, after checking around, he was directed to the small room underground. He stepped down the short

150

crude stairs and pulled the floor door down over him.

"Bosman?" he said in the half glow from the monitoring screen. Bosman turned to look at him. "Where's Dietrich?"

"He hasn't come back yet."

"Not yet? He can't have much fuel left. Did he radio in when he was coming?"

"No. He hasn't come on the radio in thirty minutes. I'm worried."

Landau sniffed. Then he said, "What does the monitor show?"

"See for yourself," Bosman said shortly.

Landau leaned over his shoulder and saw the two points of light no more than a half inch apart. "Bosman!" he said in awe. "He's almost touching Thorsen. How—how far away is he now?"

"Under a mile, maybe a few hundred yards. We calibrated it as close as we could figure."

"You mean, any time now those two lights will converge and we will have them?"

"When they converge, yes."

"You expect it now?"

"It's getting dark up there. If Sebastian knows he has Thorsen in front of him, I am not sure he will try for him in this poor light. We have to wait and see."

"Ah! Ah-ha!" Landau crowed. "So it is now about to turn out well?" Bosman did not respond, so Landau added, "It is impossible that Sebastian should get so close to Thorsen. We shot his dogs, crippled him, even if we did not get him."

"Get who?" Bosman asked, turning to look at him.

"Sebastian, who else?" Landau went on. "I took my own helicopter up there. I was not about to let him survive for the Thule crowd. But the weather was too bad —so maybe now it is good I missed?"

"Does Dietrich know you did that?" Bosman asked skeptically.

"Don't be such a fool, Bosman," Landau snapped. "Dietrich will play footsie with all this to our undoing.

151

Even now he is flying hopelessly around up there when he should be here directing the destruct. Did you radio him and tell him about the lights converging so rapidly?"

"Yes."

"What did he say?"

"That he would return immediately."

"That was thirty minutes ago? And he hasn't transmitted since?"

"I said he hasn't."

"Then it will have to be up to us to blow the destruct," Landau said flatly. "But we are helpless without the key to activate the circuits. Is he the only one with a key?"

"I think we should wait."

"Wait for what?" Landau demanded, sniffing nervously. "If that converging takes place now, are you going to let it pass? If you do, you will have to stand against Zukov later."

"What do you want me to do, Mr. Landau?" Bosman asked, disturbed now.

"Tell me if there is another way to activate those circuits!"

Bosman said nothing, thinking, watching the lights on the screen that stayed stationary now, so very close to each other. "There is a way," he said finally, hesitatingly. Landau waited. "I can unscrew the plate, turn the circuit set screws, create a spark . . . it's a clumsy way."

"Then we will do it!" Landau replied with finality.

"Dietrich should be back."

"It is now five o'clock and getting darker," Landau countered. "Dietrich must be down. We will go after him later. Right now I want to stay on those lights. And I want you on that monitor as long as it takes, ready to spark those circuits, Bosman. Is that understood?"

Bosman said nothing as Landau took off his parka and threw it aside, pulled up a stool, and sat on it, never taking his eyes off the screen. Bosman knew Landau was not going to leave the room. He picked up the phone next to him, hit a button, and asked, "Any radio contact from Dietrich?" He listened, then put the phone back on the hook. He didn't have to tell Landau there was no word. Landau blew his nose and went on sniffing in excitement. It was coming down to only Landau and him, Bosman thought. It was not what he wanted, but there was little he could do about it.

7

He stayed a long time there in the rafter ice watching the two snow houses, waiting to see what Big Bay and the other dogs stirred up. His eyes still burned and watered, and he had to keep wiping at them with the ice-coated mitten of his right hand. He noticed that the dogs had finally roused a team of dogs that had been lying in the snow by the farther snow house; he could hear the yelping and snarling even from here. Still there was no sign of a human figure coming out of either igloo.

The light was fading rapidly, and he knew he could have no more than a half hour at best in which to see where he was going. The air seemed to be getting colder, too; his body was so stiff already that he wasn't sure he could move another inch, let alone twenty yards to that nearest snow house or the seventy or so that it would be to the other. But still he waited. He wanted Thorsen to come out first; to be out there on the approach when the scientist finally appeared might cause the older man to act rashly. Sebastian knew he had to appear to be staggering into the camp area in such a state of exhaustion and exposure that Thorsen would not consider him a threat. He grunted in an almost animal way as he thought of the irony of that; the way he felt now, it wouldn't take much pretending.

He stayed there for five more minutes. When no one appeared, he took off his snowshoes, laid them aside

154

carefully, and then began to move slowly over the ice ridges directly in front of him toward the open plain of sea ice. He paused again with the nearer snow house directly below. He saw a snowmobile parked next to it, partially covered with a tarp on which snow had been thrown to make it blend with the ice. Why a snowmobile? Thorsen certainly had no such equipment.

He glanced around, just to make sure, and saw another igloo to his left, one he hadn't seen from the ice ridges behind him. So that made three snow houses. Which one was Thorsen in? Suppose whoever occupied the other igloos were to come out just when he got on that ice? What then? He'd have to play it as carefully as he could so they wouldn't find the gun on him. He paused again, shivering from the cold and the apprehension of the moment, trying to shake the exhaustion from his brain, not sure just how to play this. But as the light began to fade even more and the white snow took on a pastel color, he knew he would have to move.

He heard the sound of the dogs yelping from out by the farthest igloo. The pungent smell of cooking seal meat was still in the air. He was about to slide down the last shelf of ice when he caught a movement to his right and maybe a little to the rear. For a few seconds his mind tried to tell him that no one should be in that position in relationship to him. He turned his head slowly to the right, to make sure, and at the same instant he heard the crunch of snow directly behind him. He whirled around, but he wasn't quick enough. Something caught him hard in the back of the head—he threw out one hand and grabbed onto something soft that must be a parka. As he went down, the darkness falling on him, he felt whatever he had hold of fall on top of him. The last thing he remembered thinking was that whoever it was did not weigh much and that it must be an Eskimo. . . .

He was in a deep well, trying to climb the walls, his hands slipping on the scummy sides. Around him

155

was the heavy, thick feel of water hanging onto him with silken arms. Up above was the small narrow hole of light he was trying to reach; it was too far away, way too far. But someone was up there calling to him, shouting some kind of instruction at him, over and over again.

"What are you trying to say? What are you trying to say?" he kept shouting back. And again he reached up, trying to find a grip, only to slide back again into mucky water that seemed to be getting thicker and heavier around his legs and waist. He heard the voice again, louder this time, repeating the message, and there was urgency in that voice now, as if whoever it was sensed that he was going under. He fought to get his mind to rise to hear that voice, to understand the instruction, because he knew if he didn't understand he wasn't going to make it.

"O Lord, thou hast searched me, and known me. . . . Thou knowest my downsitting and mine uprising, thou understandest my thought afar off. . . . Thou compasseth my path and my lying down, and art acquainted with all my ways. . . ."

The words faded out, and he shouted for the voice to come on louder.

"Whither shall I go from thy spirit? or whither shall I flee from thy presence? If I ascend up into heaven, thou art there: if I make my bed in hell, behold, thou art there. . . ."

"Tell me, Mr. Sebastian, which of these is from the Bible?" Another voice jammed his brain. Who was that? He saw the image of the card flashed before him. He didn't know for sure . . . but that voice, now, those words. . . .

"If I say, Surely the darkness shall cover me; even the light shall be light about me. . . ."

The voice went away again, fading out, and he shouted back, not wanting to lose that sound, "I will praise thee; for I am fearfully and wonderfully made: marvellous are thy works; and that my soul knoweth right well. . . ."

156

"How precious also are thy thoughts unto me, O God! how great is the sum of them!" The voice spoke again, encouraging him, as if there was a way out of this place, a way up to that small shaft of light hanging so far above him.

"Search—search me, O God," he shouted back again, "and know my heart: try me, and know my thoughts. . . ." His voice trailed off, because he could not remember all of it, but that other voice, coaxing, not pushing but leading him gently, making sure he understood, went on.

"And see if there be any wicked way in me, and lead me in the way everlasting."

"Fourscore and seven years ago," he yelled, "our fathers—"

"No!" The voice broke in on him, warning him. And after a pause, during which he felt the fright of sinking, it came on again, "Remember: 'Blessed be the Lord my strength . . . my goodness and my fortress; my high tower, and my deliverer; my shield, and he in whom I trust; who subdueth my people under me—' "

"Lord, what is man, that thou takest knowledge of him!" he cried, knowing the path the voice was trying to outline for him. "Or the son of man, that thou makest account of him!"

"I will sing a new song unto thee. O God: upon a psaltery and an instrument of ten strings will I sing praises unto thee. It is he that giveth salvation unto kings: who delivereth David his servant from the hurtful sword." The voice was stronger, more firm now.

"Rid me, and deliver me from the hand of strange children; whose mouth speaketh vanity, and their right hand is a right hand of falsehood." He picked up the refrain, and now it seemed that that small shaft of light was beginning to grow. He was climbing!

"That our sons may be as plants grown up in their youth; that our daughters may be as corner stones. . . ."

"Yes!" And he shouted it in sudden realization. "Happy is that people, that is in such a case; yea, happy is that people whose God is the Lord!"

"For God hath not given us the spirit of fear; but of power, and of love, and of a sound mind." The voice was beside him then, and there was no darkness, no pull of the water, no prison of slick mud walls.

He opened his eyes.

The face remained before him, caught in a golden yellow glow. It blurred, then reappeared in clearer focus. He saw the eyes, soft blue and tranquil, carrying the portent of gentle, warm breezes, eyes that caressed him in concern and held on to him with the embrace of possessiveness. The nose was small and straight, cut cleanly against the face. The mouth was a pout of soft pale orange-red, showing slight bruises from chapping, delicate, but carrying a firm line that said there was resolution somewhere there . . . and command? The lower lip was slightly fuller than the upper, and when the smile came slowly, uncertainly, there was an explosion of light that flooded the face and brought out the brilliant gold of the short blond hair. At the same time, the eyes lit up in a coruscation like a shower of falling stars breaking up over the canopy of night. And what he saw was something close to angelic.

" 'Lord,' " he whispered, and he reached his good hand up to that face and touched the skin of her cheek that was smooth and soft, untouched by the ravages of the Arctic, " 'now lettest thou thy servant depart in peace. . . .' What—what are you doing in this—this hell of a place?"

"Shhh," she said quietly to him, and the flickering flame from the primus danced in her eyes as she bent down and kissed him lightly on his cracked, bruised lips; and he reached up and touched her hair that felt rich and gentle and yet filled with energy from her body that seemed to flow through him. Her lips were warm on his, a little uncertain, perhaps. And he reached up and gently pulled her head down, returning the kiss, and there was that feeling of drift for him, a loss of gravity almost, a dizzying sense of euphoria. He let it take him, because all the needs of his life, spawned by the loneli-

158

ness of his commission and the miles of endless uncertainties, rose up hungrily for fulfillment.

She sensed the urgency in him and lifted her mouth from his just an inch, her breath warm on his cheek, her eyes looking into his so that he felt total immersion with her.

"I hurt you," she said, touching his lips gently with hers.

"Then hurt me again," he said, reaching for her.

She held her head up from him, smiling down at him, restraining him gently. She had on a heavy brown turtleneck sweater that emphasized her blond hair. It was warm in the igloo. He sensed now, too, without even checking, that his own outer and inner parkas were off, and he was lying there in his blue cardigan and fur-lined trousers. The feeling of being free of the heavy outer parka lent a new sense of lazy comfort he had no intention of disturbing.

"I gave you a nasty crack on the head," she went on, trying to apologize, and he touched her cheek again with his good left hand, quieting her.

"The last time I saw you, Barbara Churchill, was in the Negev desert," he said, feeling the heavy hand of exhaustion still pressing down on him. His voice sounded hoarse and cracked. "What are you doing on this ice? And how come you manage to look like Miss Universe?" Before she could answer, he said, "Never mind. It doesn't matter. I don't want to get off the immediate subject we were just beginning to explore, if you don't mind."

She smiled at him, trying to roll away from him. He held her there, close to him, with his left arm. Knowing she could not remove herself that easily, she threw her arm across his chest and kissed him again. Then, almost as if she suddenly became aware, she pulled back from him, with a quizzical frown working between her eyes.

"This is not the place," she said in that quiet, easy tone he had remembered—how long ago now? Three years?

159

"Where is the right place then?" he replied. She didn't respond, sensing there probably really wasn't any right time or place for them. He lifted his bandaged right hand and felt his own face, prickly with the scraggly stubble of beard. He grunted. "I guess I don't blame you," he added. "I'm not exactly a leading man for this scene, am I?"

"Love sees only beauty," she said simply.

"Well, you look just as beautiful in that bulky turtleneck as you did in a stewardess's uniform in the Negev three years ago."

"But I'm still about to freeze to death," she returned lightly.

"Okay, so you are coldly beautiful, how's that?"

He pulled her down beside him again. "Do you intend to make love to me here, at fifty-six degrees below zero?" she asked.

"I didn't get the chance when it was a hundred and thirty in the shade in the Negev, remember? And I've been waiting a long time. . . . Anyway, my father once said that making love in the cold is better."

"We could freeze to death—"

"We could freeze to death if we don't."

She remained next to him, within the circle of his arm, her breath still warm on his cheek, her blue eyes intent on his, the closeness of her a magnetic thing, stirring him so deeply that he was sure he was going to do that very thing he knew could only fulfill and heighten their love. And at this moment, he knew it was right; it was only the two of them before God in this lonely place. He looked at her again and saw the two color marks on her cheeks, under her eyes, coming up over the tan from the Palestinian sun.

"I never asked you before, but where did you get such magnificent eyes anyway?" he said. "As—as blue as the Mediterranean and as deep as—"

"The Arctic sea?" she finished for him and sat up. "Come to think of it, you really don't look lovable. . . ."

"You're making excuses."

160

She paused, sitting next to him, her arms hugging her knees, looking down at him. "There will be a time for us, my love . . . but this isn't it."

"When the war is over, you mean?"

"I don't want to love you between crises. . . ."

"I'll take it when it comes, thank you—otherwise we may wait until we are both old and cold."

"It will be just as beautiful for us," she said quickly.

"You never answered my letters. . . ."

"That is a kind of slow torture, too."

"It's worse not getting any answers. After Berlin I almost flew out to Israel to check on you. Then, I thought, well, she may not feel the same way I do."

"I thought of you incessantly, night and day, after the Negev," she replied, putting her head down on her knees. "I—I found it hard to concentrate. I decided I finally had to, if I was going to do my job. Your letters —they made me want to run to you. . . . I knew answering them would make me run to you. . . . Do you understand?"

"It's enough that you're here," he said. "For once, it's a nice ending."

"It's not ended. There's more. . . ."

"Oh, with you, I always know there is." He tried a bantering tone. She didn't reply. He put his head back on the sleeping bag pillow and stared up at the ceiling, trying to bring time and place into some coherent whole. "You brought me out of a pretty steep dive a while ago. . . . I didn't know you could quote scripture so well."

"Do you still want to kill Thorsen?"

He turned his head to look at her. "I don't know. . . . How did you know I was—?"

"You jumped up three times in the last few hours and tried to find that mean-looking gun of yours, shouting, 'Kill Thorsen!' as if you were a bounty hunter."

"How'd you stop me?"

"You stopped yourself . . . as soon as you stood up you got dizzy and passed out again."

"So what about the scripture you used?"

161

She reached down on the side away from him and came up with a pocket Bible and placed it on his chest. He looked down at it. "That belongs to Thorsen," she said.

He reached for it, opened it to the flyleaf, and read the inscription:

To a great man of science.
R. Sebastian

"I gave this to Thorsen last year when I visited him and his son," he said in awe, flipping through the pages, noticing whole blocks of passages underlined in red, more of them in the New Testament. "He took it then as if I were offering him a bag of week-old lunch. But this —dear God, this is a well-used, consumed copy. Does this mean he's done a complete turnaround?"

"I don't know anything about Thorsen's religious background," she confessed. "All he told me is that it kept him from going insane during the past months."

"He's here? You talked to him?"

"Yes . . . in the igloo across the ice."

"The rest of his party—where are they?"

"Left behind two days ago, unable to keep up. The Eskimos were afraid to go on."

"So he's alive?"

"If you mean, did I kill him, no. But he came down with pneumonia, as he told me, back in Smith Sound, fought it all the way. Yesterday he couldn't get up. I found him in the snow house, unable to move, burning with fever. I did all I could for him. But I don't think he has much time."

"You were going to shoot him, though?"

"My orders were to take him alive, if at all possible. He knows too much about that rock just to wipe him out."

"Dietrich sure didn't—"

"I can't answer for Dietrich. That's all Interpol told me to do. Anyway, when I crawled into that igloo and saw him, and he didn't try to blow the rock on me, I knew he wasn't going to."

Sebastian made a move to get up, ignoring the pain in his head where she had hit him earlier.

"Lie down," she said sharply, and pushed him on his chest so that he fell back onto his elbows. She had that look that said this was all business, the kind he remembered in the Negev. "He probably won't know you anyway; he's delirious with fever."

"Who's with him?"

"Montoos, my guide. All he can do—or any of us—is make Thorsen comfortable. I treated him with what I had . . . but it won't do much good."

"You know, I've come a long way just to talk to that man about his soul."

"You don't want to kill him?"

He paused, suddenly realizing that other part of him was still standing in the wings of his mind, the part he had dragged across the ice from Eureka. "I—I really don't know for sure," he said uncertainly. "I don't think so."

"Who sent you to do it in the first place?"

"Dietrich . . . Otto Dietrich." She didn't reply so he added, "I can't remember too much, only long black nights somewhere out there. . . ."

"You were probably programmed to kill Thorsen," she returned shortly.

"How are you so sure?"

"You are capable of many things, Sebastian, my love, but assassination is not one of them. Do you remember anyone else at Eureka besides Dietrich?"

"Landau. . . ."

"A thin, wiry man with bad sinuses?"

"That's the one."

"Best man the Kremlin has, according to Interpol, in neuropsychosomatics."

"If you knew that, why didn't you tell NASA?"

"We weren't sure of anything, still aren't. . . . Do you remember anything unusual happening at Eureka?" He explained the revolving light over his bed and the electronic tapes feeding his brain while he slept. "It's

163

the pattern, all right. Thorsen was probably programmed in the same way, or at least Landau thought he was programming him. . . ."

He was watching her carefully now. "Programmed? Thorsen? For what?"

"To run up here with the rock."

"And to blow it?"

"I'm not sure, at least not now. What he managed to tell me, and what he put into this"—she lifted the pocket-sized black looseleaf notebook beside her—"would indicate something else."

"Well, is he or isn't he going to blow it?"

"He's seen me . . . and he hasn't blown it, has he?"

"He still has the rock?"

"He's lying on it over there. It's in a hole dug into the ice."

"Well, Dietrich is pretty convinced, and the Thule people as well, that he's going to blow it."

"Dietrich's loyalties are already suspect," she replied flatly.

He looked at her, trying to fit that revelation in with everything that had happened to him. "That's nice to know," he said, but not really that shook by the possibility. "So was Thorsen programmed to blow it or not?"

"Well, what he says, and what this notebook of his bears out," she said in a preoccupied tone, as though not too sure either "is that he was and he wasn't."

"Nice games we play," he said with a sigh. "Do you want to enlarge on that, or shall we have tea?"

She flipped open the notebook, scanned it, and said, "The way it looks is that Thorsen deliberately planted the idea that he was going to blow it." She sounded as if she were still piecing it together. "Way back a year ago he made an entry in this notebook that he was sure the Russians were going to try for the rock inside Houston—"

"How'd he know that?"

"He doesn't say. But he thwarted two attempts on their part to grab it and finally took to sleeping on the rock to protect it. In October of this past year he made an entry that he was sure he was being put through thought-control sessions and that he was being programmed to run with the rock to Arctic ice. He says he knew he would have little chance of eluding them in the open. So if he had to go out, he had to attract the attention of other agencies like Interpol and the CIA, so he planted the evidence that he was emotionally out of control and bent on destruction."

"Couldn't he tell someone in NASA or the CIA even if he felt he couldn't trust Dietrich?" Sebastian asked.

"Thorsen told me earlier today, in between his states of semiconsciousness, that Dietrich had him boxed in. He says so here in his notebook, too. All his phones were monitored by Central Control, and he was always under surveillance, with a man practically at his elbow all the time. Besides, Thorsen says, even if he wanted to try to tell someone of his fears, Dietrich would have discredited him on the grounds of his mental imbalance, which was quite obvious by then as Landau's thought control took hold."

"Seems funny that Dietrich would let out the word that Thorsen was going to blow it," Sebastian argued. "He must have known that such information would attract others, and he surely didn't want that."

"I can't answer that fully either," she replied in a preoccupied tone. "I can only surmise that Dietrich's plot to intercept Thorsen failed. When Thorsen got through to the ice, Dietrich had to find some rationale for calling in the Russian ice teams. The only way to do that was to sound the alarm that there was a threat of worldwide proportions in the making . . . and on that the Russians made their move."

Sebastian dropped his head down on the sleeping bag again and stared up at the ceiling. "You know, that doesn't make sense even yet. Landau is smuggled in to program Thorsen to go out to Arctic ice, but all the time Thorsen figures on going anyway, for reasons I am sure you are going to let me in on but which I don't want to know yet, because it will spoil what looks like the consummation of a beautiful relationship."

165

She looked up from the open notebook and gave him a small smile but then added, flipping through a sheaf of papers, "Do you want to read about the struggle of Professor Thorsen to avoid that journey?" He looked at the notebook extended to him and saw that she was dead serious now, almost intent.

"My eyes," he said lamely, still aware of their blurring and watering from the partial snow blindness.

"All right," she went on, as if having made a point. "Two pages tell of his fear of the Arctic at his age, the fear of dying before he finished what he had to do. His battle was to keep himself mentally aware at all times so that he could stay one step ahead of the Russians. And anybody who knows anything about neuropsychosomatics knows that once you go under the hypnotic powers of the controller, you are not your own man any more. Even you proved that."

"*Even* me?" he said in a half-wounded tone.

"*Even* you as a clergyman, yes," she replied shortly. "Because you should have had the spiritual barriers to resist Landau, but you did not."

"Score one for Landau," he said almost petulantly, wanting her to put the book aside, interested only in her and not the case he knew she was building for him. When she didn't reply but kept on reading from the notebook, he asked, "You're saying that the Bible staved off Landau's complete command of his brain?"

She shrugged. "It was all he had, even as he says here. He writes a scripture verse on every page. Sometimes there are half a dozen pages of verses written in. And when I found him in the igloo last night he was hanging on to this Bible as if it were the family jewels."

"So why did you take it from him?"

"I went and got it after I knocked you down. When I found that mean-looking gun on you, I figured you were out to do Thorsen in, and it could be you were on Landau's brain wave too. I took a chance that maybe, just maybe, the scriptures might tranquilize you if nothing else could."

166

Sebastian savored that for a long minute, marveling again that one feeble gesture of his own long ago could now be so critical to the way things progressed here, both for Thorsen and himself. "Clever of the old boy," he said finally. "By convincing everyone he is deranged, he could carry the rock as far as he wanted to and nobody could touch him for fear he'd blow it. Then he could play a waiting game until the right party came to him—which was you, the way things stand now. How come they picked you, of all people?"

"I was security coordinator for him when he visited Tel Aviv eighteen months ago. We got to know each other pretty well then." She got up on her knees and reached over to dip out a cup of hot soup from the pot sitting on the primus. "Here, eat while you can."

He sniffed at it. "That the seal meat I smelled cooking sometime back?"

"Be glad you have it. It's the best source of calories in the Arctic."

They said nothing to each other for a long time. He watched her reading from the notebook, studied the shape of her delicate nose, the contour of her mouth. Finally he said, "Well, now that Thorsen is here and the rock is here, all you have to do is radio Thule and ask for a pickup."

She glanced at him from her reading. "That's out," she said bluntly.

"Why? Or maybe I shouldn't ask, is that it? Anyway, if Thorsen is going under, the least you can do, for his sake—"

"If I try to communicate to Thule, you can be sure Eureka will pick it up, and who knows whether the Russians have broken my code by now? Once they knew Thorsen was down and out—even if I were to ask for nothing more than a pickup from Thule—you can bet they'd be here within the hour."

"So we head back south toward Greenland, then. We're sure to bump into American military on the way."

"I can't trust anybody," she said, and her voice

167

trembled, and for the first time he realized that the strain she had held behind that beautiful composure was very close to the surface.

"You believe everything Thorsen says in that—that notebook of his?" he ventured, feeling the shadow of the bigger issue hanging over them.

"Considering everything that has happened, and what he tried to tell me before he slipped under, yes, I believe him."

He paused, sipping his soup, hearing the dogs howl in the distance. "It all comes down to the big question, then?" he asked, deciding he might as well have it all.

"Not unless you are prepared to face the answer," she replied candidly.

"Well, I'll tell you one thing, I'm really quite comfortable here, you know that," he said, trying to play it light, not wanting any tension to come between them. "Besides that, I've got sore eyes, a frostbitten nose, frostbitten feet, and my hand may go into gangrene if I don't get off this ice pretty soon. And what's more, I can't make love to the woman of my life in a lousy six-by-six igloo! How's that for openers?"

"You don't have to go any further," she replied, not lifting her eyes from the notebook. "Anyway, the fact that Thorsen is reading his Bible is all you want anyway, correct?" Her voice remained toneless, almost polite; he hated it when she used it on him. When she glanced up at him, he saw the small chips of light in those blue eyes, and he knew he had ignited the old fires again.

"Well, what do you want me to do?" he appealed, coughing up a short laugh to let her know he didn't want to draw the old battle lines on which they had tested each other in the Negev. "Go to the North Pole to prove that Thorsen's theory that Cook might have indeed traveled to the Pole is correct?"

"That might be the grandest gesture you ever displayed," she said bluntly, "even for God." He saw her shift back a few inches from him, as if to get better light from the primus, but he interpreted the move as symbolic of her withdrawal from him.

168

"Peace, sweetheart," he said, wanting only her nearness. "Let's not go over that ground again." He reached over and closed the notebook in her hands and held hers in his good left one. "You know I'm not looking for a way to cop out now, so let's have it: Why did Thorsen come out on the ice when he knew he was going to die trying it, presuming Landau's thought control was not his reason?"

She hesitated, keeping her eyes on his hand holding hers. "You know I can go this alone if I have to—"

"Don't play with me now," he interjected quietly. "You and I are destined for the lofty, noble ideals, while other men and women simply go on their honeymoons. So what's the plot?"

She gave him a quick toss of her head, sending her blond hair into a storm of light, that familiar gesture of hers which translated her defiance and independence of any male, even of him. But it only stirred his love for her all the more.

"All right," she said with a sigh. "Thorsen is apparently the only man who knows that the rock must be left at a consistent temperature of at least minus forty degrees for at least three years in order to neutralize it." She said it precisely, as if wanting him to get the full significance of it.

"Well, there are deep freezes in Houston," he suggested.

"The poor man was practically sleeping on that rock in Houston—and most of the time *not* sleeping for fear someone would walk off with it," she said impatiently. "He had to get it out to some place that had a temperature constantly on the minus level and yet where no one could find it."

"So why must it be neutralized? As long as it is kept away from oxygen—"

"You want to read why?" she said, lifting the notebook toward him again.

"Give me the condensed version," he said, smiling at her.

She shrugged. "I'm not sure I can. . . . Anyway,

169

Thorsen claims that the moon rock, this one in particular, is a rare combination of minerals. As he puts it, and I think science verifies it, the moon has both a lunar night and a lunar day. The lunar day, which lasts as long as two weeks, heats up to three hundred degrees Fahrenheit. The night, which is about as long, goes down to two hundred ninety-three degrees below zero. Thus there is a balance of temperature between equal heat and cold. This rock has the capacity to expend in energy mass in heat, but without a supply of oxygen it remains neutral. Do you follow me?"

"Old paper moon is not so paper," he commented.

"Thorsen believes," she went on, "that the craters on the moon are not due to inner volcanic action or the collision of meteors but rather due to these rocks which, after a period of exposure to the excessive moon-day heat, finally do explode . . . but since they have not grown to the full energy mass they are capable of, because of the moon's counter temperatures and lack of oxygen, they do not create the havoc that they could. Now, however, he says he has proven in his experiments that the rock, once kept at higher temperatures on a full oxygen base, is capable of rapid growth and can then reach an energy mass quite beyond anything we have seen in atomic explosions to date."

"You're saying then that it could be growing now?" Sebastian cut in. "Did you get a look at the capsule that rock is in?"

"No. . . ."

"Well—"

"But Thorsen's last words to me today were that the rock is growing, yes," she came back quickly, her voice sounding subdued by the immensity of the fact.

He looked at her intently, but her eyes did not waver from his. "But in an oxygen-free container, sealed as it is—"

"Temperature is the critical factor," she interjected. "The rock was never kept in a low enough freeze in Houston, because neither Thorsen nor anybody else knew

170

that it fed on higher temperatures until a few months ago. When Thorsen found out, he improvised a cooling system in his private lab, because he couldn't trust it with anybody outside. That system was not fully adequate. And the run from Houston to Greenland, though the rock was kept in the capsule within a low-temp cooler, did not help it any. Even here on the Arctic ice, the uneven temperatures of coming spring—"

"But are you sure temperature is more critical than oxygen?" Sebastian insisted. "Is Thorsen that sure?"

She didn't respond to that, flipping a page in the notebook instead.

"Do you know what you are playing with here?" he added. "This kind of thing ought to be in the hands of world scientists to do a proper job of analyzing it and neutralizing it."

"Do you think a rock of this cosmic power is going to stay in anybody's hands for long?" she countered. "Do you think those Russians and Chinese closing in on us are going to listen politely while we tell them the rock needs to be disarmed?"

"All right, what do you intend to do with the thing?" Sebastian demanded. "What did Thorsen have in mind in coming out here with it in the first place?"

She hesitated, closed the notebook carefully, and with her eyes on it said, "He was on his way to bury the rock on Ice Island T-Three, roughly thirty-five miles north of our present position. It used to be occupied by American military ice teams, but nobody is there now, just empty Quonsets."

"And if he were to get there, how did he expect to dig a hole deep enough?"

"There will be a man there."

He gave a short laugh at that, and she glanced at him quickly, uncertainly. "A man?" he jibed. "*One* man?"

"That's what Thorsen told me: one man who will have the shaft ready."

"You believe that too?" She didn't reply. "If he

171

risked communicating with one man, why hasn't that man gone to the big boys about it?"

"Don't ask me to stitch it all up nice and neat," she replied abruptly. He felt the rebuke and knew she was seeing him as he was back in the Negev, trying to get it all in front of him.

"Thirty-five miles?" He went on trying to shift gears away from the point of testiness. "Only thirty-five miles?"

"It may seem a long way—"

"For us?" he said lightly, trying a smile on her. "I mean, we have no means of navigation, and we have to try to hit a drifting ice island in weather that is supposed to get nastier as the Arctic spring comes in, right? Frederick Cook couldn't cut it with five dog teams and twenty men, but we're going to pin the tail on the donkey, blindfolded, when we don't even know for sure what wall the donkey is on, right?"

"I love you for that," she said, and her eyes enveloped him.

"What?"

"I love you for saying it like that, which I know by now is your way of telling me you're going to do it." He let out a low groan of exasperation, and she added, "Besides, I have a sextant."

He shook his head at her. "Presuming you can use a sextant, which I don't doubt, and you know the bearing of the ice island, you still have to have a sun to shoot by, right? Supposing we get a couple more days with no sun?"

"Supposing we get sun all the way?" she quipped. "And since you are in touch with the One who controls the weather—"

"That's a presumption on Deity."

"Is that a new way of saying you have no faith? The scriptures say, 'If we ask any thing according to his will, he heareth us'—right?"

"You've come a long way with scripture since the Negev," he teased her.

"You taught me that." She smiled at him. "And I shall love you forever for it."

172

He grunted, dropping his eyes from hers, because he felt a little apprehension in the tense she used, as if maybe she wasn't sure she had many more times to say these things to him.

"And the bearing of T-Three? What about that?"

"Thorsen gave it to me. There's a Norwegian ice team on the far northern edge of it," she explained. "Every night they radio their bearing to Point Barrow, Alaska, their supply base. We fix on that."

"I passed an ice island south of here about fifteen miles—"

"Arlis One." She came back quickly, as if anticipating the suggestion. "Thorsen told me it's dissolving too quickly. T-Three is two hundred feet thick and will hold for at least five years."

"And if we get the rock buried up there, what's to keep the Russians or the Chinese or whoever from trying to get their grubby hands on it?"

"The American military will have to reoccupy the island, obviously," she came back shortly.

"But if you don't use that radio and call Thule, we're going to be the only ones to face those people up there—and, of course, the one superman who is supposed to be there waiting—and I don't think either the Russians or the Chinese will feel like roasting marshmallows with us."

"We cross that bridge when we come to it," she concluded.

Sebastian sighed, knowing it was useless to throw red flags in front of her now. "Good thing God is on your side," he said rather laconically, because he wasn't sure if He was on his own in this. "Or maybe it's a good thing you are on His?"

She smiled at him, and her face lit up in the way that made him more conscious of the longing he felt for her. "The Eskimos say that Ano, the spirit of the ice, commands their destinies," she commented, jabbing him a little.

He looked up at her quickly. "What did you say?"

"What?"

173

"Just then . . . what?"

"I said Ano, the spirit of—"

"Ano," he repeated, and something leaped into his brain, and he got out of his sleeping bag, pushing back the pain that grabbed his head in the effort.

"Where are you going?" she asked sharply.

"I left an Eskimo ten miles back on the trail," he said, pulling on his inner parka.

"You can't go back for him now," she protested. "Not in the dark! What about Thorsen?"

"I'm going over to see him first," he replied, pulling his face mask over his head, then putting on his mittens, not wanting to take a chance outside in the cold while he got his outer parka. "My parka is outside, I presume?" Before she could answer, he picked up her flashlight from the floor next to his sleeping bag and bent down to crawl through the entrance to the outside. The Arctic night hit him with the usual wallop of subzero air, but he felt it more, dressed only in his inner parka. He threw the light around and saw the Eskimo standing a few feet to his right.

"This your man?" Sebastian asked her as she came out behind him.

"What is it, Montoos?" she asked. "Thorsen?"

"Uh," the Eskimo replied in the familiar grunt. "He go bad now."

Sebastian flashed his light around and caught sight of Big Bay a few feet away, curled up against the cold. As the light moved over him, he got up, wagging his tail expectantly. Sebastian saw his parka hanging from a tent pole a few feet to his left. She had put it there, apparently to dry it out. He moved over to it, shivering, as Barbara said from behind, "Don't go charging in there too fast on Thorsen."

He pulled on one sleeve of his parka as Big Bay jumped up on him, nuzzling his hand playfully. Sebastian tried to push him away with his foot, and in that instant the dog reached up and jerked the parka out of his hand, turned, and started running with it across the ice toward the igloo of Thorsen's and the other dogs.

"Hey!" Sebastian yelled, trying to jump after the dog but falling flat on his stomach on the ice.

"Montoos!" Barbara yelled, and the Eskimo obediently took off after the dog, in his short-legged, gimpy run. Barbara followed, and Sebastian got up, stumbling after her, keeping the flashlight beam far enough ahead for the Eskimo to see.

"Dumb dog!" he yelled at her back, as if it was so important to explain now. "Always grabbing anything off me that's movable!"

She didn't answer him but kept running, half hopping in the tricky footing. Sebastian saw in the flashlight beam that Big Bay was now at Thorsen's igloo, trying to tear the parka apart as if it were meat, and the other dogs were joining in. The Eskimo was not more than twenty feet from the dog when Sebastian fell again. He kept the light on Big Bay, though, and Barbara hesitated only a few seconds, looking back at him. At that same instant, everything changed over by the igloo. There wasn't any unusual sound, except maybe a hollow thump as if the ice were breaking up close by. But as Sebastian stumbled to his feet, he saw that Big Bay and the parka had dissolved, and there were splatterings of red against the igloo wall.

"What happened?" he yelled at Barbara, who stood there staring ahead, very still, almost as if she were transfixed by the sight. Then, suddenly aware, she started running toward the igloo. He followed her, throwing his light over the bloody snow, seeing only the shredded remains of Big Bay. The Eskimo was lying on his back a few feet to the left, very still. Barbara was down beside him, examining him, but she got up quickly and said over her shoulder, "He's dead! And you better get inside before you freeze to death!" She disappeared inside the igloo, but he took another minute, still shaken and confused by the sudden carnage, shivering in jerks from the cold and maybe the shock, playing the light around, wondering where the explosion had come from, if it was an explosion.

Finally he turned and crawled inside the snow

175

house, pulling off his face mask and mittens. He caught the odor of death first as he moved inside. Though it was warm in the small enclosure, the damp, musky smell was close, almost asphyxiating, mingling with the pungent odors of medicines. She was already opening the sleeping bag in which Thorsen lay, then his gray sweater and his red woolen shirt underneath that. When she got down to his thermal underwear, Thorsen opened his eyes and looked up at her with an unseeing stare. Sebastian wasn't sure he recognized the old man at all. His cheeks were gaunt, his skin pale, his hair almost snow white. His thin lips moved, trying to say something, but nothing came except congested breathing that sounded like a death rattle.

Meanwhile, Barbara was feeling around his upper torso, until finally she pressed down gingerly on an area over the chest. She unzipped the underwear, felt inside, then folded the suit back. A blue patch of about four square inches showed up. She examined it carefully and then leaned back with a sigh, saying nothing.

"What is it?" he asked, his voice sounding hollow in the igloo and still a little shaky.

"Some kind of sound sensor, I think," she said in a preoccupied tone. "That blast was meant for Thorsen, and you were supposed to deliver it; that's my guess."

Sebastian thought about that, realizing suddenly how deadly serious all this really was, even beyond his own comprehension.

"So I had one of those blue patches on me too?" he asked.

"In your parka, probably, hooked up to the explosives."

He nodded. "All right, so whoever hooked me up, Dietrich, probably—does he know what happened just now?"

"Of course. They wouldn't use a sensor if they didn't."

"Okay, they know I'm dead with my sensor gone, but Thorsen's is still going."

176

"Correct," she said, and zipped up Thorsen's underwear, the blue patch remaining inside.

"And you're going to leave it on? They'll know he is still alive, and that they failed in getting him."

"I want them to think that. If they know they've failed, that means the Russians will still go slow in trying to jump him . . . and we need that margin of time to get on the move."

"You leaving Thorsen behind?"

"We can't carry him. The weight will slow us down."

"Leave him for them?"

She didn't answer. He glanced at her and saw that her face looked drawn in the light of the primus, a sign that she had been shook by all this, though it was unlike her to show such emotion.

"Nice guys, Dietrich and company," he said aimlessly, still numbed by the monstrosity of the attempt. She didn't reply.

"Help me lift him so I can get the capsule," she finally said.

Thorsen groaned feebly as Sebastian rolled him over onto his side, watching her feel around until she found the gouged-out hole in the ice and then lifted the capsule up carefully in both hands. The green plastic container was wet and the glass on top was fogged up, but he could see down into it when she showed him, catching the black shadowy shape of the rock within.

"It looks testy," he said, as she carefully tied the leather thongs hooked into the capsule around her neck, tucking the capsule itself inside her parka belt to keep it from swinging.

"What about Thorsen?" he asked. "Can you do anything for him?"

"The best hospital couldn't save him, that much I know. I gave him the strongest antibiotic there is, tetracycline. He's just too old and tired to fight it."

"I'd like to talk to him."

"Prayer would be more like it."

"I should have come sooner—"

177

"Yes, and blown yourself and him up," she retorted in a clipped voice. "And the rock with you, for all we know. . . . He needs your life now, and mine; we better start thinking about that."

He didn't look at her, keeping his eyes hopefully on the old man's face. He saw the cruel ravages of the grief Thorsen had endured for so long over the loss of his family, and now the corrosive lines added by the Arctic. Sebastian tried to arouse him, but the eyes did not flicker. The mouth finally dropped open and the breathing came in labored gasps. Finally all was silent. The face dissolved into total relaxation, sagging away from the high cheekbones and craggy forehead.

"He's gone," she said evenly, feeling for a pulse in the older man's wrist. Sebastian leaned over and put his head down to the chest. There was no sound there either. He rose and gently closed the eyelids over the fixed stare, drew the sleeping bag up over the face.

He cleared his throat, not knowing how to say it. Then, "Lord"—and his voice sounded like a child's in the wonder and loss of the moment—"may the Truth he read and seized on in his final days, that which helped him to make this final journey for mankind, may that Truth carry him home to You now. . . . Amen."

"Amen," she echoed, her voice subdued to a whisper. "And may we finish the journey he began," she added. They said nothing to each other for a long time, as if lost in the awesome moment of death.

Finally she reached over, picked up Thorsen's parka, and handed it to him.

"What time is it?" he asked, pulling the parka over his shoulders.

"Nearly three in the morning."

"We could get on the move even now, I suppose."

"What about your friend on the back trail?" She asked almost indifferently, as if wanting that settled in his mind.

He didn't respond right away. "There probably isn't time. . . ."

178

"I think you should go," she said abruptly.

He glanced at her. "Why the change in tune?"

"You've got three hours yet to sunup," she went on. "That snowmobile can go ten miles an hour, and if you hit a good run on the ice you can be there and back in plenty of time, provided no ice rafters have torn it up."

"You trying to get rid of me?" he asked. She glanced at him, looking innocent and uncomprehending. "I mean, it's going to get thick around here by dawn with Russians and Chinese—"

"Well, I'll tell you," she came back in some detachment, "nobody has more positive God-signs hanging over him than you in the last few hours. I just don't want to take a chance violating that Presence. Besides, to put it more practically, if that Eskimo of yours is still alive, he could be a big difference in our finding the ice island. . . . How's that?"

He wasn't sure even then. He felt a sense of withdrawal from her then, even dismissal. "I don't want to leave you here alone."

"You are underestimating me," she replied, giving a toss of her head, trying a smile that was wan, tired, uncertain. "You should know by now that I can take care of myself."

As he looked at her, she seemed small and fragile in the bulky fur parka for some reason. It was strange seeing her in that dimension. He felt a shaft of nagging doubt. "How long will you wait?" he asked.

"I must be gone before first light," she replied. "I'll take Thorsen's dog and sled, if I have to."

"You know I could run into trouble on that trail," he reminded her. "I may not get ten miles an hour out of the machine—"

"You can catch up," she replied shortly.

"Maybe I should take the dogs—"

"Look, I'm just telling you to do what your tormented soul tells you to do!" Her blue eyes were snapping again as she railed at him. "If you want to keep arguing about it, we'll forget it!"

He didn't like the sound of her voice, harsh and brittle. He hesitated. "All right," he finally conceded, "but always remember, I'll catch up, no matter what. I'll be right behind you. . . . Okay?"

She pressed her lips together as if to throttle some emotion deep inside her and nodded. He leaned over and kissed her, and she did not respond at first. Then she lifted her right hand and touched his face, returning his kiss with that soft warmness that was her. He pulled back and looked into her eyes, trying to see within.

"You know I'm quite willing to forego it," he said adamantly. "I can see the larger picture here too."

"I want you to go," she insisted. "Please. . . ."

He kissed her again, wanting to linger, but she pushed at him, urging him out of the igloo. He got up and followed her out. Outside he counted five dogs dead and two wounded. He asked if she had a gun; she handed him a .38 special. He shot the two dogs and handed the gun back to her. He counted eight dogs left from Thorsen's team.

"Do you know how to hook up a team and run with them behind a sled?" he asked.

"Montoos showed me," she replied confidently. He watched her walk away from him in the light of his flashlight, that easy, athletic rhythm of hers so perfectly coordinated, telling him she was in command of her own forces now. But he sensed, too, that she wasn't carrying herself in the usual head-high pose that was so much a hallmark of her spirit.

When they got inside the snow house, she insisted he take a day's supply of tuna and bacon bars and a can of pemmican.

"There is hardly enough here for even a couple days as it is," he protested. But he rolled up the food with his tent.

"I have extra pemmican," she said. "Also, take this vial of tetracycline. I have one of my own. If your man is still alive, get two of those capsules into him right away. It's the best antibiotic in the business." Then she

180

turned and picked up a pair of sunglasses and handed them to him.

He took them, and their hands touched, and for a moment she hesitated, almost as if she were confused. Then she moved on outside, telling him without further words, that there was no more time to talk. He followed her out and pulled the tarp off the snowmobile. He sat down and kicked the starter lever. It took a while before the engine clattered doubtfully to life. He flipped on the high beam and saw that it gave good light at least thirty yards in front of him, enough for him to see well ahead.

"If it looks too tangled out there, I'll be back," he shouted at her.

"Godspeed," she said, lifting her voice above the sound of the engine.

He hesitated a few seconds, pulled by the need to help Ah-Ming if he could and yet held there too. Finally he opened the throttle and moved out, keeping his eyes in front. The light was good enough for him to find the trail he had come up on, the tracks still frozen in the crusted snow and ice. He knew that what he was attempting, a night ride on Arctic ice, was considered stupid by anyone acquainted with conditions here. He felt an urge to abandon the idea, wanting to go back to her anyway. And yet he knew, as she put it, that if he didn't at least make the attempt, the rest of the journey wouldn't make sense either. So he didn't look back at her; he was afraid to, feeling the tug on his heart. He kept his mind on the sound of the engine and the beam of light opening up the trail ahead of him. But all the time he was conscious that every minute took him farther and farther away from her.

8

He had come as far as he should, he knew. The trail had not changed that much, and he had had no problem following it despite the snow that had fallen on it the day before. But all the ice mounds looked the same in the dark, and he knew it was a foolish assumption that he could ever spot the orange pennant marker that he had left near Ah-Ming's snow house. He had stopped several times to play his flashlight over the silent hulks of rafter ice, looking for that sign. And all the time he was aware of the diminishing element of time, the urgency to return to Barbara. And yet, having come so far, he felt that other pull, the need to find Ah-Ming, to be sure. . . .

He decided to make just one more move down the ice, maybe a hundred yards or so. If he didn't spot the pennant then, he would head back. He moved carefully, keeping the snowmobile at eight or ten miles an hour, wanting to be sure he knew what was ahead in the trail. After a few minutes which revealed nothing, he decided that he would swing back, thinking he might have missed it. He turned the machine around. As the light swept over the cathedral-like shapes of ice, he caught a glimpse of a black object against the ice wall to his right. He turned back quickly, poured the juice to the machine, and moved over to it. It was the sled, all right, but the pennant was gone, blown away probably. He found the snow house then, looking the same as he had left it.

He killed the motor, jumped off, and tried pulling the ice blocks out of the entrance. They were frozen solid. He went back and got the heavy knife, returned, and hacked at the entrance in the light of the snow-mobile's beam. His right hand was useless and he had to work only with his left, which made it slower. Finally, after what seemed a long time, he cut through, shoved the blocks aside, and crawled in.

He caught the familiar odor of death again, even as he had with Thorsen, but above that was the gagging smell of rotting flesh. It was dark inside the igloo, and he threw his light around the form lying there a few feet away. He moved in quickly, passed the light over the face, leaned down and said, "Ah-Ming," and slapped his cheeks once or twice. There was no response. He unzipped the sleeping bag, reached in and felt for the pulse. Only faint, hardly there at all. He found the primus, refueled it, and lit it. The light helped him in his further examination. The Eskimo's fingers were worse, carrying a purple-green cast, the skin broken open and oozing pus.

"Ah-Ming, come on, my friend," Sebastian coaxed, almost frantic now, anxious for even a minute with him to let him know. Know what? What good was even a minute to convey the whole love of God? But he went on fighting for that life anyway, until finally those eyes opened just a crack. "Ah-Ming?"

The eyes opened wider, until those black thumb-tack pupils were there, almost as clear as the color of black water against the snow. But somehow, though they fixed on Sebastian in recognition, they also seemed to be looking beyond him.

"You kill Torsen?" he said then, his lips hardly moving, the words coming on a whisper.

"No, Ah-Ming. I found him but I didn't kill him."

"Good," the Eskimo said weakly, and he sighed, as if a load had been lifted from him.

"Ah-Ming—"

"Go now . . . wife of Innuit calling . . . children calling . . . go now. . . ."

"Ah-Ming, wait—" But the eyes closed and the body in his arms sagged. Sebastian stared down at the small face that seemed to have shrunk even more in death. It was done, and there was nothing he could say or do but hold the Eskimo, trying to communicate something to the still form, unable to think beyond the loss. Then slowly he let the body down into the sleeping bag again, covered it with the few furs, found Thorsen's Bible in his pocket, and read aloud, sniffing loudly now and then between the words. When he was done, he blew out the primus, picked it up, and went back outside, laying the blocks of ice back in place.

Satisfied, he stood up, looking around. It was nearly four-fifteen by the luminous dials of his wristwatch. As he stood there in the silence of the frozen wilderness, trying to reconcile the mystery of the timing of the death of Ah-Ming, so close to his own arrival, he saw a light flash across the sky over the snow ridge directly south behind the snow house. Half curious, he dragged himself up the ice mound and studied the back horizon through his binoculars. The light came up again, hanging stationary in the distance and then drifting slowly back to earth.

Flares. But whose? Russian? Chinese? American? There were magnesium torches too. . . . Whoever it was, was risking travel at night on the ice, like himself.

He didn't bother to ponder it. Suddenly he realized it was late, maybe an hour or so from first light. He slid back down the ice mound, ran to the snowmobile, kicked it to life, and moved out quickly, heading up the trail on which he had come. It was beginning to snow, and he pushed the throttle up another notch, moved now to get back to Barbara before he got lost in the whiteout. He felt the sting of rebuke, that he should have come all this way from her when he could do nothing for Ah-Ming in the end, and he glanced back over his shoulder and saw lights again, maybe closer now, and he knew it was all coming together too fast. Was he going to make it back in time to find her? The first honest fear of losing her in this vast waste of death moved him to open the throttle wider, putting caution behind him.

Since 2:30 that same morning, when Lt. Bob Hestig reported that one of the laser sound sensor ripples had disappeared from the ice, the Operation Moon Rock general staff had remained in the plot room. It was still snowing and gusting outside, but Buckner had committed his commando team for a dawn liftoff to Eureka regardless. Meanwhile, weather ops reported that the squall, moving from the south, would hit the Arctic ice later in the morning. Chances of clearing were marginal and not anticipated until tomorrow evening at the earliest.

The six people of Thorsen's party, in the meantime, had been picked up by the American military ice team earlier that day, frozen, half starved, and bewildered by the hostility of the elements to the point of shock. But they had admitted seeing Thorsen with something hanging around his neck during the journey, though none of them had any idea of what it was. The news coming back to Thule at least confirmed what Morton had said earlier and posed the very problem they had hoped to avoid.

As they kept their vigil through the sluggish hours, waiting hopefully for some radio report from Little Bo Peep, which was long overdue, Admiral Fish, and even Morton, was pretty sure that the kamikaze had delivered his payload. But if that was the case, it appeared he had not knocked out Thorsen, whose sound sensor was still bleating away up there. And certainly, at the same time, he had not penetrated the rock with shrapnel.

The question was which presumption to make. Was Thorsen dead and the rock up for grabs for whoever got there first? Or were they to presume that Thorsen was alive and would yet blow the rock if anybody tried to break in on him? Who was going to make the first big mistake up there? Only Little Bo Peep could answer that one, and Fish was puzzled as to why she didn't break radio silence to inform them, unless she had been zapped somehow in the middle between Thorsen and the kamikaze.

At 4 A.M. Major Collins, who headed the American ice team, called in to say he was four miles behind Thorsen's projected position and faced a half mile of open water forcing him to make a three-mile end around. Did Thule want him to charge into Thorsen's camp when he did make it?

Fish looked at Morton, who had been leaning against the map table for hours, puffing slowly on his pipe like a locomotive sitting quietly on a spur, boilers fired, waiting for the first jerk of the throttle.

"Does he have canvas boats with him?" he asked.

"He does," Fish said. "But putting twenty-five men across in those—"

"Tell him to put a six-man advance team in one of the boats and get them over and on a beeline for Thorsen's camp," Morton said with finality. "Tell the advance team to travel on snowcat high beams only, no magnesium flares. I don't want the Russians to plot our every move at this point. When they get to the camp, proceed with caution. . . . Now, how soon can they be in there?"

Hestig went back to radio for a check. Fish and Buckner said nothing to Morton. It was obvious that Morton was going to go on the presumption that Thorsen was too far gone to blow the rock or, as Fish had already concluded himself, that if he had intended to blow it, he would have done so by now. Since he hadn't moved from his position for thirty-six hours, the scientist had to realize he wasn't going to make it to the Pole anyway.

Finally Hestig came back and said, "He says by first light he should be there."

"Why so long?" Morton demanded.

"Well, the lead is half frozen."

"Pushing a canvas boat in a lead with ice segments is tricky, Mr. Morton," Fish explained. "Those flimsy things puncture easily . . . and he'll have to work by magnesium flares until he gets across."

186

"Tell him to just get across," Morton snapped, jamming his pipe back into his wide mouth. "I want him in there *before* first light; otherwise the Russians have it. . . . Got that, Lieutenant? *Before* first light."

"Yes, sir," Hestig said and went back to his radio.

Nobody said anything. Buckner looked at Fish once as if to say it was too close, trying to push Collins in so short a time and on high beams only. But Fish did not raise any issues. Morton had opted to go it his way. It was probably the best choice.

So it was nearly 5:40 in the morning when Hestig came back with the radio signal. Fish was half dozing in his chair when he heard Hestig say, "Mr. Morton, I have word from Collins." Fish opened his eyes and stood up, going over to where Hestig stood by Morton, who hadn't moved from the map table yet. "He made Thorsen's camp. The Russians were there ahead of them, already gone, heading straight north—"

"Thorsen?" Fish asked.

"Dead, sir . . . but no mark on him."

"The rock, man, what about the rock?" Morton insisted.

"It's gone, sir."

"Damn!" Morton exploded and walked immediately to the huge wall to stare at the map intently.

"Did he say anything about seeing the Interpol girl or the body of the kamikaze?" Fish asked Hestig.

Hestig glanced at his radio copy. "He says he found Thorsen's body, the body of an Eskimo, a lot of dried blood splattered over Thorsen's igloo, and a bunch of dead dogs, one of which is mangled to shreds."

"The kamikaze was there," Fish concluded. "But where did his body go?" he added, more to himself than to anyone else.

"How about the Chinese?" Buckner asked then. "Has he seen them in the area?"

"He said he spotted a snow cloud about a mile or so southeast, and he's sure it's a number of snow machines moving up on him—"

"Tell Collins to move out," Morton said suddenly.

"Sir?"

"Tell Collins to push his six-man unit off on a heading east by northeast, the way the Russians came in," Morton insisted. "I want Collins to try to sucker those Chinese into thinking he's the Russians, making a run for it with the rock in their possession."

"The Chinese won't sucker for six men, Mr. Morton," Fish said doubtfully.

"Maybe not. But I am going to try everything now to get those Chinese out of the hot zone, all right, Admiral?"

Fish turned and nodded to Hestig to send the message.

"That's only six men against maybe twenty of theirs," Buckner suggested, but Morton did not respond to it.

Instead Morton said, "Admiral"—and he was rising on his tiptoes to look at the map—"if you were the Russians in possession of that rock, which way would you try to go to get off that ice in a hurry?"

Fish went over to the map and looked up at it, following an imaginary course he figured the Russians might be on. "I surely would not go three hundred and seventy-five miles back the way I came in," he mused. "Not with that payload. What I'd do is try for the nearest point where I could get a plane in to pick me up."

Morton grunted in confirmation. "All right, if they are heading north as Collins suggests and not east, where would that place be?"

"Ice Island T-Three, sir, right there." Fish put his finger on the small oblong insert on the map. "It used to be our scientific station until a year ago. Nothing there now but a couple of empty Quonsets, but there *is* a kind of runway."

"Well, that's where they have to be heading," Morton concluded.

Fish waited for him to go on; when he didn't, Fish said, "Are you going to intercept them, Mr. Morton?"

"Intercept?" Morton turned his intense blue eyes on Fish. "The worst threat is over; the rock is out of

Thorsen's hands, right? The next worst threat is a shoot-out . . . and maybe if we can get the Chinese chasing Collins, that will save us the problem."

"Are we just going to let the Russians walk off with the biggest piece of nuclear power the world has ever known?" Fish insisted.

"Yes, if it's got to be out of our hands, we'd rather have the Russians holding it than the Chinese," Morton replied. "And my job and yours is to avoid any showdown with that rock hanging out, okay?"

Fish hesitated, not knowing how far he could push with Morton. "Mr. Morton, there is still the matter of that Interpol girl and the kamikaze," he suggested. "It seems odd to me that they dropped out of sight without a trace—"

"Neither of them is relevant to the issue now, Admiral," Morton replied in a tone of dismissal. "Are you perhaps thinking that the Russians might be carrying them along—or what?"

Fish shook his head. "No, sir, not that, but—"

"Well, then, let's put it to rest," Morton replied with finality. "All we can do is wait and hope for the best. Right?"

"I've got Eureka!" Hestig called out from over by the radio panel. They turned toward Hestig as he got up to walk over to them, reading his copy.

"How come they decided to break silence now?" Morton asked. "What have you got, Lieutenant?"

"Agent Foxtrot, sir," Hestig read, "says he is holding five civilian personnel under gun in the communications shack at Eureka. He says they were making preparations to dismantle and jump out. He does not know how long he can hold. . . ."

"What are their names, does he say?"

"Bosman, Landau, Riley, McDain, and Barnes."

"Dietrich?" Morton demanded. "What about Otto Dietrich?"

"He says Dietrich has been absent from Eureka for the last twenty-four hours since he took a copter out for a patrol over the ice."

189

"Absent?" Morton said with perplexity. Then he turned to Buckner. "General, are you ready to make your jump into Eureka?"

"Yes, sir," Buckner said and started moving for the door.

"You better hurry it," Morton called to him. "He may have more on his hands than he can handle! And find Dietrich!"

"I better check with weather," Fish said, still feeling out of sorts over the T-3 escape route of the Russians. Morton did not stop him, and Fish was glad to be out of the room, away from the heavy atmosphere of pipe smoke and the drag of the hours that had left him logy and somewhat disenchanted.

When he got into his own plot room, Buckner was there, pulling on his parka. Fish went over to his own wall map and stood there looking up at T-3.

"What are you going to do about it?" Buckner said to his back.

"What?" Fish said, wishing Buckner would leave and let him think this through on his own.

"You going to let the Russians walk off with it?"

"You heard the man, General. The CIA gets the word over the military, in the final analysis."

"Sure, but who will have to come up with the magic when the Russians make that rock into a number-one nuclear power? Morton?"

"That's not enough to buck the State Department on either."

"You're not really military here anyway," Buckner went on, in his reasoning tone. "You're in charge of ice operations, which means you can commit a multitude of sins and not involve the military at all, right?"

Fish turned and looked at him. "You're late for Eureka, aren't you, General?"

Buckner nodded and smiled thinly. He hesitated, moved for the door, paused, and looked back. "It's a hell of a way to end it, that's all I'm saying, Admiral." And then he was gone.

Fish stood there a long time looking up at the map

and Ice Island T-3. Finally, with a shrug, he turned and walked out, heading for the weather ops room.

It was 5:30 when he got near the Thorsen camp. He didn't drive all the way in, parking the snow machine near a clump of ice mounds a few hundred yards to the left of the place where he had gone in before. He paused long enough to check his back trail through the binoculars. The two snowmobiles were there, staying close enough, maybe six men, no more. He wouldn't have much time to get into the camp and get Barbara out, but he was sure, with daylight already flooding the ice, that she was gone.

He climbed up on the ice mounds that overlooked the camp proper to survey the open ice in front of him. Putting his binoculars on Thorsen's snow house beyond, he saw the snow machines first, at least eight of them, parked there. Then there was a cluster of men huddled around Thorsen's snow house, dressed in white snow suits, blending into the background. As he scanned further he saw the hammer and sickle painted on the engine housing of the nearest machine.

He could not see Barbara at all among them as they hunched down into a circle talking to each other. Thorsen's dogs were gone, and so was the sled. That told him that she was safely out of the camp, but how much of a jump did she have on them? With a dog team she would never be able to stay ahead of them with their faster snow machines.

He watched them climb onto their snowmobiles and move out quickly, picking up the trail that was still fresh in the falling snow. Sebastian did not wait any longer. He backed out of the protective cover of ice ridges and ran back to his own machine, kicked it to life, and headed out on a course westward, away from the camp, hoping to get out of range of the Russians and those ice teams coming up behind him and later get back on Barbara's trail.

The going was rougher in the new terrain. He kept urging the laboring machine through uneven clumps of ice and snow, feeling it drag, the engine sputtering now and then as it gamely fought to push the machine under his prodding. The snow was heavier, too; he was afraid he would not be able to pick up Barbara's trail at all if the snow kept coming like that. Even as he drove, he felt the wind buck at him, the cutting snowflakes slashing through his face mask and stinging the already sensitive flesh. He had to figure that she was probably an hour ahead of him. If she made the usual time with dogs, he could surely catch her within the hour, but only if the weather and the terrain allowed it.

Now he found himself getting into more impassable screw ice, so he had to slow down. Finally, frustrated at not finding an easy way through, he backtracked, heading in the direction of Thorsen's camp and then north again. But he was becoming more confused about directions, with the increasing snow making a whiteout no matter which way he looked. Finally he had to stop to put the last five gallons of gas that he had into the machine. Then, with a growing sense of immediacy, he pushed on again, plowing through drifts of snow that began to pile up from the increasing wind.

"God, there's just so much any man can take in a day," he said out loud as he drove. "Get me on track . . . somehow get me on track, God. . . ."

He continued bouncing over ice mounds and dragging heavily through snowdrifts. He put the sunglasses on to protect his eyes from the stinging ice chunks that were hitting him. They helped some, but after a while they clouded up hopelessly. He took them off and pushed the machine on, ignoring his eyes. He moved through a forest of ice pinnacles, feeling the snowmobile scrape its sides and bottom on it, and then he came into an open plain of ice again. He opened throttle and pushed the machine as fast as he could, hoping beyond hope that he was heading north. With no sun, he could not really tell.

He had no idea how long he went on this course, whipping by huge icebergs on either side, trying to ignore the wind and snow hitting him, the cold that cut through him, pushing the mocking voice aside that told him he would never find her. All he was conscious of was the sound of the snowmobile's motor, the bump and heave of the machine on the rough ice and dragging snow that threatened to throw him. He kept seeing her and those beautiful moods of hers—teasing, puzzled, coy, warm, tender, and briskly angry—the storm of her hair tossed in loving defiance of him . . . everything blended with the frozen sentries of ice moving by him, billboards all telling him the same thing: that there was more to come, endless miles of it, offering nothing but the same grave markers all the way.

And then, as he came up to a low barrier of ice on his right, the machine quit. Frozen and stiff and numbed by the contemplation of being finally immobilized here, he fumbled under the engine hood, trying to spot the trouble. He finally saw that the carburetor valve shaft had bent so badly that it was not opening the feeder line to allow the gas to come through. He had to remove it and straighten it. He worked a long time, trying to do the job with clumsy mittens, telling himself that he should put up the tent, light a fire, and work at it out of the horrible cold that whipped through him with the heavy gusts of wind. But he stayed with it, knowing that time was not on his side, that every minute he wasted here put him that much farther behind her. . . .

His watch showed it to be nearly noon when he managed to get the valve shaft back into shape well enough to function. Now he was miserably cold, and he felt that lazy feeling of sleep grab him, telling him he was close to deadly exposure. He shook free of it and climbed back on the snow machine, started it up, and moved out again.

He lost track of time, conscious only that he was running alongside a long line of ice ridges on his right, forbidding him any passage through. He kept watching it, looking for a break, a spot to climb up and get a look eastward with his binoculars. By now he knew he didn't have more than a gallon of gas left. If he didn't spot her soon, he would have to abandon the pursuit. The wind was stronger, the snow thicker, the visibility poorer. He had to be wary of ice crevasses or open leads of water which he might not see in time. The snow was almost blinding him now, so he tried the sunglasses again for a while, but they soon became too smeared to use. He stopped, unable to hold into the wind, feeling totally dejected by what looked to be an impossible attempt. Then he saw that the ice wall was sheared off a few yards ahead. There was only a small passageway, but maybe it was large enough.

He moved ahead, stopped, and pulled himself up the smaller ice mound to a point where he could get a fairly decent view of the flat plain of sea ice. The lenses of his binoculars started freezing the moment he took them out, but he managed to make one sweep from right to left. Nothing. He moved back from left to right, trying to see through the curtain of white, gusting snow. Maybe he had a hundred yards visibility, maybe less. He kept moving his scan across the open ice, praying she would be there, praying he would see her. There was a clump of ice at the center of his vision, and he held his binoculars there a minute, not sure . . . and then he saw it, a faint, blurred piece of black moving across that background of cluttered ice and blowing snow. His heart leaped. But even as he watched her pushing behind the sled, suddenly she disappeared! He waited, swinging to the right, expecting her to come up again against that ice wall. He saw the dogs first, then the sled. But she was not behind.

He slid back down the clump of ice and jumped on his snow machine, ramming it through the narrow passageway in the ice, ignoring the scrape on the engine housing. He headed on a line he figured would intercept the dogs, but even then he had to make detours around mounds of screw ice, and he was afraid that he would not find them. Frantically he pushed the machine around those jabbing bayonets of ice, praying the gas would hold. Finally he swung past a huge castle of ice and saw the dogs standing still in the snow twenty yards ahead of him, nipping at each other and looking over their shoulders, wondering what had happened to their driver. Sebastian tore by them on the snow machine, moving over the trail that the sled runners had made, hunting for her.

He found her a half mile back, lying face down in the snow. He stopped the machine and ran to her, bending to lift her into his arms, first pushing the snow off her face, terrified by the stillness of her. He took off his mittens, disregarding the pain of the cold on his bare skin, and rubbed her cheeks, feeling the stiffness of the flesh. Finally her eyes opened a little and fixed on his face, then closed again. She was going into that "willful freeze," her body shutting down the circuits one by one, yielding to the mastery of the cold. He picked her up and moved over to the snowmobile, but he knew there was no way to prop her up on it. So he walked with her in his arms back to where the dogs were, staggering into the wind that blinded him with slashing attacks of hard snow. He put her down by the sled, found an extra parka, and threw it over her, anchoring it with the five-gallon jerrican of gasoline from the sled. He tried to get the tent up, but the wind tore it from him when he tried to peg it to the ice. He had no choice but to try to put together a snow house. He went back to her first, lifted her head, and slapped her cheeks gently, then harder, until her eyes flickered open again, squinting up at him against the wind and snow. Feebly she raised her right mittened hand and touched his face.

"You've got to stay awake!" he yelled at her above the sound of the wind. "Help me now! Stay awake! Do you understand me?"

She managed a faint smile, enough to let him know she would try to do her part. He carried her to the lee side of the ice ridge, away from the wind, laying her down in the snow, covering her again with the parka. Then he went to work cutting the snow and ice blocks, using both hands, disregarding the pain in his right one, bent only on getting up the shelter before she yielded to the quickest death in the Arctic, that long, easy, sliding sleep.

He had no idea how long he worked, fighting the

wind and the snow, blinded at times so that he could not even see what he was doing. But somehow he got the blocks together. It was not perfect, by any means. But it was enough shelter to keep out the storm and the cold.

He carried her inside and put her down carefully on the sleeping bag. She let out a low gasp as he did so, and he looked down into her face quickly. He lit the primus hurriedly and turned up the heat. Carefully he undid the leather laces from around her neck that were attached to the capsule and took the capsule from her parka belt, putting it carefully over by the entrance, covering it with ice chips to keep the temperature down over it. Next he took off her outer and inner parka. It was then that he saw the blood smeared on his hand, and he looked down quickly to see the darker outline against her brown turtleneck up on the right shoulder and spreading down on her right side. A shaft of alarm stabbed at him as he realized that she was in more critical shape than he had imagined.

"God," he whispered, making it an appeal, overwhelmed by this new implication. "I've got to get that sweater off," he said to her, touching her face. "You'll have to help me, Barbara. . . ."

"Taking advantage of me?" she said, trying that usual salty banter of hers to cut his concern, but her voice was shaky, catching on the pain she felt. He finally got her sweater off and laid it aside. There was a bandage where she had tried to do her own patching. He removed it carefully and looked down at the jagged hole, maybe not bigger than a dime, above her right breast, close to the area of the right lung. Small as it appeared, he knew it was deep, because there was still a steady ooze of dark blood coming from the wound. She kept watching him all the time, waiting for his reaction. He didn't look at her or say anything, trying not to show the beat of his own fear for her.

"You got this back at Thorsen's camp, didn't you?" he said, trying not to sound accusing while he fumbled for the first-aid kit behind him. "You were hit back there, but you bluffed it and sent me on that hopeless chase

196

down the ice for an Eskimo I could do nothing for. . . . I could have helped you back there. How far did you think you could go with this?"

"I'm made of good stock, you know," she said. She reached up to touch his face with her right hand, but he went on tearing strips of adhesive from the roll. "Anyway . . . you had to go back for him. . . . Besides . . . if I had told you I was hit, you would never have moved from there. . . ."

"You can bet your life on that," he said abruptly and tore off the end of a sulfa package and poured the contents into the wound, the yellow powder mixing with the red flux and turning to an ugly brown paste. Then he put a sealing bandage over it, locking it down with adhesive strips. He found two tetracycline pills in his kit and lifted her head to put them into her mouth, giving her a cup of melted snow water. Then he made some tuna and bacon soup from the meager supplies that were left and fed it to her a spoonful at a time. When she tried to push it away, he said, "If you eat, it'll help." She dutifully finished it. Then there was nothing else to do. He stayed beside her on his knees, praying between the slamming gusts of wind that shook the igloo, feeling the cold puffs of air come down on him from the holes he'd so clumsily left between the ice blocks.

He had no idea how long he stayed in that position, just watching her face while she slept, now and then reaching over to touch her cold cheek. He dozed off, finally, and awoke with a jerk to see her looking at him, studying him, her eyes half closed, just a trace of a smile on her pale lips.

"You're just as handsome asleep, did you know that?" she said to him, her voice hoarse.

He tried to rise to her attempt at banter, but the encroaching pressure of time prevented it. "We've got to do something," he said, "besides just sit here, waiting—"

"Like what?"

"Like maybe trying that radio and see if we can get help."

"You know you can't do that."

197

"I'm in command now," he told her bluntly.

"And you know . . . you have to go on with the rock. . . ."

"The rock be hanged," he replied petulantly, hating it more than ever for what it had done to both of them. "I am not leaving you here to die . . . okay?"

"Whether I die or not is really not up to you to decide."

"In your case, it is my rightful concern. . . . Besides, I've used up my quota of people who die with me. So right now I'm going to fight to save a life, the one that counts most to me."

"You put the two of us before millions—"

"That's right," he interjected, anticipating the remark. He looked down into her face then, sensing that the skin had gone even more white, intensifying the feverish glow in her eyes. He reached down and kissed her lips; they were cold and almost waxy, and he felt a jab of alarm. "You know—I have never loved you, caressed you, touched you as a lover? I have never communicated anything to you except arguments about my theology or some Cold War strategy. Is it so wrong to fight for the communion we have been denied?"

"Then . . . love me now," she said. He sensed the urgency in her voice, as she reached up her hand slowly to touch his face lightly. He took it in his own, feeling its coldness, its fragility, sensing in it the slim margin of life that was left in her.

He shook his head in the sheer hopelessness of the moment. "With that rock ticking over there?" he said, knowing he was arguing with himself, not her. "With life seeping out of you an ounce at a time, and those— those faceless millions reproaching us for using up their time? Anyway"—he tried to put it lightly—"I know you would give me yourself, you would give me anything, to heap coals of fire on my head about that rock."

She pressed her hand over his mouth lightly, checking him, then removed it, keeping it on his bearded cheek as she said, "I know you will go on with that rock any-

198

way . . . you cannot deny what you instinctively know you must do in the end . . . but . . . you should know now, because you are still so unsure of yourself . . . that I love you as any woman can love a man who has filled the horizon of her life, not . . . not because of your vows alone, which are like mine . . . not only because you are willing to die like I am for something meaningful . . . but . . . but because you are to me what is right, good . . . and beautiful. . . . I love you because you are afraid to go on, and yet you will go. . . . I love you because you have given me faith that is pure even in your uncertainty. . . . For . . . for all of that and more, I long to know your touch, your caress, and I would give you all of myself in order to say that to you. . . ."

He saw a frown dig between her eyes then, and he knew the pain was back again. He leaned down and kissed her in the hollow of her neck, feeling her pulse fluttering there as her body tried to fight off the tightening stricture of death. Reluctantly he raised up from beside her, feeling the compelling urge within him, yet knowing there wasn't time. He reached over and carefully peeled off the blood-soaked bandage, saying nothing, sensing her eyes on him. He noticed that the wound was not bleeding as much, but it was still oozing. He put on a fresh bandage and sat back looking at it, noticing the skin around it, the rich tan of it, the smooth perfection of it, what belonged to him, what he had every right to protect as his own, but now all torn and blood-streaked, terrifyingly symbolic of his own ripped spirit.

Then, avoiding looking at her, he said, "You know it's a hundred to one that I can find that ice island?"

"Those odds never bothered you in the Negev," she replied quickly, eager to meet his doubts. "Besides . . . you are not more than twenty miles from it now. . . ."

"I could be twenty feet from it and still miss it; you know that too."

"I . . . I could show you how to use the sextant," she offered.

He looked at her, gave her a quick smile, then turned

199

to pull a few things together into an emergency pack. "How many times does a novice have to use a sextant before he gets an accurate reading? You know I have to hit that island on dead reckoning."

"Well . . . here is your position," she said, pushing a yellow-lined paper over to him. "The island . . . is eighty-six degrees thirty-one minutes north—"

"I see it," he mumbled, looking at the paper dully, hating the thought of going, of leaving her. "How will I know when I'm there?"

"You'll see the outbuildings first . . . and Thorsen said his man will keep an American flag on the pole . . . sometimes . . . that will stand out against the ice."

"Sometimes," he said, not wanting to destroy her hopes, but knowing she had to be aware of the immensity of the task. "Does . . . does this ice island stick up over the ice like a huge berg or what?"

"No. . . . The two hundred feet thickness is mostly under the Arctic. . . . It may rise gradually like any big ice ridge . . . so you can't tell it that way; you must keep your eyes out for the flag."

He went on working on his pack, and when he was finished he turned toward her again. Her eyes were closed. He moved over to her, felt her pulse. It fluttered in weak response. Her face seemed to glow like a madonna's, the flame in her burning fiercely against the threat of the cold death winds that surrounded her.

He held her in his arms, touching his lips to her warm forehead. "God—" he said. The words would not come at once. Then, "You took Ah-Ming and Thorsen from me . . . forgive me if I ask you to pass on this one?" He held her closer, feeling the cold around him, the mocking silence, only the howl of the wind outside. Finally, feeling her stir, he put her back down into her sleeping bag. He turned then and went over to the radio a few feet away. He switched on the power, picked up the mike, and said, "CQ . . . calling CQ. . . ." He repeated the call letters for anybody who might be tuned in. Nothing came back but the deadly whine of static from the wind outside. "Mayday! Mayday!" he yelled into the mike then. He found the yellow paper in his pocket and read off his position. "Need help . . . urgent . . . need help. . . . Out of food, fuel, critically hurt. Do you read me? Over." Nothing. He turned off the transmit button but left the power on. Maybe the power signal might be picked up and homed in on if anyone was tuning in.

He waited. It was 3:00 A.M. He would wait for light, hoping the storm would let up to allow him to travel. He moved back to her, feeling her face, noticing it was hot. She did not respond to his touch. Her breathing was more labored, each breath she took a shaky effort.

"Is this what it always comes to in the end?" he shouted at the ice walls around him, his voice bouncing back in shrill vibration. As it died off in empty commentary, he heard another sound coming over the wind. He sat there listening, caught between the hopeful expectation of U.S. forces and the possibility that it might be the Russians. He listened again, and he was sure he heard the whine of snow machines over those wind gusts. Who could have heard his radio signal and come that fast? It had to be the Russians. Nobody else was close enough. Quickly he reached over and turned off the radio. If they were homing in on his signal, they weren't going to come in on him that easily.

He went back to sit beside her again. Now her eyes were open, fixed on him intently. And he knew. That's the way it was always going to be in the end, he was sure. He had seen that look in the Negev, in Cuba, and in Berlin—eyes that mirrored the face of God, telling him that whatever he wanted for himself was beneath what had to be the larger picture. *God, have I not learned that yet?* And that look, coming from her now, meant again that he could not sit there watching her die with those eyes forever questioning him. Or—if the Russians were kind—to see her come to life again, but maybe never again trusting him . . . or loving him. If she had to die—dear God!—then she should know he had at least made the attempt.

So with the whine of snowmobiles sounding louder with the wind, he turned quickly and pulled on his parka, face mask, mittens. He picked up his pack and tent roll, paused, and looked back at her before going out. She was still watching him as he tied the capsule strings around his neck and tucked the capsule inside his parka belt as she had done.

"I'll be back," he called to her, noticing that her eyes were closing again. "God keep you until I get back!"

He moved out into the icy wind and flying snow, to the darkness of the Arctic that held a thousand surprises for him. He stuck the tent pole with the orange distress pennant into the snow house roof. If the Russians came up on the other side of the ridge, they wouldn't see it; but he hoped it would help him find her when he came back. *If* he came back? He cut the dogs loose, giving them a chance to find their own forage and maybe their own way home. He poured the last five gallons of fuel into the snowmobile tank as he caught sight of flares in the distance behind him. The storm was not holding the Russians back . . . which meant they were deadly serious about this game too.

He kicked the start lever, praying that the fuel valve would hold. After six attempts, the motor came to life. He flipped on the high beam, turned once to glance back at the snow house, and moved out, cutting back around the ice ridge and onto the trail where he had found her yesterday. He would push the machine for all he had, putting caution behind him. He had to hope that if he made T-3, he could get help back to her in time. . . .

9

His intent now was simply to keep running in the direction of T-3, trusting only in that Divine Presence to guide him. In the dark he knew he would not see the island or the flag or the buildings. But there was always the outside chance that "the man," whoever he was, if he was there, would spot his lights and come out to meet him.

He hadn't gone far before he knew he was in a battle worse than he had yet experienced. Ice mounds loomed up in front of him like tank traps, some of them tangled into shapes that poked out with pointed lances, any one of which would run through him cleanly if he hit them in the dark. Snowdrifts stalled the snowmobile, forcing him to watch his speed. By having to go around the ice and cut back on speed, he realized that he was using a lot of gas but gaining little ground. Behind him he could see the glow in the sky where the Russians were, seeming to get brighter as they closed the gap. And always he wondered if they had found her. Would they mistreat her, trying to get information on the rock? Or would they give her medical help? He dared to believe the latter, but he would never know until he got back to her.

Something else was beginning to dawn on him too as he moved along. It was not as cold. In fact, when he stopped once to push the snowmobile through a huge drift, he took off his face mask and noticed the wind was not harsh on his face at all. In the light of his flashlight he examined the capsule hanging inside his belt, checking the bulge in it, realizing what any rise in temperature could do to it. Beyond that mounting crisis in the making was the possibility of ice breakup with the thaw. He wasn't thinking of himself so much, but what would happen to Barbara if the ice tore off around her in that snow house?

He continued moving as best he could, knowing he had no choice, sometimes crawling at five miles an hour, all the time trying to see through the blowing snow. Finally, he came to a level strip of open ice and pushed the machine to full throttle, mindful now that every yard he clicked off brought him closer to help for her. He poured it on for a good half hour that way, taking the ice ridges and snow mounds with complete disregard for the machine or himself. There was only that nagging, urgent beat within him, the need to win, to turn everything around, to once again be with her. . . .

He was so intent on that vision that he did not see the crevasse in front of him until the last second. Instinctively, he threw himself off the machine, knowing he could not stop it in time. He made sure he landed on his back, protecting the capsule, but his backpack dug into him, knocking the wind out of him. He lay there in the snow, gasping for breath as the sounds of the snowmobile plunging down into the open crevasse tolled a clanging finality to his efforts.

He rose slowly, fumbled around in the snow for his flashlight, found it, and moved over to the edge of the crevasse. He shined the light down into it, but he could not see bottom. The snow machine was gone somewhere, who knew how deep, and he sat back to ponder just how close he had come to that bottomless pit himself. What had she said to him? "You have a Presence about you." Yes. . . . How many close ones had he missed?

He stood up unsteadily in the wind and snow and with a very real sense of that other presence now too,

the Arctic itself, that swirled around him with the glee
of a sure kill. On foot, it said, he was at the mercy of
all the destructive elements it could muster. And if the
Arctic enemy didn't do it, the Russians would soon be
along. . . .

"God, I tried," he mumbled, feeling only the sick-
ening waves of exhaustion and defeat grab him. He
glanced back to see the lights coming on, closing on his
trail. He was tempted to let them come, to explain the
rock to them, and hope to get them at least to go back
with him to help her.

But instead he turned and faced that open chasm,
running his light the length of it, noticing that it ran
back west a good hundred yards, maybe more. Why was
he going to walk around it? Maybe, again, it was what
she had jabbed him with back there, that if he didn't
push to the limit, all that she and the others had gone
through was meaningless. If he didn't, would he only be
making a mockery of her death? Death? God! *Not her
death!* He refused to allow the thought and quickened
his pace, as if his extra effort would somehow change
the reality of that possibility, as if maybe God would move
on his behalf if he clocked so many miles in the attempt.
He walked around the crevasse and moved on, half
stumbling, keeping his face into the wind. The snow was
turning to sleet; it hit his parka with a steady tattoo and
turned to ice crystals, dragging further on him. Sometimes he ran, not knowing why, trying to put distance
between himself and his pursuers, sometimes figuring
in his clouded mind that he couldn't be far off now . . .
and all the time the sound of those snow machines
stayed with him, tearing jagged holes in the night, crowd-
ing him, telling him they were not fooling either.

He didn't know exactly when his flashlight quit. He
suddenly realized that he had been walking in the dark,
but he didn't know for how long. He checked the flashlight beam. It was dead. He stood there in the enveloping
darkness, and a crazy kind of laugh came up in his throat,
dying in a kind of feeble groan. The sleet was soaking

through him, and chills racked his body as he stood there. His right hand hurt so much that at times he let out a shaky sigh, more like a gasp. His legs were wooden, his feet unfeeling clumps of ice. He tried to move them but fell down in the snow, tried to get up, then fell over flat on his back. He felt the capsule pressing into his body; something warned him to get up. . . .

But he didn't. He lay there, ignoring the warning. He took the moment to rest, unable to do anything else, beaten physically, drained emotionally, and with maybe only a flicker of faith left, not enough to drive him back to his feet. He tried again, out of instinct, but he fell down once more, feeling the cold rain hit his face.

"God," he croaked, his lips hardly moving. "I take my hands off. . . . I—I can't do anything more. . . ."

He lay there, hearing the snow machines back of him. They were probably at the crevasse now, looking for a way around. And as he lay there, he saw a slash of light on the far horizon. Dawn. What did it matter? But he thought of her again, bleeding to death and yet pushing that team of dogs, and he pushed himself upright again with sheer effort of will, standing unsteadily on his feet. Now he could see ahead. He saw a sheet of flat, smooth ice, all the snow blown off so that the light bounced off its black sheen; he could see the ice mounds far beyond reflected in it. He stared at it, trying to figure out what it could mean, not sure it wasn't an open lead of water. Then, carefully, he started walking. It was hard, solid ice. He slipped and fell again, holding on to the capsule as he did. But he got up quicker now, because an idea had begun to form. He noticed that as he walked he left no tracks on the ice, nothing for them behind to follow . . . so there was just a small possibility he could yet carry it off.

He kept walking, sometimes slipping on the ice, until he had reached those ice mounds beyond, maybe a half mile ahead of him. When he got there, the light was coming up stronger, and he rolled over an ice ledge to the other side, huddling there, waiting for them to pass. They came on, in nine snow machines, pushing at a good pace, one machine out front with a single man aboard checking for his trail. They went on by him, two men to a machine, which meant, counting the single man, seventeen in all, automatic weapons slung over their shoulders.

He waited until they were a good distance ahead and moving out of sight. Then he moved painfully around the snow ridge and started following. He picked up their trail in the snow line ahead and stayed close enough to smell the hot engine grease and exhaust, but never close enough to be seen. The clouds were still heavy over him, and the sleet was half snow again. The wind was gusty but not as strong. The temperature, though, was still going up, and he could hear the familiar thump of ice breaking up around him, the rumbling under his feet as the shock waves passed.

He had to believe that they would keep going on to T-3; maybe they wouldn't. If they were following him, they would surely double back to look for him; maybe not. No one came back to check, so he slogged on, as the sun broke through the heavy clouds.

He kept walking, half stumbling, watching the marks in the snow from the machines, now and then squinting against the glare of the sun to the horizon, looking for anything that might indicate T-3. But there was nothing, nothing but the same jutting pinnacles of ice mounds that looked like a ruin out of Fantasia or a prehistoric city frozen to pillars of salt.

He didn't stop walking until he bumped into an ice wall. He stood there, not comprehending, until it dawned on him that he had been half asleep while he walked. That meant his body was shutting down its circuits as his circulation became sluggish with the cold and the heavy beat of fatigue. He looked around. He was in a maze of ice mounds, and as he stood there looking for some sign, he smelled the engine exhaust from the snow machines again. He waited: no sound. He started walking again, following the scent of that exhaust more than any specific direction. As he moved, he felt himself breathing heavily, his body leaning slightly forward as he climbed over the piled-up snowdrifts. The sun was moving up in the sky, casting a saffron glow across the ice and snow. The snow stopped. The wind was only a mild breath on his cheeks.

He fell down again, and he fought the usual struggle to get up; as he pushed himself up on all fours, he glanced up and saw them.

They were clustered in a loose circle by their snow-mobiles, maybe seventy-five yards ahead of him. He skittered off to the left, looking for ice cover before they spotted him. He debated whether to wait for them to go on, and follow, or strike out around them. It was imperative he make T-3 soon, because he knew he hadn't much left to go on.

He finally got up and, using the ice ridges as protection, made a circuitous track around them and moved back on some kind of imaginary line that he felt would take him north. He had very little willpower left to think ahead, to plan; if they spotted him, he really didn't care.

Then he stopped.

To his right he saw the line of Russians and their machines. They were looking his way, not more than a good stone's throw away. He saw one of them point toward him, and some of the others turned to look. At the same time, he saw someone else coming toward him, running, and behind the runner was the flag, snapping out in the breeze that was still there higher off the ice. "God," he croaked, and it was an animal sound in his throat, a cross between a laugh and a cry. He watched the running figure get larger in his vision. Something was happening over by the Russians, but he couldn't keep both of them in view. He didn't have the strength. . . .

Sebastian waited, watching through painful, blurred eyes, trying to bring that figure into focus. Then, with a stab that cut deeply into his brain, he knew! He would know that face anywhere! It was too much! He fell down on his knees, too weak to stand against another shock, and his painful right hand sought for the capsule, hung on to it.

"Dietrich!" he shouted, all the fury of his feelings about this journey rising up in his throat. He saw the figure slow down, hesitate, and then move closer. "Dietrich, if you . . . if you make another move . . . you'll have to kill me to get the rock!"

It was very quiet. Nobody moved. He swung his gaze toward the Russians. They were closer, taking one careful step at a time, their guns slung down at the ready.

"Now listen to me, Reverend." The familiar voice came to him from thirty feet away. "There isn't much time to talk. . . ."

"I'll—I'll never give it to you, Dietrich," Sebastian warned. "You'll have to take it. . . ."

"All right." The voice soothed him again; he hated that patronizing tone. "Now, you see that flag over there? No, no, not the big one on the pole; the one to your left, behind me." Sebastian swung his gaze beyond Dietrich. "Low to the ground, on a stick. It's red. See it?"

"I see it," Sebastian said, and he looked at Dietrich, not sure whether the man had moved a few more feet toward him.

"All right. This is your chance to make a hole in one. Understand?" Dietrich's voice stayed on that same even, academic tone, unhurried but insistent. "I want you to walk over to that flag. There's a hole there. All you have to do is drop the capsule in the hole. Will you do that?"

"I said I won't give it to you, Dietrich—"

"No, you don't have to do that. Just take it there yourself and drop it in. Only you haven't much time, do you understand? Those people over there—you see them?"

Sebastian looked toward the line of Russians again, moving a little closer. "I see them."

"Any minute they are going to try to get a shot into you. . . . You must go toward the flag now, but walk slowly, as if you were coming to greet me. Do you understand?"

Sebastian didn't understand. He wanted to protest. Instead, he knew he had to obey that voice, because his own mind was incapable of functioning on its own. He glanced once more at the white-suited men to his right and rose slowly from his knees, hesitated a few seconds, and then started walking toward Dietrich. As he approached, Dietrich said, "Go on by me now to the flag and the hole—but don't hesitate!"

Sebastian came close to him; he saw the familiar face, the glasses, the gray, languid eyes behind them. For just a second or two, he paused as if to stop. "Don't stop!" Dietrich's voice barked at him in a harsh, throttled voice, as if he didn't want the Russians to hear. Sebastian went on by him, reached up to loosen the leather lace from around his neck, and then gripped the rock in his good left hand. It was about twenty yards beyond Dietrich to the flag. As he walked, he saw just the flag—the end of the journey, whatever that meant. And even as he walked, he heard the sound of a motor from somewhere overhead, but he did not look up. Dietrich was walking beside him, one step behind but coming up closer, as a kind of shield between him and the Russians. Now he was over the hole, and he reached out and dropped the capsule into the metal chute. At the same instant, a shot cut the silence, and he felt, rather than saw, Dietrich go down next to him. Immediately, instinctively, he dropped prone on the snow by the fallen man, conscious of the whirling snow around him, the stench of hot engine grease, the clatter of those familiar rotors.

The helicopter settled swiftly on the ice between the two men and the Russians, and in a few seconds Sebastian saw the doors open and helmeted troops jumped down to spread out in a long line to form a barrier between them and the Russians, who were still trying to move in. Sebastian continued to lie there, one arm thrown across Dietrich's chest, as if to protect him. Dietrich was looking at him, his face a litle gray, his right mittened hand hanging onto his smashed left arm. There was a real smile on his mouth now, not the little spasm of one that Sebastian remembered back in Eureka.

"Welcome home, Reverend," Dietrich said.

Sebastian simply stared at him, not comprehending the words or the spirit behind them. He looked up to see a man bending over him. His parka hood was back, revealing a U.S. Navy officer's cap. He was peering down, almost disbelievingly, at Sebastian and Dietrich. Lying there, Sebastian felt the overpowering desire to sleep; instead, he got up shakily and said to the officer, "I need your copter, sir."

"What?" the man shouted back above the sound of the copter rotors that had not yet died off, continuing to whirl snow around them.

Sebastian fell to one knee, feeling dizzy. "Glad to see you, Admiral Fish," he heard Dietrich say. "You better give this clergyman what he wants."

"This—who?" the Navy man shouted as he leaned over Dietrich to make sure he'd heard right and then glanced at Sebastian with some awe.

"I . . . have a party on the ice!" Sebastian yelled. And he fumbled in his pocket until he found the yellow paper. "That bearing. She's hurt badly. Hurry!"

"The Interpol girl?" the admiral shouted, and without waiting for the answer turned to yell at somebody, calling out orders.

Sebastian only vaguely remembered getting into the copter and lifting off, his mind whirling with the rotors. Somebody was stripping off his mitten with a pair of shears and applying some cool ointment and a bandage. Somebody else put a paper cup of hot coffee in his other hand, and as he lifted it to his mouth, catching the warm, rich odor that signified friendship, his throat closed with the constricting emotion he felt. But nobody paid any attention, all of them suddenly very busy with other things.

They didn't find her. Some time later he sat in the cockpit next to the admiral as they made pass after pass over the same ice, moving outward in concentric circles from the bearing. Below them was nothing but huge open leads of black water, chunks of ice broken off and floating as if a lot of garbage had been dumped into the

211

Arctic. The admiral even went south a long way, following the possible line of drift of an ice floe on which she might be marooned. But there was nothing. They went down several times, dropping on the firmer masses of ice, trying to pick up the snow house that might have been missed from the air. Still nothing.

"This sudden spring thaw has torn the hell out of the ice!" the admiral shouted at him. "We ought to try east, the flow of the drift, but we have to go back and refuel now! Okay, Reverend?"

Sebastian opened his mouth to protest, staring down at the broken ice, symbolic of what had forever broken within him. He felt nothing. As they lifted from the shambles of exploded ice, he had no will left to fight the grip of darkness that fell on him. He only wanted the pain to go away, the knifing stabs deep inside him, the cold shaft of awareness that she was gone.

It was five o'clock by the dial of his wristwatch. He glanced at the window and noticed that the light was a half glow on the panes. Dawn, then. He had slept for twelve hours straight. And now he lay there, feeling his body tingle with the tension he had lived with for what seemed a long time, and listened for the familiar sound of rumbling ice. He finally got up and dressed, anxious to find out if there was any word on Barbara Churchill. He looked at the heavy bandage on his right hand, not sure where he got that, unable to piece everything together. He walked outside to a larger room that was drafty. The medical orderly stood up, expecting to help him, but Sebastian said, "Will you get Otto Dietrich for me?" The man hesitated, then nodded, put on his parka, and went out.

Sebastian sat at the rickety table, poured himself a cup of coffee from the iron pot, and waited. He didn't look up from his full cup of coffee when the door opened and someone came in and sat down at the far end of the table. Finally he turned and saw Dietrich, his left arm in a sling.

212

"Did they—?"

"Nothing yet," Dietrich said, pouring himself a cup of coffee and sitting down a little way from Sebastian. "They've gone off for one more run this morning."

Sebastian said nothing and went back to staring into his coffee, not really caring to converse with Dietrich.

"You wanted to see me?" Dietrich asked, clearing his throat, his voice pleasant enough but carrying the usual shortness, as if he were anxious to be off on other matters.

Sebastian wasn't sure what to ask, being preoccupied with the increasingly dismal possibilities of finding Barbara Churchill.

"I—I guess it was about that rock," he said finally, wondering why it should matter now. "Will it be neutralized in that—in that hole out there?"

Dietrich did not reply. He sat there stirring his coffee with a blackened spoon, looking down into it with interest.

After a long time, Sebastian looked at him again and said, "Mr. Dietrich?"

Dietrich sighed, lifted a spoonful of the black coffee, and tasted it gingerly. "Mr. Sebastian, at the expense of breaking security—"

"Mr. Dietrich, I don't want any of that schmaltz about security. People died to get that rock up here, and I want to know—"

"Well, I can tell you this," Dietrich broke in. "*That* rock, Mr. Sebastian, will have no problem being neutralized." He paused.

"*That* rock?" Sebastian said, and his hands trembled now as he gripped the coffee cup harder. "Mr. Dietrich—"

"Look, Mr. Sebastian." Dietrich took off his glasses with his right hand and laid them carefully on the table in front of him, as if they were his armor and he wanted peace. "In order for us to get the real piece of the moon safely out of Houston and into a sealed, oxygen-free, temperature-controlled neutralizing vault, we had to convince the Russians, and everybody else, that it was on its

213

way to the North Pole in the hands of a deranged scientist. Do you get the picture?"

Sebastian stared at him, hardly comprehending the immensity of the statement. "You're—you're saying people died out there for a useless, harmless chunk of dirt?"

"A piece of Nebraska clay, to be exact," Dietrich corrected, almost lightly. "And people have died for worse. The main thing is that it worked."

"It was a game we played all the way, you mean," Sebastian went on, still dumbfounded.

"But a necessary game, Mr. Sebastian—and you all played it well."

"Thorsen . . . he knew?"

"Of course. He was the one who suggested we go that route. He knew, as we did, that Russian agents were infiltrating Houston, setting up a grab—"

"We?"

"Well, I worked both sides of the line, Mr. Sebastian, but I was strictly CIA all the way. I can tell you now, since my cover is blown anyway and I can never go back to it."

There was a pause, during which Sebastian studied Dietrich's face guardedly, looking for a hint that he was joking.

"Well, then," Sebastian said at last, almost demanding to know, "why couldn't you have found a way to do all this without making an assassin and a human bomb out of me? Couldn't you have told me the real facts about the rock at the start?"

"I couldn't take that chance with you," Dietrich replied flatly. "The Arctic is the worst territory in the world for testing a man's resolve—and that's taking nothing from your earlier accomplishments in equally tough places. If I told you the truth, there was always a chance of a weak moment coming, as it does to all of us, when you might conclude that a phony rock was hardly worth it."

"But—"

"Besides that," Dietrich continued, as if he were anxious to vindicate himself, "I couldn't even trust passing on that info to the CIA. Too many double agents hanging in between us. You see, when Zukov, the KGB man, insisted I take Landau into Houston to brainwash Thorsen to make a run for it so they could grab the rock, I had to tip off Thorsen to prepare him. At that point Thorsen suggested to play the game their way and take the opportunity to use a decoy rock—but to pull that off, we had to keep it close to ourselves."

"Was there no other way?"

"You have to remember that I had to convince the Russians—and everybody else, for that matter—that that was the real rock out there on the ice with Thorsen. To build my case, I had to use the extreme measures I did with you. And it worked. Those Russians who saw you drop that capsule in that hole are reasonably convinced it's the real thing. It will take them a while to prove otherwise, and maybe by then the real piece of the moon will be neutralized and of no use to anybody. . . . But don't get the idea I enjoyed making you into an assassin or wiring you with a destruct package."

"I almost got to Thorsen, Mr. Dietrich," Sebastian insisted. "I only missed him by a hair."

"So Admiral Fish told me. I don't know how it blew, because I alone had the key to the circuits. And I never intended to use it; it all was for show."

"Yes, but if I had converged on Thorsen, what then? How could you be so sure I wouldn't get to him?"

"Well . . . it was a big chance, I know. I knew something of your religious zeal, Mr. Sebastian, and how it could take you that extra mile. But I had my hopes pinned on Ah-Ming."

"Ah-Ming?"

"Yes. His job was to delay you as much as he could, keep you from getting to Thorsen."

"Delay?" Sebastian snorted. "He got drunk on the primus fuel and fell through the ice. That your idea of a delay?"

215

Dietrich appeared to be struck by that news. He frowned. "I didn't know that."

Sebastian looked down into his coffee, not sure he wanted to go on. But then he said, "So how come you risked telling Interpol about the operation if you couldn't risk the CIA or NASA?"

"We didn't tell Interpol anything. As soon as the word was out that Thorsen was on a destruct mission, they dispatched their agent after clearing with Washington. I then saw an opportunity to get a safety valve on the ice for Thorsen, in case he did bog down and I couldn't get to him. I took the risk and put through a contact to Interpol."

"What was she told?"

"About what?"

"The rock, for one thing."

"That it was loaded, the real piece of the moon."

"Why didn't you tell her the truth?"

"Supposing the Russians got to her and sweated it out of her? Where would we have been then?"

"Well, did Thorsen know she was out there?"

"We told him. He was to tell her when she found him that the rock had to get to T-Three, that's all."

"And if Thorsen had died before she got to him?"

"Well, then we had a new ball game, right, Reverend?"

"But she did know about Landau, even you—"

"She got scraps of that from Interpol," Dietrich admitted.

"You told Interpol to tell her to take him alive?"

"Yes, obviously. Like I said, Thorsen knew she would be out there looking for him. When she found him, he was to tell her to get that rock safely to T-Three."

Sebastian paused, feeling gritty over the way this all seemed to fall so carelessly together. "It would have been only fair to tell her the truth," he went on. "Must all human relationships in your world of espionage, your machine men, be reduced to mere utility in the end? Can't you trust anybody—ever?"

216

"Hardly," Dietrich replied with a sad smile. "Anyway, do you think it would have changed anything, even if she did know?" Sebastian looked at him quickly, sensing the truth there. "She was trained to see the larger picture in everything. Whether the rock was phony or real, she would have seen the importance of playing the decoy if necessary. But then, if you'll pardon me, Reverend, would you have gone all the way if *you* knew?"

"You're saying she would have told me if she had known?"

"I take it you had more going with each other than the international brotherhood of spies?" Sebastian said nothing to that. "So you see," Dietrich concluded, "we always try to anticipate, Mr. Sebastian. Though we could maybe have trusted her, we weren't sure about you. . . ."

"Anybody has a right to know what he or she is dying for," Sebastian insisted.

"In your profession, maybe . . . but in ours, to wait to find out means we are dead ducks."

Sebastian wasn't satisfied, but he let it go.

Dietrich went on. "But to the other question, then— could we not pick up Thorsen earlier and fly him to T-Three if possible—I wanted the Russians there when he dropped that thing down the chute—"

"Would they have been convinced?" Sebastian interjected.

"If I was there, as their man, yes, that was one of the main reasons for my going. Anyway, when I saw Thorsen was stalled out there, I was worried that the Russians would overtake him too soon. If they took the rock off him, they'd know within a week that it was a phony. So we'd be right back where we started, and they'd be pulling out all the stops to find the real thing again. And since we have only one neutralizing vault set up for something as unique as that rock—well, it wouldn't take them long to zero in. So I had to move to get Thorsen off the ice, even if it meant leaving a cold trail."

"You would have had to shoot him, Mr. Dietrich,"

Sebastian countered. "Even I know that. To convince them you would have had to shoot Thorsen and leave his body there so they would know this was a serious game. Am I right?" Dietrich hesitated, cradling his coffee cup in his hands in a peculiar posture of appeal. "Well, Mr. Dietrich?"

"It doesn't matter now," Dietrich replied with detachment. "You saved me that; you made it simple all the way around."

"So you couldn't find Thorsen or me. Then what?"

"I had no choice but to go to T-Three and sweat it out, hoping that Thorsen would revive and get on the move, or that the weather would lift to allow me to find him—or, better yet, that the Interpol girl would find him and finish the journey."

"What about Thorsen's radio?" Sebastian went on, peeling one layer off at a time, inwardly recoiling as each new bizarre dimension came into view.

"He didn't have one." Dietrich was replying as if he were in the witness box, almost as if he were anxious to tell the truth, the whole truth. "He said he didn't want anybody tracking him on his radio signals. Besides, a deranged scientist bent on blowing up the North Pole wouldn't worry about a radio, would he?"

"And what about Admiral Fish? Did you have him primed to drop down on us just on cue like that?"

Dietrich chuckled. "That brassy old salt really took it on himself to play his hunch, even over CIA orders."

"What would have happened to us if he hadn't?"

"We'd probably be dead. Zukov was out there with those Russians. He shot to kill me, not just wing me. When he saw what I was doing, with that rock and all, I can't say I blame him."

"You were willing to die?" Sebastian asked. "I mean, you knew it could be that?"

"So was Thorsen. Sometimes you pay, right, Reverend?"

Sebastian still hadn't touched his coffee. He got up from the table and walked around the room once, trying to work off the tension, the confusion. He stopped by the table again, putting his finger down on a wet circle left by his coffee cup.

"I really didn't intend to tell you this," Dietrich went on. "You must understand that this is confidential. Anyway, sometimes the less said, the better."

"It doesn't change anything, does it?" Sebastian mused. "You know, just knowing the rock was a phony." He walked over to the window and looked out at the brilliant sun tearing at the mounds of white granite. "But no matter how important this was—this decoy and all— there is still something of unutterable waste in it anyway."

"Of course."

"I mean, if we had known about the rock, the Russians maybe would not have found us in that igloo anyway. And even if they had, so what? So they had a phony rock. By then the real one was locked in a vault in the United States. It might have taken them five years to get it, how do we know? I'm saying that knowing it was phony—well, it could have saved her life."

"Maybe." Dietrich's voice carried a note of sympathy.

Sebastian leaned his cheek up against the cold glass, trying to reach her across those miles of emptiness. "Well, I'm not so naïve either, Mr. Dietrich, about all these things," he went on, speaking to that frosted glass in front of him. "I guess I've learned by now what it means to be used and misused in these years of chasing the good, the bad, and the ugly. At times I've been living in what someone called the idiotic mockery of the universe, when sometimes I thought God was laughing at me. You know what I mean?" Dietrich did not reply. "I've been confused and repelled before at the end of one of these journeys, but not like this one, not quite. You ought to know that five minutes ago I could have taken a swing at you, if my profession as clergyman had allowed it. Because sometimes the architects of these sadistic comedies need a reminder to search for more human ways to achieve their ends. . . .

219

"But in the worst of darkness there is some light, Mr. Dietrich," Sebastian continued. "And I just thought how Jesus must have felt climbing up on that garbage heap to die a couple thousand years ago—and of the millions and millions of plugged nickels he did it for. Maybe that doesn't lead to acceptance of all this, but it will have to do."

At first Dietrich did not comment. Then Sebastian heard him move from behind and come across the few feet to stand at the window with him, looking out. "I think I should tell you about Ah-Ming," Dietrich said. "Maybe it doesn't make any difference, but I feel I ought to anyway. . . . I knew Ah-Ming years back when I was on assignment here at Thule. He and his family came into a very fine religious experience at the chapel in Thule several years ago. His wife and two kids had it first, but Ah-Ming felt a definite change too. . . . Well, when the chaplain was transferred, a new one came in, younger, less experienced in Eskimo ways, but Ah-Ming's clan took to him anyway. One day Ah-Ming took his family out on the ice to fish, and the chaplain asked to go along. Once out on the ice, Ah-Ming told his wife to stay away from a particular stretch of ice which the Eskimos refer to as being not fully born, meaning too thin. . . . Eskimos, regardless of Christianity, still believe in omens and spirits, and Ah-Ming told his wife to respect Ano. Well, the chaplain, eager to prove the Eskimo superstition a hoax, decided to make that the test. When Ah-Ming went over an ice ridge to hunt seal, the chaplain went out on that ice, taking Ah-Ming's family with him. . . . Ah-Ming heard the ice splinter. He got over the ridge in time to see them disappear into a black hole of water. . . .

"After that, Ah-Ming fell apart. He lost his faith altogether and became mean, a hopeless, murderous drunk." Dietrich paused and turned, folded his arms, and looked at the floor. "So I thought you ought to know that the reason Ah-Ming didn't want to go out on that ice with you was that he was afraid of another contradiction from a God-man—and it explains why he got drunk out

220

there and tried to beat it. Once an Eskimo is crossed, he either kills the man who did it or stays ten miles away from him."

Sebastian nodded, sensing in Dietrich a strange tone of longing, as if all that happened to Ah-Ming was his fault. At the same time, he also sensed something emerging from his tired brain, something flashing from the black panorama of the journey.

"Well, Mr. Dietrich," Sebastian said, "maybe that explains what happened on the ice. You see, Ah-Ming stayed alive long enough to ask me one question: Did I shoot Thorsen? When I told him I had not, he seemed to relax, as if it were all right to die then. It seemed even as if he were eager to go, saying his wife and children were calling him. . . ."

Dietrich said nothing right away but was very still, pondering it all. Finally he took off his glasses again and peered at them intently. "Then let me add one more thing," he went on, clearing his throat uncomfortably. "You see, Ah-Ming saved my life five years ago when I was up here. . . . I had fallen through the ice off Cape Colombia, even after he warned me about the uncertainty of that ice patch. He risked his life to pull me out. I told him then that someday I would repay him, but I could never come up with anything in kind." Again he paused, as if carefully charting his way. "Maybe—who knows?—he saw something straight coming from you."

Sebastian wanted to reach out and hold on to that possibility; he wanted something tangible to emerge to balance the sense of failure he felt. "Could it be, then, that it was you who told Ah-Ming I was a clergyman in Eureka?"

Dietrich put his glasses on again, still staring at the floor. "I remembered Ah-Ming when he had faith; it was a beautiful thing to see. I owed him something, like I said, and if there was even a remote chance he would get it back—"

"But—"

"I know." Dietrich lifted his hand to acknowledge

221

the discrepancy. "I knew that having you brainwashed out of your spiritual memory and into becoming an assassin wasn't going to help you any. But I hoped even then that something would come out of it for Ah-Ming. When I told him you were a clergyman, I had to risk his refusing to go at all—you'll never know how much I promised him to pay him for going—and I had to tell you he knew, you see, because you had to have your guard up too. . . . Anyway, that ethanol fuel for the primus you took was not on our requisition; he must have switched to that fuel at Eureka, because he probably intended to get drunk out there and leave you."

Sebastian simply stared at him. "Do you know you could have helped me by giving me my pocket New Testament back at Eureka?"

"Landau had that," Dietrich replied. He reached inside his wide belt and pulled it out, extending it to Sebastian, who took it. "I lifted that out of Landau's effects when I took off to look for you. I figured if I found you I'd give it to you, and maybe it would de-program you as Landau suggested it might. It was a weak gesture at best, but it was all I had."

There was an awkward silence between them, and finally Sebastian said, "It's incredible . . . what strange bedfellows we all are in the end, Mr. Dietrich."

Dietrich smiled. When he looked at Sebastian, his eyes no longer carried that shadow of uncertainty against the illuminated screen of his mind. "Well"—and he was speaking with some hesitancy now, unsure of himself —"sometimes we so-called unfeeling men of the machine need something to make it all worth the tight turns, too." Then he looked embarrassed. The moment of honest exposure and confession was too much for him, something he had been trained to guard against, so he straightened quickly and moved over to the table to pull on his parka. "You are scheduled to fly out of here at eight this morning to Thule for debriefing," he said, his voice back to a crisp professorial tone. "You will be ready?"

Sebastian was still caught in the enormity of what

had been said. He felt a need for clarification, even amplification. Beyond that, of course, leaving also meant the end of any hope he had still burning feebly within him regarding Barbara Churchill.

"May I ask, Mr. Dietrich, if there is any possibility yet that—that she might be alive out there?"

Dietrich frowned at his mittens as he pulled them on. "According to Admiral Fish, who is our best expert on Arctic ice, bar none, there isn't much hope. I'm sorry."

Sebastian felt the finality in that, bumping up hard against the wonder of these other things he'd just shared with Dietrich. "Well, then," he said, trying to sound resigned, "I'll be ready at eight, as you say."

Dietrich nodded and hesitated a moment as if he wanted to add something; then, without further word, he turned and walked out.

Sebastian stood by the window a long time, feeling the chaotic forces shifting within him, trying to reach a point of balance for him. He was caught between the cresting sense of wonder over what had happened to Ah-Ming and the mysterious and encouraging dimension Otto Dietrich had shown him and the void that grew in him over the loss of her. Finally, knowing he was reaching out for too much, he said, "Well, Lord, it is enough . . . enough. . . ." And he went back to the table, sat down, and drank his coffee, unmindful that it was ice cold.

At exactly 8:00 A.M. he walked with Admiral Fish and Dietrich to the waiting helicopter. The sun was now a blinding brilliance, and the ice was beginning to break up as far as he could see out on the Arctic Ocean. The air was crystal clear and clean. The thaw brought new portents of life and hope. Sebastian paused a good ten feet from the copter to look across those miles he had come, still searching every hummock out there, as if maybe he might yet catch sight of her snow house or the orange pennant sticking out of the roof.

"Arctic spring," he heard Admiral Fish say reflectively behind him. "The old Arctic winter has to let go

223

sooner or later, right, Reverend?" Sebastian did not respond, because the winter still clung to his heart and probably would never lift completely from him again. Then, as the copter engine started up its usual whine, the admiral added, "The Eskimos up here say that only in the Arctic can you see how death finally gives life, how without the winter there can be no joy in spring. . . ." The admiral paused again, and Sebastian felt him come up closer to him as the rotors began to turn, building to a loud clatter. Lifting his voice above it, the older man continued, "Somehow there ought to be a lesson in that for us Florida beach bums, wouldn't you say?"

Sebastian slowly turned his head and looked at him, seeing in those steady, commanding gray eyes a stitch of uncertainty about the adequacy of what he had said for what he had to know Sebastian was feeling right then. But for some strange reason, at that moment, it was as if Barbara Churchill had reached out to Sebastian and touched him. And some of the ice around his heart melted, and he knew that the warm winds of spring would yet flow his way too.

He smiled at the Navy officer and nodded, unable to express himself in the mystery of the moment, and the admiral took him by the arm and led him to the copter, willing him to leave behind what had to be left.

And then they were lifting off the ice, and the world of yielding death grew smaller below them. A polar bear far out across the ice plodded along looking for game. Seals dived playfully into open leads of water, no longer having to fear the sneak attacks of the bear on their snow holes, rising in gratitude to the friendly sun. The sea had turned blue, discarding its hostile, wintry black.

It was indeed resurrection spring; he knew he would always remember it like that. And in time the pain would be gone forever, like the ice, and it would never be winter for him again.